# HER

Jane was sure<br>
fax that there<br>
between them<br>
about being alone with him in the music room.
That was why she agreed to sit by his side to play a
lovely piano duet with him.

But now the music had died away. And the viscount had pulled her to her feet. His right arm went
arond her, his left hand along her cheek. His
mouth opened over hers, his left hand along her
cheek. His mouth opened over hers, instantly demanding, hungry for more than a mere outer
touch.

Clearly Jane had not succeeded in convincing the
viscount.

Even more clearly, from the way her mouth opened
under his and the way her body responded to his
ever-bolder hands, she had not convinced herself. . . .

## About the Author

*Raised and educated in Wales, Mary Balogh now
lives in Kipling, Saskatchewan, Canada, with her
husband, Robert, and her children, Jacqueline,
Christopher, and Sian. She is a high school English
teacher.*

# An Unacceptable Offer

## Mary Balogh

A SIGNET BOOK

SIGNET
Published by the Penguin Group
Penguin Books USA Inc., 375 Hudson Street,
New York, New York 10014, U.S.A.
Penguin Books Ltd, 27 Wrights Lane,
London W8 5TZ, England
Penguin Books Australia Ltd, Ringwood,
Victoria, Australia
Penguin Books Canada Ltd, 10 Alcorn Avenue,
Toronto, Ontario, Canada M4V 3B2
Penguin Books (N.Z.) Ltd, 182–190 Wairau Road,
Auckland 10, New Zealand

Penguin Books Ltd, Registered Offices:
Harmondsworth, Middlesex, England

First published by Signet, an imprint of Dutton Signet,
a division of Penguin Books USA Inc.

First Printing, May, 1988
11  10  9  8  7  6  5  4  3

 REGISTERED TRADEMARK—MARCA REGISTRADA

Printed in the United States of America

# 1

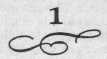

Joseph Sedgeworth yawned and held up his brandy glass to his eye to observe the inch of liquor still left in it. "I must have been mad to accompany you here, Fairfax," he said. "After two weeks in London I shall feel hemmed in and restless. And I have agreed to spend two months here with you."

The yawn was contagious. Michael Templeton, Viscount Fairfax, waited until it had passed before answering. "I have no sympathy whatsoever, Sedge," he said. "It was your idea that spending the Season here would be good for me. I would not have given the matter a thought, left to myself. And if I have to be here for a couple of months, my friend, then you will just have to suffer along with me." He grinned and raised his glass in a mock toast to the man seated opposite him.

"What I do for friendship!" Sedgeworth complained. "You know perfectly well that being in one place for any length of time always did set my feet to itching, Fairfax. Now, with you it is different. Until you married Susan, you were always in your element being here. You had all the females from the cits on up panting for your favors. It isn't at all fair, you know, for one man to be allowed to be such a handsome devil."

"Oh, come," his companion said with a laugh. "You aren't about to tell me that it is a sense of inferiority as a man that has made you so unsettled, Sedge. You don't exactly resemble the back of a hansom cab or anything like that."

"Good Lord!" his friend said, his brandy glass pausing on its way to his lips. "Where did you dream up that comparison, Fairfax? The truth is that I am just not interested in the muslin company or any female company for that matter. Females are too silly. I can't drum up any enthusiasm to talk about bonnets and the latest *on-dits* and other equally feminine concerns. Give me a bachelor existence any day. No ties, and freedom to do whatever I please."

"You might find that some mamas will have other ideas for the next few months," the viscount said.

"With you running loose? Hardly," his companion said. "They will all be so intent on trying to ensnare you that they will be quite unaware of my existence. And who can blame them? Good looks, a physique that most of us males would kill for, wealth, a fine home and estate, a title."

"And two infant daughters," Fairfax said with a grin. "Don't forget them, Sedge. They come with the package."

Sedgeworth made a dismissive gesture. "Most females dote on small children," he said, "provided they don't have to spend all their time looking after them. What kind of female are you looking for anyway, Fairfax?"

"It was your idea that I come here in search of a new wife," the viscount pointed out. "To me the plan sounds rather cold-blooded. Susan has been dead for little more than a year. And there is something distinctly distasteful about coming all this way to shop for a wife. Almost as if she were a piece of furniture or a horse."

"Nonsense!" his friend said. "Are you going to offer me more brandy, Fairfax, or aren't you? Because if you aren't, I am going to help myself." It seemed to cost him some effort to haul himself to his feet and cross the library to the desk, where a half-empty brandy decanter stood. "That is just the way our society works, as you well know. Why not call a spade a spade? Why do all the young females come flocking to London each spring? To be presented at court? To enjoy themselves? Not a bit of it. They come to find husbands. And why do all the males leave their estates to the doubtful care of bailiffs just at the time when crops are being planted? To find wives, of course, or at least to look over that new crop to find if there is anyone worth getting leg-shackled to.''

''The Marriage Mart!'' Fairfax commented. ''You are right, of course, Sedge. You have a very blunt way of speaking. But then, perhaps that is why I have tolerated for so long a friend who drags me protesting from my home and children and proceeds to drink my town house dry of brandy. What kind of wife am I looking for? I don't know. What does any man look for? Beauty, charm, a good body, good lineage, youth. Not too talkative. Cleanliness. Good teeth. I am running out of ideas, Sedge. It is too late in the day for thought.'' He yawned hugely again.

''Love?'' his friend prompted. ''You haven't mentioned love, Fairfax. That sweet nothing that all the females dream about. Are you looking to be knocked speechless by that one-and-only lady who was made in heaven for you?''

Fairfax grimaced. ''I chose my first wife that way, Sedge,'' he said. ''That sort of thing happens only once in a lifetime. No, if I marry again, it will not be for love. And if I do marry again, my friend, it will have to be someone I meet in the next few months or someone from close to home. Whatever I was like five years ago when I met Susan, now I am a homebody. And I am missing Amy and Claire already, though we left home only three days ago. I don't think London will see much of me after this Season until it is time to bring Amy to market. What a ghastly thought. It calls for more brandy.'' He jumped to his feet and was soon busy at the decanter.

''You should be able to choose within a week if you so wish,'' Sedgeworth said, swirling his drink in his glass and taking a mouthful. ''That one little miss at your godmother's this afternoon was clearly rendered witless by the sight of you. I thought her eyes would dislodge themselves from their sockets.''

"Miss Crawley?" Fairfax said in some surprise. "A mere schoolgirl, Sedge. Though I suppose she must be out, or she would not be paying afternoon calls with her mother. Good God! I must be getting old. I scarcely even noticed the chit. Was she pretty?"

"Passably, I suppose," his friend replied. "I didn't observe her too closely either. What a bore of a day. Nothing but visits and more visits. Is that to set the pattern for the next few months, Fairfax?"

His friend laughed. "You brought it on yourself, Sedge," he said. "Besides, I don't believe you hate socializing as much as you pretend. After all, you must do plenty of it with all the traveling you do. You charmed my godmother and my aunt quite outrageously."

"They are sensible females," Sedgeworth commented. "And then, there was the visit to Joy. My sister and I were very close to each other when we grew up. Now I rarely see her. Good Lord! Three children already. It seems scarcely possible."

"Anyway," Fairfax said, "our duty calls have been made now, Sedge. All that is left for us to do is enjoy ourselves for the next two months. Starting with Aunt Hazel's ball the night after tomorrow. There is nothing like starting with a flourish, eh?"

His friend pulled a face. "You have decided to go then?" he asked in a voice of gloom. "You did not give your aunt a definite acceptance."

"Why wait?" Fairfax said with a shrug. "The market has been open for business for a few weeks already, Sedge. We must begin to bid before we are doomed to everyone else's leavings."

Sedgeworth put his empty glass down beside him. "You have changed, Fairfax," he said, eyeing his friend with a slightly tipsy frown. "I never knew you so cynical."

"Five years is a long time," Fairfax said. "Remember that we have not seen each other for that long, Sedge, except for the last month, of course. But for that month you have seen me only in my home setting. I am nine-

and-twenty now, no longer the eager boy I was still when I met Susan. Marrying and begetting are serious business and tedious business. I am not thoroughly convinced that I would not be better off to remain a widower. But then, the girls need a mother, of course. Curses, Sedge! Why did you have to arrive to shake me out of my comfortable gloom and force me to start living again? I was quite contented the way I was."

"You looked it!" Sedgeworth said scornfully. "I did not once see you smile in the first two weeks of my stay at Templeton Hall. You cared nothing for anything except your daughters. It is time to live again, friend, even if life is painful. It comes along only once for each of us."

"Pearls of wisdom, indeed!" the viscount said with a grin. "When you begin to become reflective, Sedge, I know it is time to take ourselves to bed. What time is it, anyway? How many hours past midnight? Ugh! I'm just not used to late nights these days."

"You had better get some practice, then," Sedgeworth said. "Balls and such events, Fairfax. Beginning the day after tomorrow."

Fairfax grimaced and got to his feet. "To bed, Sedge," he said. "Or if you wish to stay up, you will have to be content with the brandy decanter for company. I am off."

Sedgeworth yawned loudly. "That sounds like a good idea," he said. "Bed, I mean. One day gone and how many to go? No, don't answer that question, Fairfax. I'm not sure I want to know the gloomy total."

Four young ladies were sheltering from the unseasonable heat of May the following afternoon. There was a garden party in progress and many guests basked in the bright sunshine on the lawns, conversing, drinking cool beverages, strolling perhaps to the cooler shade of the terrace before the house. Three young men who had been with the four ladies for a while had just strolled back to the house to join a few other guests who had taken shelter from the glare of the sun.

The four ladies were all sitting in the shade cast by two large oak trees, their light muslin dresses arranged carefully about them. Miss Honor Jamieson held a frilled blue parasol above her head, but it was quite unnecessary as protection against the sunlight. Its use perhaps owed more to the fact that it matched exactly the shade of her slippers and sash and complemented the lighter blue shade of her muslin gown and bonnet. She was noticeably the loveliest of the four, having been blessed with a small but shapely figure, dark glossy curls, and a face whose features were faultless.

"When I marry," she said, continuing a discussion that had been in progress for several minutes, "it will be to the most handsome man in London. I do believe I could tolerate extravagance or even some of the lesser vices, but I really do not think I could bear a plain man."

Prudence Crawley brushed some grass from her skirt. "Oh, but love is so much more important, Honor," she said. "Handsome features do not last very long, you know, especially if the man indulges too heavily in drink or eats to excess. But love continues to the grave and even beyond."

"Well, of course love is important, Prue," Honor agreed. "But I believe I can love only a very handsome man."

"I have little choice of whom I will marry," Alexandra Vye said with a resigned sigh. "There is no point in my dreaming of either handsome looks or love. Papa says I must marry a title, and Mama says I must wed someone from home. Do you have any idea how few single titled gentlemen live in the West Country? And even fewer of them happen to be in London this Season. I sometimes despair of ever finding a husband."

Honor shuddered and twirled her parasol. "Thank heaven Mama and Papa are more enlightened," she said. "I have a large enough dowry that I need not look only for wealth. They have said I may choose whom I will, provided only that he is not a chimney sweep."

All four young ladies laughed.

"And what about you, Jane?" Honor asked, turning to her cousin, Miss Jane Matthews.

"I do not ask for wealth or good looks or love," Jane replied. "I ask only for an amiable gentleman with whom I might be comfortable."

Honor pulled a face. "How dreadfully dull!" she said. "Surely you would not marry just anyone, Jane."

"Absolutely not," her cousin agreed. "Amiable gentlemen do not abound, you know. And even those there are do not necessarily flock to make me their offers. I do not have your beauty, Honor, or the freshness of youth that all of you have. I am three-and-twenty. Quite on the shelf and almost a confirmed spinster." She smiled cheerfully.

"It must be just awful to be that old and not married," Alexandra said with lamentable absence of tact. "Have you never wanted to marry, Jane?"

"Indeed I have," Jane replied. "Ever since I was eighteen and brought here for my first Season, in fact. Unfortunately, wanting and achieving are vastly different things. I had an offer during that Season that I would now accept cheerfully. But at that time I was as you three are now. I dreamed of making a dazzling marriage with a handsome gentleman with whom I would be head over ears in love. I went home to Yorkshire still dreaming. And that is where I have been ever since, until Aunt Cynthia and Uncle Alfred invited me to join them here for Honor's come-out."

"How dreadful!" Prudence said, wide-eyed.

Jane smiled. "The years have not been wasted," she said. "I have grown up since I was here last and now realize that amiability is the most important quality in a gentleman. Good looks, as you said, Prudence, quickly fade, and I am sure that romantic love does too. Character traits are longer-lasting and are something on which a good marriage can be built. Respect and affection can grow in a marriage if husband and wife like and respect each other."

"Well, if that is the sort of attitude that age brings,"

Honor said feelingly, "I hope I am never three-and-twenty, Jane. Give me a handsome man and I will promise to live happily ever after. Really, though, there are so few to fit the description in London. I am mortally disappointed. They must have all enlisted and are wasting themselves with the armies in Belgium or in America. Only the plain, ordinary ones remain. Look at Ambie and Harry and Max." She waved a hand in the direction of the house, into which the three young men had disappeared a few minutes before."

"You should not complain, Honor!" Alexandra said indignantly. "Wherever you go, a trail of lovelorn gentlemen follows. If that would only happen to me, I should not care that they looked ordinary. Anyway, Max is quite handsome, I think, though not very tall."

"You are not right about one thing, anyway, Honor," Prudence said. "The most handsome man in all England happens to be in London at this very moment. At least, I would wager he is the most handsome."

"Pooh!" Honor said scornfully. "Then he must be that chimney sweep Mama and and Papa warned me against. If there were such a man of our class in town, I should have found him long ago, Prue, and raced him off to the altar before the rest of you could even catch your breath."

"Ah, but he has only just arrived," Prudence said. "And I have first claim on him, Honor, for I was the first to see him."

"I daresay the midwife was the person to have that pleasure," Honor said with a tinkling laugh. "But tell all, Prue, my love. I do believe you are just teasing. And it is a most cruel joke."

"He was at Grandmama's yesterday when Mama and I were visiting," Prudence said. "Grandmama is his godmother, and he had come to pay his respects the day after his arrival. I declare I fell in love with him the instant he walked through the door. I could do nothing for the remainder of our visit but gawk at him with my mouth hanging open. I still do not believe he can be real. Tall and built like a god. Dark, thick hair that would make any girl's fingers itch to touch. The most perfect face I have ever set eyes on. Blue eyes—really blue, not gray. And one expressive eyebrow—the left, I think. Anyway, it made me turn quite weak at the knees. And he is here for the rest of the Season!''

"You must have been imagining things,'' Honor said. "I have quite given up hope of meeting such a paragon this year, Prue. You must not raise all our hopes like this unless you are quite sure of your facts.''

"You will see for yourself soon enough,'' Prudence assured her. "Though I shall probably be very sorry when you do. You will doubtless take him right from under my nose, Honor. He is bound to admire you. He is in search of a wife, Grandmama says.''

"This becomes more and more promising,'' Honor said, her parasol twirling wildly above her head.

"Yes,'' Prudence said. "His first wife died a year ago quite tragically while giving birth to their third child. He has two little girls and is badly in need of a mother for them.''

"A definite obstacle,'' Honor said. "I am not over-fond of children, especially some other woman's. Oh well, we cannot demand perfection of life, I suppose.''

"I hardly dare breathe,'' Alexandra said. "Is he by any chance a titled gentleman from the West Country, Prue?''

"More south than west, I think,'' Prudence told her. "But a viscount, Alex.''

Alexandra sighed.

"When are we likely to meet this Adonis, do you think?'' Honor asked. "The Pendletons' ball tomorrow night?''

"Very probably,'' Prudence said. "Lady Pendleton is his aunt.''

"If he is as handsome as you say, Prue,'' Honor said, "he will be easily recognizable. But do tell his name.''

"Oh,'' Prudence said, "how foolish of me. Viscount Fairfax.''

"Never heard of him,'' said Honor.

"Oh," Jane blurted, "I have." She flushed when all eyes turned her way. "He was in London during my first Season. And I assure you that everything Prudence has said is true. He is certainly the most handsome man I have ever seen."

"And why did you not attach his interest then?" Honor asked.

Jane laughed. "Lord Fairfax?" she said. "He did not even know I existed, Honor. He had eyes only for Lady Susan Richardson. She was the most lovely creature. And is she now dead? They had a whirlwind courtship. They were wed before the end of the Season."

"He is the impulsive sort, then," Honor said. "I am beginning to really like what I hear. But were you very in love with him, Jane? Confess."

"I doubt if there was a lady below the age of thirty who was not," Jane admitted. "And I doubt if there was a gentleman below the age of thirty who did not dislike him heartily."

"A wager!" Honor said, snapping shut her parasol and regarding her three companions with sparkling eyes. "Let us wager on which of us will have him. We will refuse to accept competition from anyone else, of course. What shall we wager?"

"Now you are being ridiculous, Honor," Prudence said gloomily. "You know very well that you will win. There would be no competition at all."

"Rubbish!" Honor said kindly. "None of you are antidotes, even Jane with her advanced age."

"Not me," Alexandra said sadly. "I do not believe Mama would accept the South Country."

"Jane?"

Jane laughed. "Of course not, Honor," she said. "Why would someone like Lord Fairfax even look at a rather plain woman of advanced age, as you put it, when he might have his pick of all the lovely debutantes?"

"Jane," her cousin said crossly, "you might as well take to wearing caps. You certainly behave like a dried-out old spinster already."

"Besides," Jane said, "the viscount would not fit my requirements at all. How could one possibly be comfortable with a man like him? I should be in a constant state of anxiety whenever another female was within five miles of him. No, my dear cousin, he is all yours. If you can catch him, that is."

"Oh, I have no fear of that," Honor said, speaking with characteristic lack of modesty.

She really thought she had carried it off quite well, Jane thought when she was alone in her own room later. She had been so shocked when Prudence mentioned the name of the man she had been describing that she had been unable to stop her reaction.

She had admitted that she had been in love with Viscount Fairfax five years before, but only in a general way, in the way that any woman might be in love with an extraordinarily handsome man. They had not suspected that her love for him had in many ways ruined her life. That was perhaps a little exaggerated, but maybe not. Had it not been for her painful infatuation with the viscount during that Season, she might well have accepted Mr. Saxton's offer and been living quite contentedly with him ever since in Oxford, where he had accepted a lecturing position at the university.

None of that was Lord Fairfax's fault, she had to admit. He really had not known of her existence. Even without the presence of Lady Susan and his great love for her, he would not have noticed Jane. Even now she was no beauty. But when she was eighteen she had really been very plain. Mama had lived in Yorkshire since her marriage and had little idea about London fashions. Yet she had had all of Jane's clothes made at home instead of waiting to engage a London modiste. Her clothes had been almost embarrassingly unfashionable. And her hairstyle! She still shuddered at the memory of the masses of ringlets that Mama's dresser had thought so becoming. She had also been somewhat overweight at the time and the ringlets had only served to accentuate the plump roundness of her face.

And she had been very eager and hopeful of finding love and of making a good match. Poor young Jane, the older Jane thought now. She had fallen painfully and hopelessly in love with Lord Fairfax. Not that she had ever held out any hope of attracting his notice. She had resigned herself to worshiping from afar. But even so she had cried and cried the night after the announcement of his betrothal appeared in the *Gazette*.

After the Season was over, she had been very depressed for several months before giving up forever all the fond hopes of romance she had taken to London with her. Love was not for her. Neither was glamour of any sort. She would consider herself lucky to make a marriage with a very ordinary gentleman. Contentment was what she would aim for. And that surely would not be beyond her grasp if the gentleman she married was amiable. All she asked for was her own home to manage, companionship, a few children. A dull prospect, perhaps, but very practical. Jane soon came to pride herself on her good sense.

And was that good sense now to be put to the test? She was to see the viscount again, and by Prudence's report he was as handsome as ever. Would her stomach stay in place when she first saw him? Or would it turn over rather painfully as it had always used to do?

She would find out the evening of the next day, she supposed, provided he really did put in an appearance at the Pendletons' ball. But she must not dwell on the thought. She must concentrate on the hope that Mr. Faford would sign her card. He was a gentleman whose interest she might fix if she set her mind to it. She had realized that fact for a few weeks now. He was neither handsome nor wealthy nor particularly young. But he was kindly and he was attainable, she believed.

# 2

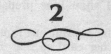

H onor was surrounded by her customary court of
admirers. She looked extremely beautiful, as usual,
Jane thought. Despite her comments of the day before
on the plainness of all the gentlemen she had met thus
far during the Season, she appeared to be enjoying
herself immensely. Her cheeks were flushed a becoming
shade of pink and her eyes sparkled. She waved a
peacock fan before her face. It matched exactly the
shade of her slippers and gloves and highlighted the
gleaming white of her lace-covered gown. Jane stood on
the outer fringes of the group, talking to a young man
who had just done her the courtesy of signing her card
for a country dance later in the evening.

Her card was half-filled and Jane was quite content.
She had danced the first two sets, although neither had
been solicited in advance. Uncle Alfred could be relied
upon to lead her out for one set, and Mr. Faford would
surely sign her card as soon as he arrived. He was late
already. And if she had to sit out a few dances, it would
not be the end of the world. Only the newest debutantes
considered such an eventuality a disaster. She would
merely sit with her aunt or find another acquaintance
with whom to converse for half an hour.

Jane smiled to herself. Honor had confided to her
before the opening set her chagrin at finding that she
had not one space left on her card.

"What if I find that there is someone else with whom
I particularly wish to dance?" she asked. "And what if
Viscount Fairfax makes an appearance and turns out to
be as handsome as you and Prue say? I shall burst with
frustration, Jane."

Jane laughed. "You must be the only female present

17

tonight to complain of a full card, Honor," she said.
"If I were you, I should be preparing to enjoy my
triumph."

Honor pulled a face. "But just look at these names!"
she said, opening her card so that Jane could see the
signatures scrawled next to the various sets. "There is
not one handsome face among them. Not one!"

"These poor gentlemen," Jane commented, her eyes
moving over the card. "You must be very demanding,
Honor. There are some very distinguished names here."

"Hm. 'Distinguished' is a word one uses when it
would be a lie to say 'handsome,' " Honor replied. "Oh
Lord, here comes Perry. At least I am thankful to be
able to tell him truthfully that I may not dance with
him. I swear, Jane, the poor boy has two left feet."

The next set was about to form. Jane could see her
uncle moving purposefully along the edge of the ballroom floor in their direction. Dear Uncle Alfred, she
thought, come to make sure that she would not have to
spend too many sets standing on the sidelines. She knew
that he would far prefer to be playing cards. She smiled.

And then beyond her uncle's advancing figure she
saw him. Viscount Fairfax. He had just entered the
ballroom and was standing in the doorway, his fingers
toying with a quizzing glass. Oh, he had not changed. If
anything, he was even more handsome now. The extra
years had added muscularity to his slender physique.
His hair was longer than he had used to wear it. And he
looked quite breathtakingly magnificent in black tight-
fitting evening coat and knee breeches, masses of
sparkling white lace at his neck and wrists. Even as she
returned her attention to her uncle, Jane felt it. Quite
unmistakably. That old churning of the stomach.

She put her hand in her uncle's and allowed him to
lead her into a set that still needed one couple. Lady
Pendleton had left the receiving line and was about to
start the dancing, but she had hurried over to greet her
nephew, Jane saw in one swift glance. He was still
standing just inside the doorway. There was another

gentleman with him, shorter, slightly stockier, his looks quite overshadowed by those of his companion.

Jane looked around for Honor. Her cousin was part of another set. She was talking animatedly to her partner and the couple beyond them. But she had seen him, Jane felt sure. There was an extra sparkle and self-consciousness to her behavior. She would be even more furious now that there were no dances to spare on her card. Poor Honor! Jane turned her attention to the music, which was beginning.

It was even more obvious at the end of the set that Honor had seen the viscount. She had her partner leave her in a part of the ballroom far removed from the spot where her mother sat conversing with a group of dowagers, and she was waving vigorously for her father to bring Jane to her. Jane saw as they approached that Lord Fairfax and his companion were quite close by, talking with their hostess.

"Jane!" Honor hissed, fanning herself so fast that her cousin could feel the breeze from where she stood. "Why did you not tell me? He is not just handsome. He is . . . handsome! I just have to dance with him. Max or Ambie will not mind releasing me from my obligation. You must partner one of them instead. You will not mind, will you?" She regarded Jane with wide, anxious eyes. "Dear Jane!"

Jane could not help smiling. "Really, Honor," she said, "you could not possibly be so rag-mannered. It just is not done to pass on your rejected partners to someone else. Or even simply to reject them, for that matter."

"Oh, but Max or Ambie will not mind," Honor insisted. "They are just like my brothers."

"I would guess that those two young gentlemen do not think of themselves in any such way," Jane said. "Besides, Honor, there are hosts of lovely girls here. How can you be sure that Lord Fairfax will even ask you?"

"But of course he will!" Honor said ingenuously.

"He has already noticed me, you know. I swear his eyes were on me for fully half of the last set. Oh, bother, Harry has spotted me and is on his way to claim his dance." She turned a dazzling smile on the tall, thin young man who was approaching.

Jane did not have a partner for that particular set, a quadrille. She looked around to see if any of her acquaintances was close by, saw that none was, and turned to make her way around the room to her aunt. However, Lord Pendleton blocked her way.

"Not dancing, Miss Matthews?" he asked. "I would lead you out m'self, my dear, if it weren't for this confounded gout. May I fetch you some lemonade?"

"No, really, my lord," Jane said. "I am not thirsty."

Lord Pendleton was in no hurry to move away. He stood and chatted amiably to Jane, watching the dancers as he did so. Jane too looked about her. The viscount, she could see, was dancing with Lady Pendleton, his companion with someone Jane did not know. Honor was sparkling, and dazzling the faithful Harry.

When the music drew to a close, Lady Pendleton joined her husband. She was on the arm of the viscount.

"Ah, Pendleton," she said in the rather masculine tones that characterized her, "there you are. You see, Michael did decide to put in an appearance after all. The scold I gave him two days ago had its effect."

The two men shook hands. "Glad you came, Michael," Lord Pendleton said. "And Sedgeworth too, I hope? Hazel would have been disappointed if you had not come. Not every woman can boast such a fine nephew, you know."

Jane felt decidedly awkward. She did not know whether she should stay beside Lord Pendleton or turn away and look elsewhere. Perhaps she should even move unobtrusively away. She took a step back and glanced toward the empty dance floor. Honor was crossing it, smiling dazzlingly at her cousin.

"Why, Jane, you naughty thing," she called teasingly as she approached nearer. "I have looked all over the place for you and only now saw that you were with Lord Pendleton.'' She smiled at the latter and fluttered her fan.

''My manners have certainly gone begging,'' his lordship said, turning to Jane and taking her by the elbow. ''I suppose you have not met my wife's nephew, my dear, since he has only recently arrived in London and has not been here for several years. May I present Michael Templeton, Viscount Fairfax? Miss Matthews is from the North, Michael. Niece of Jamieson. And Miss Jamieson is his daughter. She has been taking the *ton* quite by storm this year.'' He smiled kindly at a blushing Honor.

Lord Fairfax bowed. His eyes met Jane's briefly. They regarded her steadily and unsmilingly. She curtsied and muttered, ''My lord.'' But he had already turned to Honor, who was glowing with blushes and smiles and who must have been raising a veritable gale with her fan.

''I am so pleased to meet you, my lord,'' she said. ''You have chosen a splendid occasion on which to make your first appearance in public. I declare this is the greatest squeeze of the Season so far.''

He inclined his head. ''My aunt's ball always was one of the grandest affairs of the year, Miss Jamieson,'' he said. He did not smile, Jane noticed.

''The next dance is to be a waltz,'' Honor said, turning to Lady Pendleton and smiling brightly. ''I am so glad you included several this evening, ma'am. It is such a divine dance.''

''I have been told that no ball is fashionable if it is not included,'' Lady Pendleton said with a smile. ''I do hope you have been granted permission to dance it, my dear.''

''Oh yes,'' Honor assured her breathlessly. ''Lady Jersey was gracious enough to give me her approval almost two weeks ago.''

''You are fortunate,'' her hostess said. ''Some young ladies have to go through their entire first Season without the chance to practice the steps they have learned so diligently at home.''

"Miss Matthews," the quiet, low voice of Viscount Fairfax said, "would you honor me with your hand for this set? If you have no previous commitment, that is.''

Foolishly Jane glanced at Honor, almost as if she were about to ask her permission. That young lady's fan had ceased its motion and her mouth gaped a little. But only for a moment. She smiled brightly as Jane turned to the viscount.

"Thank you, my lord," she said. "I am free for this set.''

He held out a hand to her, and she placed her own on top of it.

"You are a lucky chap, Michael," Lord Pendleton said with a wink. "This is the supper dance.''

Jane felt as if she were in the middle of a dream. The hand beneath her own was slim yet quite firm. She was actually touching him. Lord Fairfax! He stopped when they had walked a few feet onto the dance floor. The music was beginning already. She turned to face him and found that she had to tilt her head back to look into his face. Her head reached only to his chin. She placed her left hand on one of his broad shoulders and the other in his outstretched hand. His right hand came to rest firmly behind her waist. She concentrated on following his lead as he began to dance.

It was pure accident that she had been presented to him. She really did not know Lord Pendleton well. He had merely been playing the courteous host. And Lord Fairfax must have felt obliged to invite her to dance. Her, rather than Honor. Of course, she had been presented first. Tomorrow he probably would not know her again if he met her at another function. But there was this half-hour that she was to spend with him. And supper afterward. It would be something to remember. Five years before, she would have been ready to swoon quite away at such an unexpected encounter. Jane smiled to herself at her own very schoolgirlish response to a perfectly ordinary occurrence.

"You waltz very well," the viscount said. "You must have had some practice."

"Actually I was shamed into learning the waltz," Jane said. "The first few times I tried, I tripped all over my partners' feet. Then one young man told me to relax and feel the music in my bones. He said dancing with me was somewhat like dragging around a sack of meal. I thought him impertinent at the time."

His left eyebrow rose. "And you do not now?" he asked. "I hope you gave him a thorough set-down."

"Oh, undoubtedly I did," Jane replied. "He was my brother."

She expected him to laugh at the absurd story. She felt uncomfortable when he did not even smile.

"How do you take to London after living in the North of England?" he asked. "Are you quite dazzled by the splendor of it all, or do you find yourself longing for the peace and quiet of the countryside?"

Jane considered. "A little of both," she said. "I certainly would not like to live permanently in town or even to come here annually during the Season. But once in a while it is pleasant to have all the activity and the crowds around you. I would not say I am dazzled. I was here five years ago, you see, and discovered then that nothing is essentially changed when one moves to a different setting. I suppose it is because one has to take oneself with one. It is a lowering thought to realize that."

"You sound as if you do not enjoy your own company, Miss Matthews," Fairfax remarked.

"On the contrary," she said. "I have learned a great deal in five years. And one thing I have learned is to like myself. If we cannot like ourselves, we can hardly expect anyone else to do so, can we?"

"I suppose not," he said. "Sometimes it is difficult, though. To like oneself, I mean."

Jane smiled and was suddenly very aware of his blue eyes looking directly into hers, and from so very close. She broke eye contact with him in some confusion and glanced around her. She was just in time to see Honor being led onto the dance floor by Ambrose Leighton. Why was he so late claiming her? But the answer was clear to Jane almost before the question was formed in her mind. Honor must have excused herself from her obligation to him, certain that the viscount would solicit her hand for this set. How humiliated she must feel to be caught thus on the sidelines, minus the partner she had been so sure of.

"Do you miss your daughters, my lord?" she asked, turning back to her partner. "I understand you left them in the country."

His eyebrows rose. "You know of them?" he asked.

Jane felt herself flushing. "I daresay everyone in the *ton* knows as much," she said. "You may not arrive in London and expect to remain anonymous, you know."

"I had forgotten," he said. "I thought I would be quite the stranger here for a while. It is years since I was last here. In fact, it must have been the year you were here. It is strange that we never met. But you asked about my daughters. Yes, I do miss them. They are a constant source of delight to me. The elder is only four. However, they are in the hands of a nurse who lavishes all the love of her heart on them. She was my nurse too, and I can vouch for the fact that they will receive the best of care."

Conversation between them flowed with surprising ease for the rest of the waltz and for the first part of the supper while they sat alone. She told him of her life on the Yorkshire moors, a life which was saved from loneliness by the presence of a village close by and the homes of her brother and sister and her numerous nieces and nephews. He told her something about his estate in Hampshire. She found him quite charming. Although he had solicited her company only out of politeness, he did not give the appearance of boredom or eagerness to be gone in order to find himself a more attractive partner. She had expected somehow that he would be a trifle arrogant.

Fairfax was not bored. In fact, he was beginning to relax somewhat. He felt quite fortunate in his first choice of partner. Not that Miss Matthews was the sort of female he would have chosen if he had been able to look around him freely. She was not a girl in her first bloom and there was nothing remarkably pretty about her. That little cousin of hers was far more to his taste. But sometimes good manners had to take precedence over personal inclination. His uncle had presented her first, the dancing was about to begin, and he had felt obliged to ask if she were free.

He had thought he was to be stuck with a silly partner for all of one waltz and the supper when she had told the story about her brother. But it was not so. In fact, she seemed to be a woman of some sense. Years before, when he was single, he had put up with all sorts of feminine silliness. And the sillier the female, it had seemed, the more she had to say. Strangely, he had not minded at the time. Empty-headed, vaporish girls had made him feel more masculine and virile, he supposed. But he did not think he would be able to stand that now that he was older.

Miss Matthews might not be a beauty, but at least she had something interesting to say. He supposed she had given up trying to lure a husband with all the usual feminine wiles. She was settling into the life of a spinster, no doubt. Though he must not be unkind. She could not be older than five-and-twenty at the most. Perhaps no older than Susan would have been. Yet he could not imagine Susan having matured into a life of quiet good sense.

Fairfax raised his hand in the direction of Joseph Sedgeworth, who had just entered the supper room with a young lady on his arm. That same young lady who had been at his godmother's two days before, if he was not mistaken. His friend led her toward the table. Fairfax got to his feet.

"Miss Crawley," he said with a bow, "how good to see you again. You are looking very lovely."

The girl blushed to the roots of her red hair before he turned away to present his friend to Miss Matthews. Before they could all sit down, Miss Jamieson had also arrived at their table on the arm of a young man whom she introduced as Ambrose Leighton.

Miss Jamieson did most of the talking for the rest of the supper. She was indeed very lovely with her dark hair and creamy complexion and very shapely figure. And she was very well aware of her own beauty and charm. He should be enchanted, Fairfax thought. In fact, he was attracted. There was a sparkle and an animation about the girl, although it was somehow counteracted by her obvious vanity. But he was also amused. The little chit was all the rage, his uncle had said. Yet she seemed such a very young girl. Had Susan been like this when he had fallen so headlong in love with her five years before? Probably she had, though physically the two girls did not resemble each other except in size.

Fairfax found that his amusement grew during supper. Miss Jamieson was clearly setting her cap at him. Indeed, Miss Crawley seemed very aware of him too, though she was blushing and tongue-tied and looked anywhere but at him. He felt so much older than he had five years before. He had lived through what seemed like a lifetime of experiences since then. He had not expected to draw female attention with as much ease as he had as a younger man. He had expected that the very young girls, at least, would look on him as an older man not worthy of a second glance. It might be amusing to find that he still had the old power to attract.

"Miss Jamieson," he said as the guests around them began to stroll back toward the ballroom, "I suppose it is too much to hope that there is any space left on your dancing card?"

"By coincidence, I have not promised the next set to anyone, my lord," she said, glancing coquettishly at him with her large dark eyes. "The reason being that three latecomers were arguing over which should be granted the last dance on my card. I was so cross with them that I told them that they might all take themselves off and quarrel elsewhere. I wanted nothing more to do with them for this evening."

Fairfax found that he had to make a great effort not to laugh aloud. This little creature was quite delightful. She lied without a flicker of guilt showing on her face. Who was the poor fellow that was about to be thrown over for him? he wondered.

"Then might I have the honor, ma'am?" he asked, pushing back his chair and rising to his feet.

"Oh," she said, "how wonderful! I must confess that I was not looking forward to the next dance. I was afraid that some people might think I was a wallflower."

"Wallflower?" Fairfax repeated. "You? Never, ma'am. I am sure anyone with any sense would have divined the truth immediately."

She blushed becomingly and placed a hand on his.

Sedgeworth was soliciting Miss Matthews' hand for the set, Fairfax noticed. In fact, the two of them had been talking quietly for the last five minutes or so.

"What a perfectly divine ball!" Honor said with a sigh in the carriage later.

"You enjoyed yourself, did you, puss?" her father said with a chuckle. "I should think so too. You seem to have all the young bucks in London chasing after you."

"Oh, they don't signify at all," Honor said with a dismissive gesture. "All mere boys. Now, Viscount Fairfax is what I call a man."

"And it is said he is in search of a wife," Lady Jamieson said. "His poor first wife died, you know."

"Don't you think he is just divine, Jane?" Honor

said. "And will you not change your mind now and wager with me on which of us will get him?"

"Get him!" Jane repeated with a laugh. "As if we would be the only two contestants, Honor. The man danced with at least half a dozen other ladies tonight."

"We must not be daunted by the fact," Honor said. "After all, we were his first choices. And you were his very first, Jane. Maybe he already has a *tendre* for you and I shall have to fight desperately to win him from you."

Jane laughed outright. "Honor," she said, "you are so delightfully transparent. The idea of Lord Fairfax's developing a *tendre* for me is so absurd that you know I am bound to disclaim the truth of any such suggestion and assure you that he must prefer you. And we both know that I was not really his first choice. The poor man did not have much alternative but to ask me, if he did not wish to appear ill-mannered."

"Do you really think he preferred me?" Honor asked eagerly. "Indeed it would not be so very strange if he did, would it? All those horrid plain men seem to prefer me to any other girl. It would be just too rotten if the only handsome man in town were to prove the exception. Do you think I may expect a visit tomorrow afternoon, Jane? Mama?"

"I should not be at all surprised, my love," her mother assured her. "You are easily the loveliest debutante this year and he must have an eye for beauty, for apparently his first wife was very pretty. Not that Jane is an antidote, of course. In fact, Jane, you look quite well in that particular shade of green. You should wear it more often. You could easily pass for twenty."

"Should I accept an invitation to go driving, do you think?" Honor asked in some anxiety. "Or should I appear more aloof at first?"

Jane burst into laughter. "Honor," she advised, "why do you not let the viscount put in an appearance before you face tricky problems like that?"

"Oh, but one must be prepared for any eventuality," Honor said. "Don't you agree, Papa?"

"Am I going to have to spend a fortune on a grand wedding this summer already, puss?" Sir Alfred Jamieson asked with a chuckle.

"Oh, Papa!" Honor protested. "Do not tease. I am very serious."

"Jamieson, I do wish you would have a word with the coachman about the mad way he turns this corner into the driveway," his wife said crossly, swaying against him as the carriage turned.

"You should hold on to the strap, my love," he replied mildly. "But I shall certainly speak to him."

# 3

**H**onor was doomed to disappointment the next day. Though she had her usual array of bouquets and nosegays delivered during the morning, and though several visitors arrived during the afternoon, including three gentlemen admirers, Viscount Fairfax was nowhere in evidence.

"It is not that I really expected him," she assured Jane after the last visitor had left and they were both climbing the stairs to their rooms to change for a late-afternoon drive. "After all, he has scarcely settled in London yet, and we did meet for the first time only last evening. And I am not conceited or anything, Jane. But I did think perhaps he would not consider it too forward to pay me a short call. Or to pay you a call. We must remember that he might be nursing a desperate *tendre* for you." She laughed merrily.

Honor's remaining hope for that day was that the viscount would be at Mrs. Tate's musicale that evening. It promised to be a very dull affair, but he might be there. Perhaps no one had yet told him what a bluestocking Mrs. Tate was. Honor was unusually subdued during the drive back home.

"I don't understand it," she said. "If the man is in search of a wife, why did he keep himself at home this evening? You would think that he would have wished to follow up his advantage of last evening, would you not, Mama?"

It was Jane who answered. "How do you know that he stayed at home," she asked, "merely because he was not at Mrs. Tate's?"

"What?" Honor asked, alarmed. "Do you think

some other females have had him all to themselves tonight, Jane? That would be vastly unfair.''

Jane joked with her cousin and was genuinely amused by the strange mixture of conceit and anxiety she displayed. But for herself she was not happy that Fairfax had decided to return to town just at the time when she was there. She found herself unable to put him from her mind for more than five minutes at a time. She had relived over and over the hour she had spent in his company the evening before. How very charming he had been, and friendly. She wished somehow that he had appeared cold or arrogant. At least then perhaps she could have persuaded herself that she had loved merely a handsome exterior for five years.

She was disturbed at seeing him again, excited by the fact that at last she had met him, danced with him, conversed with him. And she knew that for the next several weeks she would live for the glimpses she might have of him and the remote chance that he would recognize and acknowledge her, even talk to her on occasion. She was every bit as bad as Honor except that she kept her feelings to herself and had none of Honor's confidence in attracting the viscount's notice.

She did not wish to feel this way. It was childish to worship an unattainable man. It was demeaning. She was a grown woman who had spent painful years building self-respect. Was she to lose it now so easily in the consciousness she must have of her inferiority to him in the power to attract? She had spent those same years learning to face life with calm common sense. She knew—or thought she knew—exactly what she wanted of life. She wanted to find a husband with whom she could be comfortable, and she wanted to devote her life to that husband and to his home and children.

Mr. Faford called the afternoon after the ball and took her driving in the park afterward. He talked about his prospects. He had a comfortable income from land he had inherited from his father. He would inherit more on the death of his grandfather. And once he had married off his younger sister, he would be without dependents. His reason for telling these things to Jane seemed quite obvious to her. It was not vanity, surely, that told her that she might expect to receive an offer from him before the Season was out.

She should be preparing her mind to accept Mr. Faford. In fact, she must accept him or face a probable future as a spinster in Yorkshire. That part of the country did not abound in eligible bachelors. Marriage to Mr. Faford would offer her just the sort of life she had been looking for. Yet now, only one day after seeing Viscount Fairfax again, she was feeling dissatisfaction. Dreams of love and romance were forcing themselves on her. Ridiculous, childish, quite unrealistic dreams. Was she to give up her chance to marry merely because of that vague longing? What could she gain from such an attitude but a long and lonely future?

Jane had been quite relieved not to see Fairfax at Mrs. Tate's musicale. She hoped that perhaps they would not see a great deal of him at all. She might be safe if that were so.

It was three days before she saw Lord Fairfax again, in a quite unexpected setting. She made a visit to Hookham's Library that morning, taking a maid for company. Honor, who normally read a great deal, had given up the pastime since her arrival in London, along with painting, her great passion. She dreaded more than anything the label of bluestocking. Jane drew a copy of Mr. Fielding's *Joseph Andrews* from a shelf. She had heard of it. It was reputed to be a satire on Mr. Richardson's *Pamela*.

"Good day, Miss Matthews," a man's voice said from close behind her.

She whirled around. She would know that voice anywhere, having spent an hour listening to it a few evenings before. She smiled. So he recalled her name too.

"Good morning, my lord," she said. "Is it not a beautiful day?"

"Indeed, yes," he agreed. "Lovely enough to make me almost wish that I were back in the country. Are you wondering if that book is worth reading?"

"I have heard of it," she said, "and have been wishing to read it. I have read *Pamela* and disliked it heartily. I should be quite delighted to hear someone make fun of it."

"And Fielding does a good job of that," Fairfax said. "In fact, it is a good book in its own right. But you surprise me, Miss Matthews. Most ladies of my acquaintance swoon quite away at the sentiment of *Pamela.*"

"I would like to give the girl a good shake for marrying Mr. B.," said Jane.

He did not smile, but there was a glint of amusement in his eyes for one moment. "Indeed?" he said. "You are not a romantic, I perceive, ma'am?"

"Not in that sense!" she said decisively. "The poor girl is facing only misery in her marriage. She has nothing whatsoever in common with her husband, and she is not accustomed to the life she will be called upon to lead. Moreover, that man will tire of her quickly enough, and then what will romance have gained her?"

"And yet the book describes the first few years of the marriage as being quite idyllic," the viscount pointed out.

"I do not believe a word of it," Jane said.

"Well, ma'am," he said, "I shall be interested in hearing your assessment of Fielding's satire. I believe you will ejoy it. Do you plan to attend Lady Merriot's soiree this evening?"

"Yes," Jane said. "My aunt has accepted our invitation."

"I shall look forward to seeing you there," he said. "Ah, here you are, Sedge. Chosen your books, have you? I have discovered that Miss Matthews is a reader too."

Mr. Sedgeworth bowed and smiled at her. "How do

you do, Miss Matthews?'' he said. ''You had better make your escape while you may, or Fairfax will be pressing all the volumes from his own library on you, and you will feel obliged to read them.''

''Is that what I do to you, Sedge?'' Fairfax asked. ''I did not realize you were such a reluctant reader. But you are quite safe, Miss Matthews. My library is in the country.''

The gentlemen bowed and excused themselves soon after. Jane stared foolishly after them. Then she found herself smiling and having to restrain the urge to execute a little jig of exuberance. She turned toward the bookshelf and pretended to examine her book while she brought herself under control. Here she was again, she thought in some disgust, behaving worse than a girl of sixteen. She was wild with excitement merely because a handsome gentleman had had the civility to exchange pleasantries with her for a few minutes. She forced herself to think of Mr. Sedgeworth. He appeared to be a pleasant and well-mannered gentleman. Let her concentrate her attention on him whenever the viscount was close by.

She would see them again tonight. And he had said that he looked forward to seeing her. Mere civility, of course. She must not refine too much on it. She would very probably receive no more than a distant bow of recognition. And Honor would be turning the full force of her charm on him. She appeared every bit as infatuated as Jane herself did. Jane sighed. That thought, if any, brought her feet firmly back to the ground. Why should he pay any attention to her when there was Honor to look at and talk to and flirt with? Not to mention any number of other pretty girls, all well below the age of twenty.

Jane looked at the copy of *Joseph Andrews* clasped in her hand, shrugged her shoulders at it, and took it across to the librarian's desk.

Viscount Fairfax sat in his library, definitely his

favorite room. The rest of his town house always seemed too feminine. His mother used it far more often than he did, of course. It was not a house in which a man could relax. But here he could slouch back in a comfortable chair of faded leather, his booted feet, crossed at the ankles, resting on the desk, his hands clasped behind his head.

He had not realized how much he had missed his solitariness until now when he was alone again. Sedgeworth was driving Miss Crawley to the park for the fashionable hour. He had not escaped without a great deal of teasing and warnings that he would be caught in parson's mousetrap before the summer's end if he did not have a care. Fairfax was greatly enjoying the company of his friend. But sometimes it was good to be in one's own company. And he was used to being alone.

For the last year he had spent the bulk of his time alone or with Amy and Claire. Indeed, he had been alone much of the time even while Susan was still alive. They had not really shared a close companionship. What was it that Miss Matthews had said that morning? Pamela and Mr. B. had nothing whatsoever in common. That description fit him and Susan all too well. They had fallen madly in love during that spring five years before and had rushed into marriage even before the Season came to an end. All had been wonderful for perhaps the first year. It had taken that long for the glamour to wear off. Perhaps it would have happened sooner if there had not been the birth of a child to look forward to.

When had he first faced the truth that he and Susan were from totally different worlds? After Amy was born, perhaps? He had been so excited, so proud to have a daughter, and one who promised to be as dark and as strong-featured as he. Susan had hardly stopped crying for a week after the birth and had forced him to hire a wet nurse for the child. She had been bitterly disappointed not to have a son.

He had been touched at first, though distressed to see how little Amy's presence was welcomed by her mother.

He had thought Susan's reaction was all remorse that she had disappointed him by not presenting him with an heir. But she had told him the truth through her tears. She hated living at Templeton Hall. She hated the neighbors and the dull life of the country. She planned to have him take her back to London and travel with her to the various spas and even overseas. If she had produced a son, they could have left almost immediately. There would be no further need for her to bear children. She would see to it, of course, that the child always had the best of care at home.

Lace handkerchief in one hand, hartshorn in the other, she had bewailed the fact that now they would have to spend at least another year in the country until she had produced his heir. The prospect horrified her, though she was quite determined that it must be done. Susan had a very strong sense of duty.

He had realized, just as if scales had suddenly been taken from his eyes, just how different she was from him. She took completely for granted that he would be as eager as she to abandon his child and his home in pursuit of a life of pleasure. She assumed that he, like her, would see Amy as a child of little or no account. She had no conception of the fact that his whole life revolved around his home and his small family. It did not occur to her that perhaps he would be perfectly happy with a dozen daughters and no sons if that was the way their family developed. He was not fanatical about perpetuating his dynasty, as so many men were.

They had both changed after Amy's birth. Susan had become more openly restless and petulant. She talked with nothing but contempt and impatience about their neighbors. She became obsessed with the need to conceive again, though she seemed to have lost any real enjoyment she might have had of the sexual act itself. He began to spend more and more time with his infant daughter or alone. He read a great deal, spent hours in the music room playing the pianoforte, though Susan thought it an unmanly activity, and walked and rode about his estate, becoming far better acquainted with his hand and his tenants than he had ever been before.

It had not been a good marriage. There was nothing vicious about Susan. She was no different from what she had appeared to be when he first met her: a sociable and beautiful and essentially empty-headed young lady. He found that he could not blame her for not sharing his interests in life. Perhaps he was more to blame. He must have appeared to be very like her during the Season in London. Certainly he had thrown himself with gay abandon into all the glittering activities of the Season.

But whoever was to blame or not to blame, the fact was that they were two vastly different people doomed to spend their lives together. And the relationship had deteriorated further after the birth of Claire—beautiful little Claire, who even as a small baby had resembled her mother very closely. He had not wanted the third child so soon. Susan needed time to recover her health, he had told her. And the doctor too had warned her against having another child within two or three years. But she had been almost demented with the need to produce a son so that she could start living again, as she put it.

And she had died along with their third daughter. Fairfax found now that he was closely observing his one Hessian boot beating rhythmically against the other on top of the desk. He would never forget her screams giving place to moans as the hours passed. He had gone to her in the end and held her cold hand while she delivered the stillborn child and died less than an hour later. He did not believe he would ever forgive himself.

Poor Susan. He had not loved her after he had stopped being *in* love with her. He had not even particularly liked her. But she had been a living person and his wife. It had been his duty to protect her from harm, not kill her with the bearing of his children. She had certainly not deserved to die. He would never quite rid himself of his guilt. It would help perhaps if he could just stop the thought from constantly intruding that he was fortunate to be released so soon from an unsatisfactory marriage.

Fairfax deliberately stopped the motion of his foot. There was really no point in going over such thoughts again. He had come close to driving himself mad with them during the months following Susan's death. Sedgeworth—good, loyal Sedge, who had never stopped writing a regular monthly letter during the five years when they had not seen each other—had been his savior, coming to stay at Templeton Hall when he perceived from his friend's letters that he was mortally depressed, and persuading him finally that he needed to seek new amusements for a few months. It was Sedge too who had suggested London and a search for a new wife.

And did he really desire a new bride? Fairfax asked himself now. Would it not be disloyal to the memory of Susan to marry again, and so soon? And did he really wish to be in that situation again, bound for life to a woman to whom he might not be suited after all? Of course, there was Sedge's argument that Amy and Claire needed a mother. He supposed it was true. They were very young now and received a great deal of love from their nurse. And when he was at home, he spent several hours of each day with them, playing with them, taking them for walks, teaching them to swim, reading to them. But in a few years' time they were going to need a mother to teach them how they should behave as young ladies. Sedge had mentioned an heir too. Why did so many people assume that he was not satisfied with two daughters? He would not exchange them for all the sons in the world.

Did he wish to marry? He had avoided social activity since his aunt's ball. And yet while he was there he had enjoyed that old satisfaction in drawing female attention. He had enjoyed letting his eyes rove over all the younger ladies, imagining which would have some wit as well as beauty, which might allow one some liberties if one were to lure her into the garden, which might make interesting bedfellows. Not once during the whole evening had he considered which might offer some companionship in the restricted social setting of Templeton Hall, or which might make the most affectionate and responsible mother for his children.

If he really were going to marry again, should he not consider those things first and foremost? It would be stupid in the extreme if he chose a new bride in much the same way as he had chosen Susan, only to find a second time that romantic love wore off very fast. Now, if he were truly sensible he would select for himself someone like Miss Matthews. Old enough to have gained some maturity. Quiet. Sensible. Willing and able to speak about more than just the latest fashions or the latest scandal. She had nephews and nieces. She probably had experience in dealing with children. He did not find her particularly attractive, though when he thought about her figure—fairly tall and slender—and about her face —regular-featured, with direct, intelligent gray eyes— he had to admit that she was not at all ugly or even plain. He could not imagine himself in bed with her. But then, there had been nothing remotely exciting about his experiences in bed with Susan after that first year, for all her great beauty. He might as well have held a cold fish.

Fairfax swung his legs to the floor and stretched his arms above his head. He really did not believe he could choose a bride coldly. The heart would have to share the choice with the head. If Miss Matthews was to be at the soiree that evening, then the little Miss Jamieson would be there too. Now, there was an interesting little character, all artificiality and vanity on the surface and yet with a sparkle of mischief lurking at the back of it all. It might be worth getting to know her better.

He laughed aloud suddenly as he pushed himself to his feet. How very indignant Miss Matthews had been with Richardson's Pamela, who had very meekly accepted Mr. B. as soon as he offered her marriage, when she had fought like a tigress during his numerous attempts to ravish her. Miss Matthews had been as cross with the girl as if she were a real person. Her eyes had quite sparkled and her cheeks glowed for the space of a couple of minutes. He would be quite interested to hear her judgment of *Joseph Andrews*. He might do well to use his evening in becoming better acquainted with both cousins. Each seemed interesting in her own way.

Fairfax noticed the time and tried to imagine what Amy and Claire would be doing at that moment. Amy was probably at her paintbox. Claire was doubtless undressing or bathing that little scruff of a doll that she loved so fiercely. He smiled. God, how he missed them!

Jane was aware as soon as she entered Lady Merriot's drawing room that Lord Fairfax was already there. There was a sort of sixth sense that made her feel his presence even before she saw him. She remembered that it had always been so. He was standing at the opposite end of the room, conversing with a group of men, all recognized leaders of the *ton*. She realized as soon as her eyes came to rest on his splendid figure just how foolish was her unacknowledged hope that he really would find time to greet her during the evening. She put into practice her earlier resolve and looked about her for Mr. Sedgeworth.

He was very close by and apparently was making his way toward her. She smiled at him.

"Good evening, Miss Matthews," he said. "How lovely you look in pink. I have just been realizing how few people I know in London. I spend so much time traveling around this island and on the Continent that I have become unfamiliar with the very people I should know best. Will you do me the kindness of keeping me company for a while? Your face at least is familiar." He grinned, and Jane found that he was far better-looking than she had thought. He had kindly eyes.

"It would be my pleasure, sir," she said. "Have you tackled any of that pile of books you borrowed this morning?"

"Alas, no," he said. "There always seem to be far

more important activities to take one's time in London. One is to drive in Hyde Park at just the correct hour of the afternoon. Have you tried it? I must recommend it if you have not. You will learn absolutely everything of scandalous proportions that has happened within the previous twenty-four hours. And you will soon learn that the bonnet or gown you purchased two weeks ago is woefully out-of-date.''

Jane laughed. "You are a cynic, I perceive, sir," she said. "One must learn to take delight in observing all the great absurdities of human nature while realizing that one's very presence in the midst of it all proves one's own absurdity."

"I am justly reproved, ma'am," he said, "for having shown that I consider myself above such foolishness. You are quite right, of course. I bowed and smiled and tooled my horses up and down Rotten Row just like everyone else. And perhaps all those other people were observing me with a satirical eye. Now, there is a lowering thought."

Jane felt quite proud of herself after a few minutes. She was enjoying Mr. Sedgeworth's company, she told herself, to such a degree that she had scarcely noticed that Lord Fairfax had joined Honor and other young people at the pianoforte, where Honor was entertaining them with her dubious skills at the keyboard.

# 4

Later in the evening, after supper, Jane was sitting with a group of ladies, listening with half an ear to their conversation. She sat deliberately with her back toward the rather noisy group of young people across the room, Honor and Fairfax in their midst. It had been a great deal easier to remain oblivious of them when she had been talking to Mr. Sedgeworth. But he had been drawn away by their hostess to make up a fourth at a table of cards. Jane tried to concentrate on the story one lady was telling of the gay life she had led in Brussels until her return to England ten days before. It seemed that half the fashionable world was there, and almost all the dashing young officers.

"Miss Matthews."

Jane looked up, startled to find Lord Fairfax standing beside her.

"I have been forced to conclude that you have no intention of speaking with me this evening," he said. "Is it because you have read *Joseph Andrews* and find that my recommendation was ill-founded?"

"Oh," she said with a laugh. "I have started the book, though I am afraid I have not read very much, yet. Not enough to make any sort of judgment."

"Indeed," he said, and he drew up a chair and seated himself beside her. "Then why have you been avoiding me?"

Jane's eyes widened. "But I have not been doing so, my lord," she said. "You have been in other company all evening and so have I. This is the first time I have come face-to-face with you."

"I thought you would have been with the young people," he said. "I waited in vain for you to approach

42

the pianoforte. You did tell me at my aunt's ball that you play, did you not? Why do you not come and play for me now?"

"Oh no," she protested, blushing. "I have never felt comfortable performing in public. I play for my own enjoyment, usually at times when I can forget my surroundings and even myself."

"Do you?" he said. "Then I shall not press you. I do the same myself."

"You play, my lord?" she asked in surprise.

"Yes," he said. "But why I admit the fact, I do not know. Some people think it an unmanly accomplishment."

Jane looked blank. "Why?" she asked. "All the famous composers are men. Why should not they play as well?"

He shrugged. "Enough of me," he said. "Tell me more about yourself, Miss Matthews."

"Oh dear," Jane said. "I do hate that request. There is nothing more calculated to tongue-tie me than to be invited to speak of myself. I search frantically in my mind for something to say and find to my dismay that there is absolutely nothing."

"That is refreshing, at all events," he said. "One would not dare put the question to many ladies for fear that one might be listening to the answer for the next several hours. And pardon me, ma'am, I did not mean to cast a slur on your sex. There are as many men who find themselves fascinating topics of conversation."

Jane smiled. "I really live a quite dull life," she said.

"Nonsense!" he said. "I am sure you malign yourself. You told me you have several nieces and nephews. Do you spend a great deal of time with them?"

Jane nodded. "I believe rather more than either my brother or my sister think good for the children," she said. "They accuse me of spoiling them."

"And do you?" he asked.

"I think not," she said. "I am afraid there is always a

frightful noise and a great deal of rushing around when I am with them, for I believe that most of the time children should be allowed to express themselves freely and move about as they wish. There is a need, of course, to learn restraint and good manners. But not in the nursery. My views are not popular, of course. I am considered to be a bad influence.''

Jane was flushed. When two people conversed at a social gathering, they usually gave each other one half of their attention and the room at large the other half. The viscount's eyes and apparently the whole of his attention were on her.

"Some children find it harder than others to be quiet and disciplined, though, do they not?" he said. "Amy —my elder daughter—is almost always quietly busy about some task, even though she is only four years old. Now, Claire finds it almost impossibly irksome to sit still even to eat a meal. She is two.''

"But you surely do not try to force such a baby to sit still?" Jane asked.

"Oh, by no means," he assured her. "I am afraid your brother and sister would not allow me within a mile of their children, Miss Matthews. I am far too indulgent, so my old nurse constantly tells me. I dote on my children and spoil them quite shamefully. I merely meant that Claire is vastly different from Amy, though they have the same parents and the same home. It is strange. One imagines, I suppose, that all of one's children will be very much the same as one another and easily molded into the sort of people we would like them to be.''

Jane smiled. "Your daughters must miss you," she said.

"I believe so," he agreed. "I received a painting from Amy today. It has a band of blue sky across the top of the paper, a band of green across the bottom, and a coach and horses suspended in midair. The most ghastly face is peering out of the window. Nurse has written at the bottom of the page, 'Papa on his way to London.' ''

Jane laughed. "I would wager the painting has been given the place of honor in your bedchamber," she said, and then blushed hotly at her own choice of words.

He inclined his head. "Of course," he agreed.

Jane did not know how much time passed while they talked. She was startled when her aunt interrupted them to announce that it was time to go home. Lord Fairfax rose to his feet and took Jane's hand as she stood up. He bowed over it.

"Good night, Miss Matthews," he said. "I have enjoyed our *tête-à-tête.*"

He *had* enjoyed it too, Fairfax thought, accepting a glass from a passing footman's tray and sitting down again facing the empty chair that Miss Matthews had occupied. Indeed, the thought that had come to him almost as a joke that afternoon was perhaps not a bad idea after all. Perhaps he should marry Miss Matthews. She was very easy to talk to and really quite interesting if one enjoyed quiet good sense. Certainly time had passed quickly in her company. He could scarcely believe that he must have been talking to her for half an hour.

She liked children and even seemed to share his liberal views about child-rearing. She would probably be able to make friends of his daughters. That would not be difficult with Claire. But Amy was a strange and moody child, difficult to get close to. It was hardly surprising, he supposed, considering the way Susan had neglected her. Yes, really, the idea of marriage with Miss Matthews was an eminently sensible one.

Was good sense a good enough criterion by which to choose a wife, though? Would Miss Matthews not make a dull wife? Married to her, would he not crave someone with more verve and beauty, someone with more sexual allure? No, he really did not believe that Miss Matthews would be dull. She was quiet and sensible, of course, but did those qualities denote dullness? Was not a talkative and vivacious beauty more likely to prove uninteresting in the final analysis? He had found out to his cost in his first marriage that the whole of one's married life is not lived in other people's drawing rooms or ballrooms or even in the marriage bed. There were endless hours to be spent together in the quiet solitude of one's own home, hours during which the craving for real companionship could become quite acute.

He suspected that Miss Matthews might well be able to supply that companionship. Would it matter that she was not what one might describe as a beauty? Was it important that she lacked the power to focus the attention of everyone in a crowded room on her own dazzling person? Was it essential to find one's wife exciting in bed? Anyway, that was impossible to predict. He had certainly expected Susan to be so. He would expect Miss Matthews to be a dutiful wife. At least he would not expect her ever to refuse him as Susan had done each time she was sure she was increasing. And having a regular bedfellow would in itself be satisfactory even if not wildly exciting.

Yes, he really must consider the matter further. He must get to know her better. At the same time, of course, he could further his acquaintance with Miss Jamieson. They were cousins and lived in the same house. He found the little beauty quite diverting. She amused him greatly. He could not imagine her in his home, it was true, but he would not be averse to amusing himself with her company while he was in London. That pouting little rosebud of a mouth certainly invited kissing.

"You look to be in a brown study, Fairfax," Joseph Sedgeworth said. "Miss Vye needs someone to turn the pages of the music for her at the pianoforte. Now, I'm not a musician, you know, and would be turning pages at the strangest moments. You must come and help out." He lowered his voice. "I believe the females are merely using their wits to lure you closer, you know. Miss Crawley suggested that I come and ask you."

"By all means, let us not disappoint the ladies,"

Fairfax said, getting to his feet and smiling in the direction of the small group around the pianoforte.

"He must really like me, do you not think, Jane?" Honor asked anxiously. They were strolling in the park the morning after the soiree. "He was in my company almost all evening. It was becoming almost embarrassing. We will become the *on-dit* of the town if he singles me out for such marked attention at every function we attend."

"But it is hardly surprising," Jane said. "You have proved very popular, Honor. You must be very grateful at the way the Season has turned out for you. There are several gentlemen who spend a great deal of each evening in your company."

"Yes," Honor agreed, "but who would even notice mere boys like Harry or Peter or Ambie? They remind me of lapdogs. But Viscount Fairfax! Who could fail to notice that he has a preference for me? Oh, Jane, is he not quite divine?"

"Extremely handsome," Jane agreed. "And he did single you out last evening, Honor. I am sure everyone noticed. And I am equally sure that you are pleased that everyone did, and would be quite gratified to become an *on-dit.*"

Honor giggled and twirled her parasol. "You are unkind, Jane," she said. "I am not really conceited, am I? Can I help it if gentlemen flock around me? Do you think he will call today, Jane?"

"I have no idea," Jane said. "You will just have to wait and see."

"Well, perhaps Mr. Sedgeworth will call to see you and bring the viscount with him," Honor said. "You spent a great deal of the evening with him, Jane. Do not think I did not notice just because I was with Lord Fairfax. And he is a most proper gentleman. Nothing to compare with the viscount, of course, but he does have a very pleasant smile. He would be a good catch for you. Certainly better than that dreadfully dull Mr.

Faford. You cannot possibly take him seriously, can you, Jane?"

"I have nothing to take seriously," Jane said. "He has not made me any declaration."

"Oh, but he will," Honor said. "I know by the look in his eye. Don't accept him, Jane. You can be quite old-maidish at times, but really you would be most miserable with Mr. Faford. Indeed, I sometimes think he behaves quite like an old maid."

"Now you are being unkind," Jane said, laughing despite herself.

"Really I should be offering up prayers that you will accept him," Honor said, "to be sure that you will not win that wager you refuse to make over Lord Fairfax. He must have spent all of half an hour with you, Jane, at the end of last evening. Had you once glanced in my direction, you would have seen that my eyes sparked green with jealousy. I shall be quite out of humor with you, you know, if he makes you the second Lady Fairfax instead of me."

Jane flushed. "Now you are being absurd, Honor," she said. "You know there is not the remotest chance of such a thing happening."

"He does have two children, remember," Honor said. "Perhaps he is looking for a somewhat older, more mature woman to be their mother."

"And if you think I fit the description, thank you kindly for the compliment," Jane said dryly.

"Oh." Honor looked stricken for a moment. "I did not mean to insult you, Jane. But you are three-and-twenty, after all. And you really are a very sensible person. You never do anything silly or giggle too much in company or use outrageous tactics to attract attention. I'm afraid I do all three." She giggled to illustrate her point. "It all seems to work, though, does it not? I have told Lord Fairfax some shocking lies already, you know. Last evening I told him I was organizing a picnic and he must come. I have been puzzling all morning over how to break the news to

Mama. You must help, Jane. Say it is your idea. Then Mama will think it makes perfect good sense.''

"Not me," Jane said fervently. "Besides, Honor, in all the time we have been here I have not once heard Aunt Cynthia say no to any of your wishes."

"Oh," Honor sighed, "I do hope he comes visiting this afternoon, Jane."

"So you fancy Miss Jamieson, do you, Fairfax?" Joseph Sedgeworth teased as they rode their horses slowly through the crowded streets of London. "But then, you always did have an eye for beauty. And of course you have always been able to have your pick of any female you fancied. The little chit was falling all over herself last evening to attract you."

"Jealous, Sedge?" Fairfax asked with a chuckle.

"Heaven forbid," his friend assured him. "I would not like the task of taming that little bundle of vanity and mischief, Fairfax. Though she does have something to be vain about, I will admit. A decidedly shapely body, for example."

"Most," Fairfax agreed. "Do you not itch to see it without the encumbrance of clothing, Sedge? And touch it?"

"If she were a different class of female," Sedgeworth said, "I might be tempted to think along those lines, Fairfax. But there is no point in even teasing one's mind with such thoughts of a lady. Unless one has the intention of leading her to the altar, that is. And frankly, I consider a leg shackle far too high a price to pay merely for the pleasure of putting a female in my bed."

Fairfax laughed. "You must have an iron will, Sedge," he said. "You will not consider marriage to a lady, yet you are too high-principled to take a mistress or to hire yourself a whore. Tell me, when was the last time you had a woman?"

"That is not a pertinent question, Fairfax," his friend

said in some discomfort. "A man has to have some secrets even from his friends."

Yes, he does, Fairfax thought. Sedge took for granted that the purpose of their visit to the Jamieson house was to call on Miss Jamieson. And Fairfax was content to let him think so. He wanted to keep quite silent about his interest in Miss Matthews until he knew her a little better and had made up his mind whether he was really serious about his idea of marrying her or not. He certainly did not want his companion's teasing on the matter.

When they were shown into Sir Alfred Jamieson's drawing room a few minutes later, they found it already crowded. Mrs. and Miss Crawley were there, and three young gentlemen, all seated close to Honor. Mr. Faford was standing at the opposite side of the fireplace, apparently taking his leave of Jane. He crossed the room while the two newcomers were still greeting Lady Jamieson, and stood talking with them for a few minutes before leaving.

Fairfax was pleased to find that there was no empty seat close to Miss Jamieson, while a chair had quite conveniently been vacated next to Miss Matthews. It would therefore not look at all suspicious for him to stroll across the room and sit next to her. He did so while Sedgeworth accepted a seat close to a smiling Miss Crawley.

"May I?" Fairfax said, indicating the empty chair.

"Of course, my lord," Jane said, looking up wide-eyed into his face. And then she added in some confusion, "I do beg your pardon. I thought you would go to the other side of the room."

"It seems a little crowded in that direction," he said. "I notice that Miss Jamieson does not lack for admirers."

"She has taken very well," Jane agreed. She bent her head over the needlepoint she had picked up when Mr. Faford left.

Fairfax watched her for a while. "This is another example of that very worthless life you lead, no doubt,

Miss Matthews," he said. "You do the most delicate work. Would you like me to hold my quizzing glass between your eyes and the needle so that you can see what you are doing?"

She looked up and laughed at him. "Very definitely not, my lord," she said. "I should also be able to see the mistakes I am making."

She really was quite pretty when she laughed, Fairfax thought. And her laughter held genuine amusement. It was not the artificial tinkle that so many ladies affected. The flush on her cheeks was becoming too. She was looking down at her work again.

"Will you drive with me in the park later?" he asked. "I have been reminded since my arrival that it is obligatory to do so at least once a week when one is in town."

She looked up at him again with wide, startled eyes. "I am honored, my lord," she said, "but I am afraid I cannot. I already have an engagement."

With Faford, no doubt, Fairfax thought. Was he going to have a rival for her affections? He was going to have to make up his mind fairly soon, or Faford was going to be offering for her. And she would doubtless accept. Miss Matthews was not a young woman. She was not likely to turn down an eligible suitor.

"Ah, of course," he said. "I might have known I would be too late. Perhaps some other time."

"I would like that," she said.

The conversation in the room soon became general. Honor was seated beside Prudence Crawley and had been whispering excitedly with her for several minutes. She clapped her hands, looking around the room with flushed and animated face.

"Listen, everyone," she said. "I am going to have a picnic next week and everyone is to come. Prue's great-aunt lives in Richmond next to the River Thames. It will be the perfect site, and Prue says her great-aunt will be delighted to let us use the grounds. How does Tuesday next sound?"

There was a buzz of enthusiasm from Honor's three admirers. Prudence cast her mother a guilty look. Honor avoided her mother's eyes, though Lady Jamieson was smiling indulgently and nodding her head.

"My lord?" Honor asked, turning the full force of her charm on the viscount.

He kept his face grave though he was laughing inside. This was the picnic she had mentioned on the spur of the moment the evening before. All for his benefit, he guessed. Perhaps it was conceited of him to think so, but really the little chit was most transparent in her designs. She was taken with him. Well, a picnic might be the ideal setting for that kiss he planned to steal sometime within the next couple of months.

"It would be my pleasure, Miss Jamieson," he said.

"Mr. Sedgeworth?" she asked.

He bowed and accepted.

"And Max and Peter and Ambie will come, of course," Honor said carelessly, her eye passing over her trio of admirers. "Jane will make all the food arrangements with Cook, will you not, Jane? I have no head for such matters. And you are so good at organizing."

"Whom else are you going to invite?" Prudence asked. "You must be sure to have equal numbers, Honor."

The young people put their heads together in order to solve this thorny problem. Fairfax gave up with some reluctance his spur-of-the-moment plan to take Miss Jamieson driving. He did not wish to trap himself into a situation in which all the *ton* would expect him to make the girl an offer. He really did not think he would ever consider her seriously as a prospective bride. Certainly he did not want his hands to be tied. He had spent long enough with her the evening before. Better to wait a few days before singling out her company again.

He exchanged glances with Sedgeworth, and they both rose to take their leave.

Sedgeworth commiserated with his friend as they rode away. "You couldn't penetrate the defenses of all those lovelorn swains, eh, Fairfax?" he said. "What a waste of a visit, my friend, having to sit clear across the room from the beauteous Miss Jamieson."

"Ah, but, Sedge," Fairfax said, "did you not notice that I was the first person singled out for invitation to the picnic next week? I confess I took heart from that fact. You merited only second place."

"True enough," his friend admitted. "But I still have a place of great honor. Think how lowering it would be to have been lumped in with Max and Peter and Ambie. Poor souls. You'd think they would have more pride, wouldn't you, Fairfax? At least we are 'my lord' and 'Mr. Sedgeworth.' "

"I fear perhaps the mark of respect is only for our advanced age, though," Fairfax said. "After all, we are both approaching thirty and must appear quite aged to those very young creatures. Were we ever as young as that, Sedge?"

Jane received her second proposal of marriage later that same afternoon. The first she had refused five years before because the man had seemed impossibly dull beside the glittering personality of the quite unattainable Viscount Fairfax. The second she refused—for what reason? Jane asked herself when she was back at home again. Surely not for the same reason. She could not possibly be that foolish. Could she?

She was afraid she knew the answer. Every man she met now would be measured against the viscount and found wanting. And in a few months' time she would return to Yorkshire and spend the rest of her life repenting her extreme folly. There was nothing whatsoever wrong with Mr. Faford as a suitor. He had the means to support her. He was a man of steady character. He was kindly. And she had refused him.

He did not have thick dark hair that her fingers itched to run through or a tall, muscular body her own ached to be held against. He did not have blue eyes that looked intently into hers as she talked. He did not have a left eyebrow that lifted expressively to show surprise or amusement. He did not have the gift for conversing in a manner that made her forget herself, her surroundings, and the time. She did not throb with love for him.

But he did have a regard for her and a wish to make her his wife. And why ache for dark hair and blue eyes and a muscular body when she knew they would never belong to her? Foolish, foolish infatuation!

She surprised herself by her refusal. She hardly knew that she was going to say no until her mouth opened and formed the word. Mr. Faford was surprised too, though he was too well-bred to make much comment on her reply. They drove home from the park in embarrassed silence. He asked her at the end of the journey if her answer was final, whether there was any hope of her changing her mind if he asked her later in the Season.

But she refused even this second chance. She might have said yes and concentrated on talking sense into herself over the coming weeks. She said no.

So she was making an utter fool of herself again, pining for a man who would probably wed her cousin within a few months. She had learned nothing whatsoever in five years. She heartily despised herself. She dared not look ahead to the future.

# 5

**H**onor's conversation consisted of little else except her picnic until the following Tuesday. She was in a fever of excitement. What should she wear? she asked both Jane and her mother a dozen times. Her pink? Did pink really suit her? The sprigged muslin? She felt it was quite becoming, but what if Prue decided to wear hers? The two dresses were very similar. Her pink bonnet was her favorite. If she wore that, then of course she would be wise to wear the pink dress. But perhaps her chip straw bonnet would be more suitable for a picnic. The yellow would be a quite striking choice, though, would it not? The sun would complement it if it turned out to be a bright day. The dress would give the day sparkle if it were cloudy.

Lady Jamieson listened indulgently to her daughter's prattling. It was left to Jane to see that the picnic was properly organized. It was she who conferred with the cook about the variety and quantity of food required, the number of footmen needed to serve it, and the number of carriages necessary to convey the ladies. She guessed that the men would prefer to ride.

Jane was not at all sure that she was looking forward to Tuesday. She liked the sound of the setting, and it was always pleasant to be out-of-doors during spring and summer. But it would mean a whole afternoon spent in proximity to Lord Fairfax. And she was realizing more and more that being near to him was the worst thing in the world for her. She could not think or behave sensibly, it seemed, while there was still the chance of seeing him and perhaps talking to him. She almost wished that Honor's hopes would be realized and that he would court her quickly and marry her. At least then perhaps she would be able to face reality again.

Oh, but the very prospect was dreadfully depressing. She liked Honor a great deal. Who could not? But not as Lord Fairfax's wife. She was not right for him. Honor was good-natured, despite her vanity, and she had a great deal of intelligence and talent that she ruthlessly suppressed now that she was in London. But she was certainly flighty. She loved gaiety. She would not suit his way of life at all. She was beautiful, of course. And he seemed to like beautiful women. No one had been lovelier than Susan, and he had very obviously loved her deeply. Perhaps he would love Honor too. Some men do not require steadiness of character in their wives.

But Honor did not like children. When she had come to Yorkshire with Aunt Cynthia and Uncle Alfred to bring Jane to London, she had been quite cross with Harold's children. Jane's brother had brought them to the house to say good-bye to her. Honor had thought them unruly and had raised her eyes to the ceiling when little Andrea had shrieked as Jane lifted her, kissed her, and swung her in a circle.

Fairfax appeared to dote on his children. Honor would find life very hard if she were forced to have a great deal to do with them. Jane had overheard her discussing the matter with Aunt Cynthia one morning. If she married the viscount, Honor was saying, she would make him take her everywhere of any interest in the world. She would make sure the children had the best of care, but she would not wish to spend all her time with them at Templeton Hall.

Jane ended up sighing every time her mind strayed to such topics. She must just make sure on Tuesday that she kept herself busy. She would have to see that a suitable picnic site was chosen, of course, and she would have to instruct the footmen when to serve the tea. If she did not, no one else would. But that would not fill in her whole afternoon. She must try, if she could, to engage Mr. Sedgeworth in conversation. He had appeared quite friendly at the soiree, and he might help her keep her mind away from his friend.

They saw the viscount once during the days before the picnic. Jane and Honor were walking along Bond Street, a maid behind them, when they came face-to-face with him. He raised his hat, bowed, and would have passed on, Jane felt, after greeting them. But Honor had other ideas.

"Lord Fairfax!" she said. "You are just the person we have been needing. We are desperately in need of the services of a discerning gentleman. Do say you are not in a hurry."

Fairfax stopped and looked at her, his left eyebrow raised. "In what way may I be of service, Miss Jamieson?" he asked.

Jane too had looked at her cousin in surprise.

"It is Papa's birthday very soon," Honor said, all dimples and large eyes, "and I wish to purchase a new fob for his watch. Jane and I have been quite undecided about which one he would like. We have come very near to quarreling, in fact. What we need is the opinion of a gentleman of taste."

"And you wish me to help you make the choice?" he asked. "I would be honored, ma'am, though I am sure your papa would value anything that you selected for him."

"Oh, will you help?" Honor asked breathlessly. "I would be most grateful, my lord." She reached for his arm and turned to Jane. "You may go on to the library, Jane. You know I find that place a terrific bore. Jane is very learned, you know, Lord Fairfax. Now, I am just a giddy young girl who prefers to let the gentlemen of this world do all thinking and reading. Hatty, you may go with Miss Matthews. His lordship will accompany me to the library afterward. Will you, my lord?" She turned wide, innocent eyes on him.

He bowed. "I will certainly not abandon you in the street, Miss Jamieson," he assured her.

"But that was lying, Honor," Jane said later, taking her cousin to task. "I really do not know how you could do it."

"Nonsense!" Honor said with a peal of laughter. "I merely said Papa's birthday was soon. Christmas is not a century away, after all. And besides, Jane, I mean to have his lordship, and I shall do anything in my power to get him. He is quite lovely to walk beside. Very large and strong. And he did not hold my arm away from him. He hugged it close to his side. I am very glad you decided not to wager with me, Jane, or I should feel as if I were boasting. I mean to have him all to myself at Richmond. Prue says the grounds of her great-aunt's house are large. Perhaps we can lose ourselves sufficiently for him to kiss me. I shall blush and shed a few tears if he does, of course, and swear that he has stolen what he has no right to." She giggled again.

"You are shameless, Honor," Jane scolded, feeling a little sick.

"I know," her cousin admitted, catching her skirts in her hands and twirling around the morning room, humming tunelessly.

Fairfax was feeling quite cheerful. It was a beautiful day as, indeed, most of the days that spring had been. And they were approaching Richmond, already away from the worst of the noise and grime of London. The ladies filled two open barouches, the brightness of their clothing in the sunlight making them all appear lovely. And there was a whole afternoon ahead. An afternoon during which to get to know Miss Matthews better if he could get her alone without anyone suspecting his intentions. And an afternoon during which to flirt further with Miss Jamieson.

He smiled to himself as he glanced back to see the young lady, sitting very upright in the barouche closest to him, looking rather like a ray of sunshine with her yellow dress and parasol and her chip straw bonnet. He wondered what fantastic lies he would draw from her that afternoon. He had not been able to resist asking her as he handed her into the carriage how her father had liked the watch fob. She had glanced hastily behind her to see where her mother was and answered him archly that Papa's birthday had not come yet. When was that birthday? he wondered. He would wager that it was not before September at the very earliest.

She had really taken her time choosing that fob, taking him to three jewelers before deciding that one fob she had seen at the first shop was the one she wanted. He had made no objection, of course. She had linked her arm quite indecorously far within his so that her shoulder rested against his upper arm, and she had moved even closer when they were forced to pass other shoppers on the pavement. The little chit was offering him quite an open invitation, in fact. Perhaps it was fortunate for her that he was not in the business of ravishing little virgins. She probably did not even realize that she was playing with fire. If she were his daughter, now, and he caught her up to such tricks, he would shut her into her room and feed her bread and water for a week.

The party was turning through the wide gateways that led to an imposing house. But the carriages and horses passed it without stopping. There was no one in residence, Prudence Crawley had explained. It was a beautiful place. The grounds sloped away gradually behind the house, past extensive formal gardens, a row of hothouses, and a grove of trees to well-kept lawns that ended at the banks of the River Thames. The barouches and the baggage coach halted when they had passed the trees, and Honor rose to her feet with a little shriek of excitement.

"How positively enchanting!" she cried, focusing all male attention immediately on her person. "There is even a boathouse. Is there a boat, Prue?"

She squealed with delight when she discovered that indeed there was a boat and that they might take it out. Ambrose Leighton rushed forward to help her from the barouche, but it was Fairfax's arm she took almost as if by random choice when she was on the ground. His amusement returned.

"Oh, do let us go and look," she said.

Miss Matthews was already out of the other barouche and was walking toward the baggage coach, Fairfax saw at a glance. Doubtless she had taken upon herself the organizing and smooth running of this afternoon's entertainment. He would talk to her later. He turned in the direction of the boathouse.

Two other couples followed them. But when the boat had been lifted out and set in the water, it was Honor, of course, who demanded the first ride. The boat was large enough for only two. It was taken for granted that he would be the one to row her, Fairfax noticed as he helped her in and made sure she was safely seated before letting go of her hand.

"I do admire the ease with which you row, my lord," Honor said as he pulled out toward the center of the river. "I am sure my hands would be covered with blisters in no time at all."

"I rowed a great deal at university," he said. "It is really not a difficult task, provided one does not dip the oars too deep and try to displace the whole river with every stroke."

She looked at him wide-eyed and twirled her parasol. "I am quite sure I should never be able to learn how," she said. "I really am quite helpless about such matters."

"And what do you do at home to amuse yourself, Miss Jamieson," he asked, "when you are away from the amusements of town?"

"Oh, I manage to amuse myself," she said. "I visit whenever the weather permits and Papa can spare the carriage. My friend Julia's maid has a sister who is a lady's maid in London, and she sends copies of all the latest fashion plates. We find it vastly entertaining to look at the pictures and to try to persuade the village dressmaker to copy the styles for us. And we spend hours dressing each other's hair in the newest fashions.''

"I see," he said. "And do you paint? Do needlework? Read?''

"I had a horrid governess who made me read every day," said Honor. "I swore when I left the schoolroom that I would never open another book. I do not believe a lady should read, my lord, because then she might appear to be above the gentlemen whom she meets socially. It would not be ladylike to embarrass them so, would it? I dabble in painting, of course. What lady does not? But I consider it to be something of a waste of time. Why paint a scene from one's own estate when the real trees and grass and such are right there, and so much lovelier to look at than the picture?''

Fairfax glanced back to the bank. There were only a few people in sight. The four who were waiting for their own turn at the oars were seated on the bank beside the boathouse. Miss Matthews, easily recognizable in her spring-green dress, was walking with Sedgeworth. He wished for one moment that he could change places with his friend. At least one could hold a sensible conversation with Miss Matthews.

He turned back to his companion. "I cannot help but notice how like a ray of sunshine you are today, Miss Jamieson," he said. "It must be the color of your dress and parasol.''

"Oh, do you like them?" she asked, her eyes sparkling. "The modiste told me that not all ladies can wear yellow. It makes their complexions look sallow," she said. The parasol was given another twirl.

"That certainly cannot be said of you," Fairfax said. "The color suits your dark hair and the roses in your cheeks to perfection.''

The roses in her cheeks became even brighter, he noticed. And so the conversation continued. He was quite relieved ten minutes later to be able to suggest that they return to the bank to allow someone else to have a ride in the boat. She was Susan all over again, without the petulance. But then, Susan had not been petulant at the start. He thought, on reflection, that perhaps it would be wise not to claim that kiss after all that afternoon. He had been planning a stroll up to the hothouses after the boat ride, with a route through the trees and a kiss in their shelter.

But it would not be fair. Miss Jamieson was a very young girl obviously angling for a husband. She would give the kiss very willingly, he had no doubt. But she would probably expect an offer the very next day. And he did not doubt that despite her vanity and her rather empty head, she was a girl with real feelings. He did not believe she was in love with him, but she would be hurt and doubtless bewildered to discover that he had merely dallied with her. And dalliance was all he could offer Miss Honor Jamieson. She was lovely and eminently kissable, but she was not the sort of female he would choose for a second wife. Certainly not. He would be foolish indeed to fall into the trap of mere physical appeal again.

As soon as they were on the bank, Ambrose Leighton helped Alexandra Vye into the boat. Honor took Fairfax's arm and led him off up the lawn in the direction of the blankets, which had been set out in the shade of some trees. Lady Jamieson was there dozing, her back against a tree. Jane was also sitting there, her arms clasped around her knees, looking down on the river.

"Jane," Honor called as they drew closer, "are you afraid of the water? You need not be, you know. The boat is quite safe. At least"—she gazed wide-eyed up into the face of Fairfax—"it is when it is in the hands of someone who knows what he is doing."

"I have been walking," Jane said. "The boat seems much in demand anyway."

"You must have someone take you out," Honor declared. "I am sure Mr. Sedgeworth would be delighted to do so. Where is he?"

"He went up to look in the hothouses," Jane said. "I decided to sit here to cool off."

"Would you care to come out on the river, Miss Matthews?" Fairfax asked. "It will be my turn again soon, I believe."

"Oh, do let us eat first," Honor begged. "I am starved. When do you plan to have the footmen set the baskets out, Jane?"

"I shall do so immediately if everyone's attention can be attracted," Jane said.

Honor turned to beckon to the two people sitting on the bank and to a group that had appeared up by the hothouses.

"After we have eaten, Miss Matthews," the viscount asked, his eyes steady on Jane, "would you care for that boat ride?"

"Yes, thank you," she replied. "I should enjoy it."

An hour later Fairfax handed Jane into the boat. There was already a suggestion in the air of the coolness of late afternoon.

"Do you like water?" Fairfax asked. "Do you swim?"

"I can swim," she said, "but I do not like to do so. I am afraid to put my head beneath the water, you see."

"Ah," he said, holding her hand in a firm grip while the boat rocked beneath her, "I would guess that you did not learn as an infant. Very young children have no such fears, you know. I was taught as a young child and I have done the same for my daughters. They like nothing better than to be in water."

"Even the two-year-old?" Jane asked.

"She learned last year," he said, "when she could barely walk. I will not say that she learned quite to swim. But she learned to do a good imitation of a cork. We have a lake only a half-mile from the house and have plenty of opportunity to enjoy the water in some privacy."

The river was calm, with that glassy quality that water takes on so often in the late afternoon and evening.

"You are very relaxed," Fairfax said, "for one who is afraid to get her hair wet."

Jane laughed. "Oh," she said, "you will not find me to be a wilting creature, my lord. I trust your skills utterly. If you do pitch me into the water, then will be time enough to panic. But I shall try to keep in mind that you are a gentleman and an excellent swimmer and that you are bound to save my life even at the risk of losing your own."

He smiled at the humorous good sense that she showed. "You are a very sensible lady, are you not, Miss Matthews?" he said. "Does nothing perturb you? I wonder."

She glanced at him as if she were about to reply, but looked down at her hands instead. She looked quite pretty for the moment, her slender body bent forward slightly, the color in her cheeks somewhat heightened.

"Will you marry me?" he asked, and listened in some amazement to the echo of his own words.

Her head shot up and she gazed wide-eyed at him. She said nothing.

He had meant the words, he realized suddenly. He had decided without even quite knowing it himself. "Did you hear what I said?" he asked after a few moments of silence. "I asked if you will marry me."

Her eyes were fixed on his. Dark gray eyes. "Why?" she asked. He read her lips. Very little sound escaped her.

He looked away from her eyes. They were mesmerizing him. He noticed that he had rowed a long way from the rest of the party on the bank. "I could lie," he said carefully. "I could tell you that I have fallen madly in love with you. And I think you would know that I was lying. The truth is, Miss Matthews, that I need a wife, and I believe you would suit my needs. I choose to live most of my time on my country estate, and I choose to play an active role in the upbringing of my daughters. I need a woman to share that life with me and to manage my home. My children need the security of a mother. A nurse is unable to give them that emotional satisfaction."

"But why me in particular?" she asked. "I am not . . . I mean . . ."

"I need a woman of good sense and even temper," he said, "and one who loves children. I believe you to have those qualities."

She sat quietly regarding her hands for several minutes while Fairfax turned the boat and began to row back in the direction from which they had come. The slight twisting of her hands was the only sign she showed of emotion.

"I see that I have taken you by surprise," he said at last. "Is there someone else? Faford, perhaps? He will be making you an offer soon, if he has not already done so. Are your feelings engaged?"

"No," she said quietly, her head still bent over her hands. "I have refused him."

"I see," he said. "And am I to suffer a similar fate?" He was surprised by her near-silence. He had expected instant acceptance.

She looked up at him then. "I do not know," she said steadily.

They were closer to the bank than either of them had realized. They both became suddenly aware of the bright colors of ladies' dresses reflected in the water.

"This is really not at all fair," Honor called gaily. "You have had a longer ride than any of us, Jane. Is this the reward you claim for arranging such delicious food with Cook? And I thought you had done it out of the goodness of your heart."

"I am sorry," Jane called. "Aunt Cynthia must be anxious to start back."

"May I have the honor of calling on you tomorrow?" Viscount Fairfax asked quietly as he pulled for the shore.

"No," Jane replied. "Please, nothing so public, my lord."

He nodded. "May I have your answer the next time I see you, then?" he asked.

"Yes," she replied.

There was no further opportunity to exchange a
word. Honor took Fairfax's arm as soon as he stepped
out of the boat and began to walk with him in the
direction of the carriages. And a few minutes later, the
servants having removed the baskets and the blankets
from the lawn and some of the men having put the boat
away, they were on their way home.

So he had done it, Fairfax thought. He had made his
offer to Miss Matthews. It was irrevocable now. There
was no withdrawing. And was he sorry? He had
certainly spoken impulsively. He had intended to wait
awhile before making a final decision.

But he did not believe he regretted his words. Miss
Matthews was a sensible choice of bride. There would
not, of course, be that aura of romance and excitement
that had surrounded his first marriage. But there was
much more likelihood that this marriage would bring
him contentment. She would be an interesting
companion. His home would be well run in her hand.
Susan had been content to let the servants run the
house. Miss Matthews would be good with the children.
By her own account, she would not try to quench their
high spirits, yet her quiet, sensible approach to life
would surely have a stabilizing effect on them.

And he did not find her unattractive. Her figure did
not have those tantalizing curves that could set a man's
loins to aching, but it had a slender grace that was not
unpleasing. He felt a certain interested curiosity to find
out how that body would feel against his own. Was she
capable of showing passion? Of enjoying the marriage
act? He wanted a wife this time who would share his bed
all night and every night. Would she be willing? She
loved children. They would have some together. He
would like several more. Well spaced out, of course. He
would always live in terror of killing her as he had killed
Susan.

Fairfax shook the thought from him. He would
persuade her to marry him with as little delay as
possible. He was very eager to be back at Templeton

Hall. He wanted her to meet Amy and Claire. He wanted to see how well they would all like one another. Perhaps she would want a grand wedding. He hoped not, though he would comply with her wishes. Those matters were important to women, it seemed.

He would not tell anyone yet. Not even Sedge. He did not wish to be teased about the matter until he was quite free to divulge their plans. No, he was not sorry that he had spoken this soon. He no longer derived any great pleasure from the entertainments of the Season. He found it all somewhat tedious. And he did not really crave a woman merely for the sake of physical gratification. Lady Shenley, a quite delectable widow, had signaled her availability to him only the night before. He knew he could enjoy himself with her for the rest of the Season if he wished. He had felt only a passing interest. And he supposed the same thing had happened on a lesser scale with Miss Jamieson. The pursuit of a kiss seemed almost too trivial to be worth the effort.

No, he would marry again. And this time he would be contented because he was making a sensible choice. Miss Matthews would be a good wife. Jane. He liked the name. No nonsense about it, just like her character. He was fortunate to have found her. It was unlikely that he would have singled her out for an invitation to dance if she had not been talking to his uncle the night of that ball.

Why had she not given him her answer immediately? He glanced at her now, seated in the second barouche beside her aunt, listening with a smile to something Miss Vye was saying. Even a sensible, mature woman had her pride, he supposed. She would not wish him to think she was desperate for a husband. So she was making him wait. Well, let her have her moment of triumph. She was worth waiting for.

Yes, she really was.

# 6

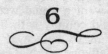

Jane was sitting up in bed, clasping her knees. She had blown out the candles, but she had pulled back the heavy curtains from her window first. Moonlight slanted into the room, making it almost as light as day.

Finally she was alone. All the while during the journey home from Richmond she had thrown herself into conversation with the ladies with whom she shared a barouche. And during dinner and in the drawing room afterward she had concentrated her mind on the chatter of Honor and her aunt. She had not wanted to think until she was alone.

Honor had been vastly excited at the success of her picnic. Viscount Fairfax had been most attentive. Had anyone noticed how much time he had spent with her? He had taken her rowing and walking, and he had complimented her on her appearance. A ray of sunshine, he had called her. She was very pleased that she had insisted on wearing her yellow. He had commented on her ccomplexion too. Had he not looked marvelously handsome himself? And was he not strong? When he had rowed the boat, one would have sworn that he had to make no effort at all. Jane must have noticed. Did Mama think she could expect an offer soon?

Jane had said nothing. She worked at her needle-point.

"I think Mr. Sedgeworth is developing an attachment to you, Jane," Honor said archly. "I saw you walking with him while I was in the boat with Lord Fairfax. What did you talk about?"

"About a large number of topics," Jane replied. "Books. Music. The Congress at Vienna."

"Oh, really, Jane," her cousin said, "you should not do so. It is no wonder you are three-and-twenty and still unmarried. No gentleman likes to believe that a lady might be a bluestocking."

Jane looked up. "Then what is one supposed to talk about?" she asked.

"Oh, fashions, gossip, the weather," Honor replied. "Anything, Jane, that suggests that we are just feather-brains. Gentlemen like that. And you should admire them. Flatter them. They cannot resist, you know."

"I would think gentlemen would be bored to have nothing more stimulating for conversation," Jane said.

"Well, there you are wrong," her cousin assured her. "Mark how successful I am, Jane. You see how gentle-men hang around me wherever I go. I have not accom-plished that by talking about books, I assure you." She giggled. "I told Lord Fairfax this afternoon that I spend all my time talking fashions with Theresa Bell and dressing hair. He was charmed."

"You did not tell him about your water paintings, Honor?" Jane asked.

"And about the French lessons you give Sir Humphrey's children?" her mother added.

"Gracious, no," Honor said. "He would have thought me decidedly dull."

Jane had finally excused herself, claiming fatigue after a busy day. And she was sitting up in bed now, convinced that she would not sleep all night. She still felt as if she were in the middle of a dream. Surely it could not be real that Viscount Fairfax had asked her to be his wife. At any moment now she would wake up and laugh at her own absurdity in dreaming such a thing.

But it was real. He had asked her. And she had given no answer! That was the most surprising fact of all. She had stared dumbly at him at first and then agreed that she needed time to think. She had not thrown herself at his feet and poured out her undying gratitude. It was amazing. She could be Jane Templeton, Viscountess Fairfax. Her wildest dreams could come true with one word from her. And she had not said anything. She had asked for more time.

Why?

Even if she did not love Lord Fairfax, he had everything to offer that she had looked for. He was well able to take care of her. He was amiable and interesting. He had a home to which he was attached and children whom he loved. She would surely be able to build a life of contentment out of such ingredients. And in this particular case there was the added attraction of the fact that she loved him.

But that was also the main problem. How could she love so deeply and yet enter into such a marriage? He did not pretend to have any regard for her. He merely wanted someone to manage his home and be a mother to his daughters. He had chosen her because she was a woman of sense. He had said as much. If she tried to look at the matter objectively, she had to admit that he had probably chosen with some care. She had neither great beauty nor popularity. She had admitted that she liked children. And he knew that she enjoyed activities that could be carried on in the country as well as in town: reading, playing the pianoforte, sewing. He had seen today that she would willingly take upon herself the organization of social functions. She must seem the ideal wife.

It hurt. That was absurd, of course. She had never looked to arouse any feelings beyond indifference in Viscount Fairfax. How could she be hurt that he offered her marriage without love? Perhaps it was his assumption that she did not desire love that hurt. Did she seem such a very dull person that love and passion were unnecessary to her? It had sounded like a business proposition that he had made to her.

She had not expected anything more of marriage, of course. Would she be equally hurt if another man offered her marriage under similar terms? Had Mr. Faford said anything about love or personal regard? He had said that he thought they would suit. That was all. And she had not been hurt, had she? She had not even thought of being so.

How would she answer when she next saw the viscount? Could she possibly say no? What was the alternative to marrying him? She would go home to Yorkshire within a few weeks and never see him ever again. Could she bear it? When she could be married to him, living in the same home as he, building a companionship with him, learning the intimacies of marriage with him, having his children? There really was no choice, was there? She could not possibly say no. She would regret her decision all her life.

His children. Of course, that must be another reason for his marriage, although it was too delicate a topic for him to have mentioned. He wanted an heir. He clearly loved his daughters, but he must have desperately wanted a son when he was married. The first Lady Fairfax had died in childbed when the younger daughter was only a year old. Poor lady. Much as he had loved her, Fairfax must have considered her a failure in that one respect. And was she now to become the bearer of his children until there was a son? It was in some ways an exciting thought. By this time next year she could be a mother, the mother of Lord Fairfax's child! But it was also a demeaning thought. While she was loving him, he would be using her merely for her reproductive functions.

Jane sighed. Her brain felt hopelessly addled. She might sit here all night long thinking, but she knew that when it came to the point she would be no more ready to give a wise answer. And since a wise choice was not to be made, she knew she would choose according to her inclinations. She would accept him. And then she would have to face Honor's terrible disappointment and humiliation. In fact, she would have to face a great deal of public reaction. Since his return to town, the viscount had quickly been accepted as the most eligible gentleman of the Season. She would be considered the most fortunate female in London.

She wished he had not come. She might now be contentedly betrothed to Mr. Faford, with no thoughts of love to tease her mind. Or she might be enjoying a friendship with Mr. Sedgeworth. But of course, he would not be here if Fairfax was not. She liked him a good deal. She had thoroughly enjoyed her walk with him that afternoon. Those two gentlemen were very well suited as friends, in fact. They had a great deal in common. She had talked easily with Mr. Sedgeworth on a wide range of topics. But she had been comfortable with him, without that physical awareness that intruded on the few conversations she had had with Fairfax.

If only she had met Mr. Sedgeworth without his friend, she might have entertained hopes of winning his regard. Now, of course, that was out of the question. Why was it that two men could be so similar in many ways and yet arouse such vastly different feelings in her?

Jane slid down in bed finally and pulled the bedcovers up under her arms. When would she see Lord Fairfax next? she wondered. Jane Templeton. She could be his wife. She probably would be. No, she could not believe it was true. She would not even think of it anymore for this night.

She resolutely closed her eyes.

Michael, she thought. Michael. She tested the name by whispering it to the moonlit room.


Joseph Sedgeworth propped one foot against the empty carriage seat opposite and settled comfortably into the corner. He grinned at his companion.

"It was to be Parker's card party tonight," he said. "Why the sudden change of heart, I wonder? Why is it so important to attend the theather tonight, Fairfax?"

"I told you, Sedge," his friend said evenly, "I like Shakespeare. I did not know until today that *As You Like It* was being performed tonight. There is always a card party to attend."

"Our going to the theater could not possibly have

anything to do with the fact that Miss Jamieson will be there, I suppose?" Sedgeworth asked, amused eyes on his companion.

Fairfax shrugged. "We do not even know for sure that she will be there," he said. "Miss Crawley said this afternoon merely that she had been invited to join Sir Alfred Jamieson's party to the theater tonight. If you will not believe that I go to see the play, my friend, then you may believe what you will. I could turn the tables, you know, Sedge, and point out that you put up no objection to the change of plan. Could that have anything to do with the fact that Miss Crawley will be one of the party?"

"Spare me," Sedgeworth said with some feeling. "The chit hangs around me only because doing so brings her nearer to you. She is suffering from a severe case of hero worship, I would guess."

"I think it is quite hopeless to try to get you married off, is it not, Sedge?" Fairfax said good-naturedly, leaning forward in his seat as the carriage drew to a halt outside the theater.

His mother's box was at quite the opposite side of the theater from that of Lord Jamieson, Fairfax discovered as he seated himself and looked around him. The other box was already occupied by several people. Sir Alfred and Lady Jamieson were there with both their daughter and their niece. Miss Crawley was indeed one of the party, as were three of those young puppies who followed Miss Jamieson around almost wherever she went.

He raised his hand to acknowledge the bright smile and wave that Miss Jamieson had just given him. She looked dazzling as usual in sapphire blue. She must have said something to the other occupants of the box. Several of them turned toward his box, among them Miss Matthews, who looked her usual calm, rather pretty self in midnight blue. He inclined his head, keeping his eyes on her the while. He was feeling more and more that he had made a wise choice. There was something quite distinguished about Miss Matthews when one took the time to look closely.

It was Sedgeworth who suggested at the interval that they pay their respects to the ladies in Lord Jamieson's box. Honor was closest to the door and stood up when the visitors entered. She curtsied and fanned herself vigorously.

"Is the play not marvelous?" she asked the two gentlemen, her eyes sparkling. She added quickly, "Though Papa had to explain to me at first what was happening. The language sounded so strange, almost as if it were not English at all. I suppose I should have paid my governess more mind when I was younger."

"Pretty heads ought not to be addled with such stuff," Ambrose Leighton assured her. He had risen too.

Honor smiled at him and then turned large eyes on Fairfax. "If it were not so very hot in here," she said, "I should be enjoying the performance a great deal more."

"Why did you not say so earlier?" Ambrose asked, offering her his arm. "I am sure it will be much cooler in the corridor, Miss Jamieson. Allow me to escort you there."

Fairfax stood aside to let them pass. He almost laughed aloud. How could a young lady convey such bare-teethed fury while smiling all the while and thanking a thick-skulled admirer for his thoughtfulness? Somehow Miss Jamieson managed it. He turned to Jane while Prudence and one of the young men engaged Sedgeworth in conversation.

"Miss Matthews," he said, "would you like to take a turn in the corridor too before the play resumes? With your aunt's permission, of course."

Lady Jamieson tittered. "Oh, Jane does not need my permission, Lord Fairfax," she assured him, "though it is very courteous of you to ask. She is of age."

Jane got to her feet, her eyes on a level with his neckcloth. She looked very pale. Did she believe that he was about to withdraw his offer? he wondered. He noticed how slim and well-manicured her hand was when she laid it on his arm.

They did not speak for a few minutes after they left the box, beyond an exchange of comments on the coolness of the corridor in comparison with the theater and on the surprising fact that the corridor was not more crowded. Fairfax wished to give her a chance to regain her composure. Not that she was outwardly disturbed. But she still looked unnaturally pale.

"Have you given any more thought to what I asked you yesterday?" he said at last.

"Yes, my lord," she replied without looking up at him.

"I must confess that I have thought of little else," he said. "Perhaps it is unfair of me to give you so little time to consider. But I am eager to marry and return home and resume normal life again. My children need me there, I believe, not enjoying myself here. They need both of us, in fact. Will you give me your answer, Miss Matthews?"

"I am greatly honored," she said quietly, her eyes on the floor ahead of them.

Good God, Fairfax thought, his eyes flying to her face, was she about to refuse him?

"But I am afraid I must say no," she finished, her voice shaking over the last few words.

He stared at her in stunned silence for a few seconds. "I see," he said at last. But he did not see at all. "Might I be permitted to ask why?"

She swallowed noticeably and glanced quickly at him before staring ahead at the floor again. "I think we would not suit," she said.

"But why not?" he was startled into asking. "I thought we had a great deal in common, Miss Matthews."

"Perhaps we do," she said lamely.

He should let the matter drop. Good manners dictated that he accept her refusal with good grace. And she was very obviously ill-at-ease, if not, indeed, quite distressed. But he could not believe his ears. It had never once occurred to him that she might refuse him. Why would a not-too-beautiful, not-too-popular spinster in her twenties refuse an offer of marriage to someone of his position and wealth? He had always believed that marriage was the one main goal of a female's life.

"Why then?" he persisted, bending his head a little closer to hers and looking directly at her.

She swallowed again.

"I am a person," she said very quietly and intensely. "I am Jane Matthews, my lord. There is only one of me. I am unique. To you I may appear to be no different from hundreds of other drab, aging females. But I am a person, not a commodity, not a footstool. Perhaps you do need a woman to look after your home and your children and to provide you with an heir. Perhaps I would contribute to your comfort. But what about me? What am I to gain from such an arrangement? I am not a servant for hire. I am an independent person, and my happiness matters—at least to me."

He stared at her in amazement. The paleness had disappeared from her face. It flamed with color now. "Did I speak so insultingly?" he asked. "I beg your pardon, ma'am. I had no intention of doing so. I thought the advantages of such a marriage to you would be obvious. I would provide you with a home, security, companionship. What more do you desire?" He was somewhat surprised to hear his own voice sounding irritable, almost angry.

"Nothing," she said. "Nothing. Please return me to my uncle's box, my lord. The corridor is deserted. I believe the play is about to resume."

He drew her to a halt outside the box. "My apologies, ma'am," he said, "for having troubled you with such unwelcome addresses. I wish you well." He really had not intended his voice to sound quite so icy, he thought as he took her hand and raised it briefly to his lips. It was very cold.

She curtsied, but she did not raise her eyes to his. "Good night, my lord," she said. She sounded as if she were about to cry.

Sedgeworth was grinning when he reentered their box. "You might have been luckier at cards tonight, Fairfax," he said. "That Leighton pup would not be able to take a hint if it were handed to him on a velvet cushion, would he? If looks could kill, the poor devil would be six feet under already. Better fortune next time!"

"I am leaving, Sedge," Fairfax said without responding to the teasing. "Are you coming or staying?"

"Oh, I say," his friend protested, "you aren't really so out of sorts merely because you could not walk with the lady of your choice, are you, Fairfax? I would say you probably had a great deal more of sense out of Miss Matthews than you would out of the little Jamieson. I want to see the end of the play. Sit down and forget your woes."

"I shall leave you the carriage," Fairfax said. "I feel like the walk."

Sedgeworth was prevented from replying by the pointed turning of a lorgnette in their direction from a neighboring box. Behind the lorgnette was a large and frowning dowager, who followed up the glare with a loud "Shhh!" Sedgeworth shrugged at his friend and grinned. Fairfax left.

Fairfax's legs took him home almost of their own volition. He wore an evening cloak, but he scarce knew whether the evening was cool or warm. He was stunned. She had refused him. It was about the first time he could remember a female refusing him anything. But this time he had expected it least of all. Had it been Miss Jamieson or one of the other acknowledged beauties of the Season, he would still have been surprised, but at least those girls must have a large number of suitors to choose among.

But Miss Matthews! She must already be well past the

usual age of marriage, and it could not be said that men flocked to her side. It was true that that Faford fellow had seemed interested when he first knew her. But the man could not be described as much of a catch. He had applauded her good sense in refusing him, little suspecting that he was to join the rejected suitor soon after.

Why had she refused him? He had a great deal to offer her. He had the property and wealth that he had mentioned to her. He was reputed to be an attractive man. He was not very much older than she. He had expected her to accept him with alacrity. Was it the fact of being a second wife that bothered her? But he had never referred to Susan in her hearing. She could not possibly feel threatened by a dead woman, surely? Was it the children? Did she find objectionable the idea of bringing up another woman's offspring? But she had said she loved children. And she would certainly have some of her own.

What had she said? She had been very upset, even angry. She had accused him of not considering her as a person, of using her like a footstool or a servant. How absurd! He had offered her the Templeton name, the Fairfax title, and she felt she was being treated as a servant? Her own happiness mattered to her, she had said. Could she not be happy with him? He had never thought of himself as a particularly dull person. Susan had found him so, of course. But Miss Matthews seemed different from Susan. He had thought that she was not particularly interested in gaiety and social entertainments. He must have been mistaken in her.

Perhaps he should feel delighted to have escaped another marriage in which his wife would be discontented and hankering after the fashionable centers. He could not feel delight. He had been in London for a few weeks already, and now it appeared to have been so much waste of time. He had very sensibly dismissed the idea of courting Miss Jamieson and had carefully chosen to direct his attention toward a woman who would be more of a companion to him and mother to his children. And it had turned out that he was a poor judge of character, after all. Miss Matthews wanted more out of life than the rather quiet, domesticated one he could offer.

He should be delighted. Why, then, did he feel so irritable? Why did he feel humiliated, as if the woman had made a fool out of him? He did feel like a fool. He had always believed that he was attractive to most women. To be refused by a less-than-beautiful one was a blow to his esteem. He had not expected ever to have something in common with the Fafords of this world.

By the time he reached home, Fairfax was feeling less than kindly disposed to Jane Matthews. Almost he was persuaded that she had deliberately led him on. Was she laughing at him now? Was the woman frigid, that she could afford to turn down two offers of marriage within a few weeks? Was she one of those rare women who were contented to go through life as spinsters? Of one thing he was certain. He would see as little of her as possible in the coming weeks. In fact, he would try to arrange matters so that he would not have to see her at all.

Fairfax was looking at a newspaper when Sedgeworth joined him for breakfast the next morning.

Sedgeworth yawned. "I should have come home with you last night," he said. "Did you go straight to bed? I accepted an invitation to supper at Jamieson's and ended up playing cards until some unholy hour this morning. On second thought, perhaps you should have stayed. You might have had your *tête-à-tête* with the little beauty after all. Young Leighton had to leave straight from the theater."

"Hm," Fairfax said, turning a page of his paper. "I was tired."

Sedgeworth chuckled and crossed to the sideboard to help himself to breakfast. "Sounds like sour grapes to me, Fairfax. The little chit is panting after you. Is it her fault that she has a whole army of males doing the same for her? You will not have an ounce of trouble ousting the opposition, you know?''

"And did you capture Miss Crawley as a partner for cards?'' Fairfax asked, folding the paper in two so that he could more comfortably peruse the top half of the page.

"Absolutely not,'' his friend said with a grin. "She and Miss Jamieson settled to a noisy game of spillikins with the two remaining followers. Not exactly my cup of tea. No, I had Miss Matthews for a partner. We won by a comfortable margin, too. She was in unusually high spirits. She looked quite fetching, in fact.''

Fairfax's lips thinned behind his paper. "I am thinking of going home,'' he said.

"What!'' Sedgeworth exclaimed. "You mean Templeton Hall? You cannot be serious, Fairfax. After all the effort I went to to drag you here in the first place? I thought you were beginning to enjoy yourself.''

"I miss the girls,'' Fairfax said. "You cannot understand that, can you, Sedge?'' He flung down his paper beside his plate.

"A fat lot of good you were to your girls when I came upon you,'' Sedgeworth said. "You were in an almost constant black mood and never even smiled. I thought it was agreed that you were to look around you for another wife.''

"I have looked,'' Fairfax said bluntly, "and I am ready to go home, Sedge. Single. And it was your idea, my friend, that I was coming here in search of a wife. I do not believe I am ready for marriage yet.''

"Is it all because the chit is not as easily accessible as you would like, Fairfax?'' Sedgeworth asked in puzzlement. "I would have expected you to enjoy the challenge.''

"Miss Jamieson!'' Fairfax said through his teeth. "Always Miss Jamieson. What makes you think I have lost my heart to that little clothhead, Sedge? She is all beauty and no brain. She is the last female on earth I would consider for a wife.''

Sedgeworth put down his knife and fork and roared with laughter. "No, really, Fairfax," he said. "You are doing it just too brown, you know. Protesting too much. You must not give up the campaign yet, old boy. At least wait until the end of next week. My sister was particularly insistent that we join her party to Vauxhall Gardens. She said, with some truth, that I am becoming more like a stranger than a brother. Of course, you could go home and leave me here, I suppose. But you have been insisting that I go back to Templeton Hall when you go. I have nothing else to do before setting off on my travels again when summer is over.''

Fairfax sighed. "I have dragged you around to all my family's entertainments," he said. "I suppose the least I can do is stay and go to Lady Dart's Vauxhall party. I used to love the place. Plenty of quiet walks in which to steal kisses. Ah, those were the days, Sedge. But I will not stay beyond that date. I want to go home. And I do not wish to spend overmuch time at Jamieson's in the meanwhile. Fair enough?''

Sedgeworth shrugged. "As you wish," he said. "But you could always spend the time with Miss Matthews, you know. That would soon make the little beauty send her other admirers packing in haste. And you must admit the time would not be unprofitably spent. A very interesting person, Miss Matthews. Not a bad looker, either, when you stop comparing her with Miss Jamieson.''

Fairfax excused himself and left the breakfast room.

# 7

The same morning, Jane was suffering a reaction from the events of the night before. Her aunt and cousin were still in bed after the late night. It had been past two o'clock when the last of their visitors left. Jane had been very glad to have the breakfast room to herself. She was back in her room now, seated on the window seat that overlooked the street. Her knees were drawn up, her arms clasping them.

So much for her matrimonial hopes, she was thinking. She had been granted a second chance to come to London during the Season, at a time when she was beginning to resign herself to a spinster life. She had had two offers and she had refused them both. She would return home in a few weeks' time and probably never have another chance to marry. Even if she did, she was not sure she would have the heart to accept it. She would live a single life, then. She would never know the joys of marriage and motherhood.

She rested her forehead on her raised knees. Was she some kind of a fool? She had refused Mr. Faford because her renewed infatuation for Viscount Fairfax had spoiled her for a loveless marriage. And yet when the impossible had happened and Fairfax himself had offered for her, she had refused him too. She had refused to marry the man she loved.

She had not been sure even when he had invited her to walk in the theater corridor exactly what her answer would be. She had expected it to be yes. She had not thought she would have the will to say no. But she had said no. He had been so sure she would accept him. He had sounded almost impatient at having to wait long enough to get past the formality of her answer. He wanted to get home to his regular life and home to his children. Almost as if it were a nuisance to have to be delayed by her. She had liked him. Since she had met him and talked to him, she had been impressed by his lack of arrogance. But last night he had appeared conceited.

Of course, he probably had good reason to be. Female heads turned in his direction wherever he went. It had been so five years ago and it was so this year. Even in the country he was probably a great favorite with the ladies. Was it surprising that such a man should have taken for granted that she would accept him? She, plain, very ordinary Jane Matthews? He had probably expected her to prostrate herself at his feet with gratitude at the unspeakable honor he was doing her.

And she had seen herself in much the same way. Ever since she had first set eyes on hm she had felt inferior, as if he were so far above her that she was presuming even to raise her eyes to him. When she was eighteen she had been contented to worship from afar. It had seemed right. She had never expected to receive even one glance from him. During the five years since, she had trained herself to aim low. She was not worthy of a man like Fairfax, she had persuaded herself, even if she had not put the idea into quite those words. She had convinced herself that she was being realistic and sensible. Right up until last evening she had kept the same attitude. She had been grateful for every look and word he had spared her, stored them up for future delight.

It was only the evening before that the scales had fallen away from her eyes and she had seen clearly. In what way was she inferior to Lord Fairfax? She was not beautiful; he was extraordinarily handsome. Did that make her inferior? She had the sort of character that could win her the affection of those close to her but that did not attract people in general; he had a charm that could focus the attention of a large gathering on himself if he chose. Did that make her inferior? She was the daughter of an untitled gentleman of impeccable lineage and comfortable fortune; he was titled and reputedly very wealthy. Did that make her inferior? She had been educated by a governess and had learned a great deal for herself through reading and listening; he had gone to a good school and university and liked to read and develop his mind. Was she in any way inferior?

These thoughts did not occur consciously to Jane's mind as she walked with Viscount Fairfax at the theater. But the sudden realization that she had made herself into an abject, poor creature did strike her quite consciously. Although perhaps Fairfax did not mean his words in quite the way they sounded, although perhaps he was nervous and not projecting a true image of himself, his urging that she give him her answer had made Jane very angry indeed. She had not wanted to give him a reason for her refusal. Indeed, she could hardly frame a reason in words even to herself. But he had pressed her, and she had become even more angry.

She had had no time to think out her words in advance, but she had found once she started that words came pouring out of her. And she had tried to convey to him her anger in being thought of by labels. She was needed as a wife, a mother, a housekeeper. She was not needed as Jane. She was not a wife, a mother, or a housekeeper. And she would never be primarily one of those things even if she did eventually marry. Primarily and always she was Jane, a unique and very real person. She could never marry anyone who would not recognize that. She would not allow herself to be treated as a commodity. Even if she loved Lord Fairfax fifty times more than she did—impossible!—she could never marry him unless he could look at her and see Jane and assure her that it was Jane he wanted, not any other woman in the world. Just Jane.

She had been very proud of herself for the rest of the evening, proud of the fact that her sense of worth had overcome her awe at being addressed by Viscount Fairfax. She did love him. She knew that she would live to regret never seeing him again. She knew she would suffer from a sense of emptiness, knowing that she could have married him and lived her life with him. But for that evening she was proud. She had watched the second half of the play attentively, her cheeks hot, her eyes intense. And afterward, she would not have been able to recall one action or one word that had taken place on the stage.

Her aunt and uncle had unexpectedly decided to invite their guests back to their house for supper. When Mr. Leighton had been forced to decline because of a previous engagement and it was seen that Mr. Sedgeworth was alone in his box, Uncle Alfred had walked over there himself and invited him to supper. Jane had thoroughly enjoyed the rest of the evening. She was glad they had company. She was not yet ready to be alone with her own thoughts.

She had agreed to partner Mr. Sedgeworth at cards. And she had enjoyed his company. She thought now that she might even have flirted with him a little. He was so thoroughly friendly and so completely unthreatening. He was a man she could like and respect and yet one for whom she felt not one ounce of physical attraction. She could relax in his company. That was what she would concentrate on for the rest of her life: building friendships with men—and women—whom she could like. Life did not have to be dull even for a spinster.

That had been the night before. Now, after a few hours of sleep, the future did not seem quite so bright. Would she see Fairfax again? she wondered. She supposed it was inevitable that they would be in the same room occasionally and glimpse each other from a distance. But surely he would be anxious now to avoid her. As she would be to avoid him. And once the Season was over, she would never see him again. Never. It was an awfully long time.

She could not feel sorry for her decision. She still thought as she had the night before. In many ways she felt like a new person. No longer would she undervalue herself. She looked back with some horror now to the attitude with which she had come to London. Almost any man would do as a husband, she had said, provided he was amiable and had no obvious vice. And she had convinced herself that it was common sense that had led her to that decision. It was not common sense. It was a conviction that she could expect very little of life.

Never again would she take that attitude. She was in fact very satisfied with herself as a person. She had developed her talents and her mind as far as she was able as a female in a male-dominated society. If she compared herself to Honor, she would have to say, even if it seemed immodest to do so, that she was inferior only in beauty. Honor was not unintelligent and she was not without accomplishments. But Honor was ashamed of both. She felt they took away from her femininity and so she lived a lie. She subjected everything that made her an interesting and a unique person to the all-important need to find herself a husband. And what was the criterion by which she judged a man suitable as a husband? His looks merely. Jane did not believe Honor loved Lord Fairfax. She doubted if the girl knew him even to the limited extent that she, Jane, did. But he was a handsome man and so Honor pursued him.

Jane looked unseeingly out the window. The rest of the Season suddenly seemed quite unenticing. She longed to go home. At this moment she would give a great deal to be able to put on a bonnet and set out on a long walk across the moors, nothing to come between her and her thoughts except nature at its wildest and bleakest. She did not want to have to continue going to balls, routs, soirees, and everything else that various members of the *ton* had devised for the mutual pleasure of all.

She did not want to see him again.

She ached with pain and emptiness at the thought that she might never see him again. And that her exile from him was of her own doing.

\* \* \*

For the following week and a half Jane and Honor saw almost nothing of Viscount Fairfax. He raised his hat to them and nodded one morning from the opposite side of the street when they were out shopping. Honor reported that he had stopped his horse to talk to her for a few minutes in the park one afternoon when she was driving with one of her admirers. But he had not stopped for long. He was on his way somewhere, not just out for the social exercise.

Honor was disturbed for a few days by his absence from their drawing room and every entertainment they attended. Then she shrugged the matter off. "It is true that he is easily the handsomest man in town," she said to Jane, "but if he chooses to be moody, I shall have nothing to do with him. It is not as if he ignores just me, Jane. We have been where everyone else of any consequence has been for the last few days, and he has not been in sight. So it seems he shuns everyone. I shall not worry my head over him any longer."

The presence in London of the Earl of Henley helped lessen her disappointment. He was recently returned from Vienna and was much in demand by people who wanted firsthand news of what was happening at the Congress there. The earl was in his forties and no match in either looks or physique for Viscount Fairfax. But he was distinguished-looking and wealthy. And he was popular with the *ton*. He was an earl. Two facts endeared him more than any others to Honor, though. He had a reputation as something of a rake. And he very openly singled her out for his gallantries from the moment of his arrival.

"I have not at all decided if I shall have him," she confided to Jane one morning while they were enjoying a quiet stroll in the park. "He is a little older than I would wish my husband to be. Just imagine, Jane. By the time I am thirty, he will be close to sixty! However, he is much more distinguished than Max or Harry or even Percy. And the idea of being a countess is quite appealing."

Jane offered no opinion. She considered it likely that if the Earl of Henley had made it into his forties without succumbing to the charms of any female or her mama, he would continue to do so. However, if his attentions would keep Honor's mind off Fairfax, Jane would be thankful. She did not wish to be forever listening to her cousin talk about him. She did not even wish to think about him.

They did not see the viscount, but Mr. Sedgeworth continued to be much in evidence. He called twice at the house during the next week and a half and took Jane driving on one of those occasions. He appeared at almost every social function they attended and always spent some time with Sir Alfred Jamieson's party. He danced with both Jane and Honor at Almack's. He led Jane in to dinner one evening and sat beside her. Later he turned pages for Honor while she played the spinet, and fetched her tea when she was finished. He sat beside Jane at a musical evening and between items described to her some of the concerts he had attended in Italy and Germany.

Both ladies grew to like him.

"He certainly proves that one does not have to be extraordinarily handsome to be amiable," Honor said. "And indeed he is quite handsome when one looks closely. He is not very tall, of course, and his hair is no decided color, just light brown. But he has a very pleasing face. His eyes and his mouth seem always to be close to smiling. I think he would do very well for you, Jane. Much better than that dreadfully dull Mr. Faford, who does not bother you any longer, thank heaven. I was very afraid you might marry him. And I believe Mr. Sedgeworth likes you."

"The same might certainly be said for you, Honor," Jane pointed out. "Whenever he dances with me, he dances with you too."

"Yes," Honor agreed, "but he does not spend a great deal of time conversing with me, Jane. I think he is one of the few gentlemen who like to talk to an intelligent woman. And I, of course, am the merest ninny-hammer.''

"If he believes so, the fault is no one's but yours," Jane said. "No one who does not know you closely would guess that there is a brain somewhere beneath all that dark hair.''

Honor laughed. "You must not give away my secret, Jane," she said. "I would lose my following instantly if anyone suspected.''

"As far as I can see," Jane said, "you seem to despise the bulk of that following anyway, Honor.''

The girl laughed again. "But it is irresistible to be the most sought-after debutante of the Season," she said. "Besides, Henley would likely not have given me a second glance had there not been a whole host of lovelorn males around me when he first set eyes on me.''

Jane welcomed her growing friendship with Mr. Sedgeworth, especially when it became clear that being with him was not bringing her into contact with Fairfax. He referred to his friend only once, and that was during their drive in the park.

"I am worried about Fairfax," he said. "He positively refuses to go anywhere where he is likely to meet ladies. That limits his activities almost entirely to visits to his clubs. I had great hopes of bringing him out of the gloom he has been in since the death of his wife. But he is being attacked by homesickness. I suppose it is not easy to get over the death of a wife one has loved. However, Miss Matthews, I must not bore you with my own worries.''

Jane had made no comment and the topic had been changed. She found Mr. Sedgeworth very easy to talk to and very interesting. When he realized that stories of his travels did not bore her, he told her a great deal about various countries.

"It must be wonderful to be free to travel wherever you wish," she said with something of a sigh one day.

"Yes, it is," he said. "I hope the political situation has settled down by the autumn. With Boney escaped from Elba and things looking as if they are shaping up to a showdown any day, the matter is by no means certain." He looked at her suddenly. "But that is not what you meant, is it? You meant that because I am a man, I have the freedom to come and go as I wish."

She smiled. "It is very restricting to be a woman," she said.

"I confess I had not given the matter much thought before," he admitted. "I suppose I have always thought that females desired no more than husbands, homes, and families. But you have avoided such a fate so far, Miss Matthews. Do you feel very restricted by the conventions?"

"Sometimes," she said. "But I was not asking for your pity, sir. I had not thought a great deal about travel until I heard you talking of different places. I daresay that in reality I would grow very tired of the constant traveling and staying at inns."

She could relax with him. She began to think of him fondly as a real friend and looked forward to their meetings with pleasure. Jane did not have a close friend in London apart from Honor, with whom she did not see eye to eye on several issues. She came to smile a great deal when she was with Mr. Sedgeworth. She was able to keep the pain of not seeing Fairfax at bay except perhaps at night, when she frequently tossed and turned, unable to get to sleep.

She hesitated somewhat when Mr. Sedgeworth invited her to join a party to Vauxhall Gardens one evening. She was terrified that Viscount Fairfax might also be of the party. But it seemed unlikely. He had been to no social functions in over a week. When Mr. Sedgeworth explained that the hosts were his sister and brother-in-law and that they had invited several of their friends, she considered it safe to agree. She wanted to go. She had been to Vauxhall once with her parents and had thought it an enchanted place. She had been unhappy there, having no one for company but her parents, while scores of friends and lovers enjoyed themselves dancing or walking along the lantern-lit paths or laughing over the fireworks displays. She wanted to go back now with a friend and in company with his relatives and their friends.

She did wonder, though, when she knew who the hosts were, whether Honor was not perhaps right in her guess. Was Mr. Sedgeworth developing an attachment to her? He certainly did not behave like a lover. She thought of him merely as a friend. Yet he was willing to escort her to a party hosted by his sister. She was not sure how she would react if he really did have a regard for her.

Her apprehension was put to rest, though, when a short while later he asked Honor too to join the Vauxhall party. Jane even smiled, in fact. Why had she assumed that she had been invited as his exclusive partner? She must be developing some vanity after receiving two offers in the past few weeks. It was a relief to know that Honor would be there too.

They were to dine at Lord and Lady Dart's house on Curzon Street before leaving for Vauxhall. Jane and Honor were to travel there together in Sir Alfred Jamieson's carriage. Honor was not vastly excited.

"How do we know who will be of this party, Jane?" she asked. "We scarcely know the Darts. Certainly I do not know who their friends are. Probably all older married couples. And you and I are to share Mr. Sedgeworth. I could think of better things to do. He probably invited me only because it might have appeared ill-mannered not to. But I shall find it humiliating to have only half a man in attendance for a whole evening. And at Vauxhall too. I have been longing all Season to go there. And the first time it happens, we are to be part of a middle-aged party."

Jane laughed. "Lady Dart is probably no older than I am, Honor," she said. "Certainly she is younger than her brother. And he cannot be thirty yet. Besides, it is unlikely that she would have arranged a party of uneven numbers."

Honor brightened somewhat. "I wonder who the extra gentleman will be," she said. "I hope he is at least handsome. It cannot be Henley or he would have told me when he called this afternoon."

Jane knew the moment they entered the Darts' drawing room who the extra gentleman was. He was standing with his back to the fireplace, a glass of something in one hand, appearing surely taller and more handsome than ever, his face pale and severe, looking as if he were attending his own funeral. She met Fairfax's eyes for a moment, long enough to see his slight bow of acknowledgment. Then her own eyes wavered and dropped, and she could feel the annoying color mount her neck and cheeks. And there was that old churning of the stomach, but far worse than ever before. Why had she not simply asked Mr. Sedgeworth if Viscount Fairfax was to be one of the party? It would have been easy to do. A mere casual inquiry would have been enough.

It was too late now. Jane smiled and extended her hand to Lady Dart, who had come hurrying toward them. And her smile deepened when she saw Mr. Sedgeworth immediately behind his sister, smiling his very friendly and comforting smile. Honor, having greeted both, smiled broadly and walked lightly across the room to talk to Fairfax.

Viscount Fairfax had the advantage over Jane, if advantage it were. He knew that she was to be of the Vauxhall party. He had personally accepted Lady Dart's invitation and felt obliged to keep his promise. But he had been furious the afternoon Sedgeworth joined him at White's Club, smirking in such a manner that Fairfax knew immediately that he was up to some mischief.

"I have just come from Jamieson's," he said.

"Oh?" Fairfax did not encourage talk of the ladies of that house.

"And have invited Miss Jamieson to be one of the Vauxhall party."

"You have what?" Fairfax was immediately alert.

"I have taken matters into my own hands, Fairfax," his friend said. "For some reason you have quarreled with the chit, and you have been in a black mood ever since. I am making a last effort to get you two together again."

Fairfax sighed. "Well, you can spend the evening entertaining her yourself, Sedge," he said. "I have already told you I am not interested."

"I can't," his friend said smugly. "I shall be escorting Miss Matthews, and I do not believe I am willing to exchange ladies. I find Miss Matthews far more interesting. No, you can have the beauty, Fairfax."

That was when Fairfax had become furiously angry. But what could he say? Sedgeworth knew nothing of his offer to Miss Matthews. And why should he be angry, anyway, and why so reluctant to see the woman again? He had merely been trying to make a marriage of convenience and had been rejected. What was so embarrassing about that? What had plunged him into such low spirits for almost two weeks? Women of Miss Matthews' caliber were easy to come by. Why did he dread having to face her? Why had he gone straight home after seeing her on the street that morning and not gone out again for the rest of the day?

Sedgeworth's manner became more serious. "It is just one evening, Fairfax," he said. "At least give the little chit one more chance. If you find that you cannot patch up the quarrel, there is no harm done. You are going home next week. If you do decide that you wish to pursue her again, then why not make her one of your house party? You have already invited Joy and Wallace and the children. Why not Miss Jamieson as well? You would be able to see her in your home setting before making an offer. And she would be well-chaperoned."

Fairfax gave him a speaking glance.

"It was just a thought," Sedgeworth said lamely.

Fairfax found it a great ordeal to wait in the Darts' drawing room knowing that she would arrive soon. It took all his presence of mind to stand with apparent unconcern across the room when she made her entrance with Miss Jamieson and found him with her eyes almost immediately. He bowed in their direction and was strangely pleased to witness her confusion. But why should he care? Why feel the same confusion himself?

She was just Miss Jane Matthews, a mildly pretty woman past the first bloom of her girlhood. He fixed his eyes on the approaching figure of a smiling Miss Jamieson, looking quite as dazzling as ever. He prepared to be sociable.

# 8

They entered Vauxhall Gardens by the river. They had gone by carriage when Jane went there with her parents. This approach was far more enthralling, the lights strung from the trees reflected in the ripples of the water, the music seeming to float out toward them. If only she could relax and ignore the presence of Viscount Fairfax.

Mr. Sedgeworth had led her in to dinner. Fortunately Fairfax held back until they were already seated and then took Honor to a place at the opposite end of the table. It was not a great deal of consolation. There were only ten at table and the conversation was frequently general. Fortunately Honor was in high spirits and focused most of the attention on herself.

In the boat, too, Fairfax and Honor were somewhat removed from Jane and Sedgeworth. But it was impossible for Jane to relax. She felt his presence as strongly as if he had a hand at her neck. She was relieved, after they had all strolled to Lord Dart's box close to the orchestra, to find that they were free to stroll or dance at their leisure. Lady Dart declared that it was too early to think of supper yet, though they must all gather later to sample the wafer-thin slices of ham and the strawberries for which the Gardens were famous. And of course they must all sit together to witness the fireworks after supper.

Fairfax took Honor to dance. Sedgeworth suggested to Jane that they take a walk. He grinned apologetically at her as they set off.

"I am afraid I have mortally offended Fairfax," he said, "and he is punishing me by staying away from me."

"Oh?" said Jane. She had a different theory on why the viscount was avoiding their company.

"I thought that his quarrel with Miss Jamieson was one that could be mended," he explained. "So I trapped him into escorting her here tonight. Do you know the cause of that quarrel, Miss Matthews? Whatever it is, it seems that Miss Jamieson has forgiven him. She is behaving most charmingly tonight."

"No, I do not know," Jane said. She had wondered several times over the last two weeks whether Mr. Sedgeworth knew of her rejection of his friend. Clearly he did not.

"I had high hopes earlier in the Season that they would make a match of it," Sedgeworth said. "She is something like his first wife, you know, though not in looks. Lady Fairfax was very blond. Perhaps it is her very similarity to his wife that makes him hesitate. I believe he loved her very dearly."

"Yes," Jane said. "I saw them together before their marriage."

"And I never did see them afterward," he said. "I was always traveling, and when I was home I did not like to intrude on a married friend. Perhaps I should not try to interfere now. But I hate to see someone I care for unhappy. And I believe Miss Jamieson has made him unhappy. He has been moping around even more in the past two weeks than when I first went to see him a few months ago."

Jane could think of nothing to say.

"However," he said cheerfully, "I cannot say that I am altogether sorry that Fairfax has decided to punish me tonight. I can think of no more pleasant way to spend an evening than wandering in Vauxhall Gardens alone with a lovely lady."

Jane smiled. She was unused to such gallantries from Mr. Sedgeworth. "I came here five years ago with my parents," she said, "and thought then how lovely it would be to walk here with a friend."

"And is that what you consider me?" he asked. "A friend?"

She looked across at him and smiled. There was a strange tension between them that she had not felt before. "Yes," she said.

"I believe I am beginning to think of you as something more than that," he said. "In fact, Miss Matthews, I would like you to be my wife. And that was very graciously said, was it not? I assure you I am quite unused to making such offers and indeed thought never to have to learn. Until the last few weeks I had every intention of living a bachelor existence."

He stopped walking and turned to her in some embarrassment, his hand covering hers as it rested on his arm.

"Miss Matthews, do forgive me," he said. "I have said it all wrong, have I not? The truth is that I have come to rely on your friendship a great deal in the last weeks. I find myself looking forward to our meetings and thinking of you a great deal when we are not together. I have come to realize that my life and my travels are going to seem very lonely and empty without you to talk to and share my thoughts with. I want to have you with me when I travel, and show you the things I have particularly loved, and experience new places with you. You have become very important to me. Am I still making a horrid mess of this? Will you marry me?"

Jane stared. Yes, she had been expecting this, had she not, or at least suspecting that such a thing might happen? She moved her head suddenly in the direction of a noisy group of people advancing down the path on which they stood. He turned too and they strolled on until they were again almost alone.

"I have come to rely on our friendship too," she said. "I feel easy with you, relaxed. Oh, I do not know what to say, Mr. Sedgeworth. I like you and respect you and greatly enjoy your company. But I do not believe I can attach the name 'love' to my feelings for you."

"I did not use the word myself, Miss Matthews," he said. "I think perhaps we are both past the age of romance, are we not? I have a deep regard for you and the liveliness and intelligence of your mind. I believe we could have an affectionate relationship, and perhaps that is not very different from romantic love. Is there any other man that you do love?''

Jane felt her heart begin to thump. She closed her eyes for a moment. "Yes," she said finally.

"I see," he said. "And is your feeling returned? Is there any chance that you will marry this man?''

"Absolutely not, to both questions, sir," she said.

"Then marry me," he said, "and know that you will be held in my affection for as long as I live. And I will see to it that you have an interesting and a secure life. I ask only your own affection and companionship in return.''

He drew her off the path to sit on a rustic bench. The sound of the music was quite faint in the distance. Light from the breeze-blown lanterns danced across the path in front of them.

"Am I pressing too hard?" he asked. "Forgive me. I want you to make a free decision. I want you to marry me because you wish it and not because I have talked you into it.''

Jane looked at him, at his kindly eyes. She really did not deserve this, this one extra chance with a man as friendly and as interesting as Mr. Sedgeworth. "I would like to marry you, sir," she said. "Thank you.''

His face relaxed into a broad smile of relief. "Splendid!" he said. "You have made me very happy, Miss Matthews. I shall spend my life trying to make you so. My acquaintances will not believe this. I shall be teased to the death. Especially by Fairfax. I was protesting to him only a few weeks ago that I had no interest whatsoever in marriage. But then, that was before I met you. I am so very happy.''

Jane swallowed. She felt a twinge of alarm. Was she doing the right thing? He was acting for all the world like a man in love. What had she done? She had betrothed herself to this man, her friend. Had she done both him and herself a terrible disservice? Friendship and marriage were two vastly different situations. Could she be a good wife to him? Oh, but she wanted to be. She wanted the warm security that marriage to him could bring her. She would have a friend by her side for life.

"Tears, Miss Matthews?" he asked softly.

She realized that they had been staring at each other for some time and that both her hands lay in his.

She laughed shakily. "This is all very new to me," she said. "I think I am very happy too, sir."

He grinned. "You think?" he said. "And will you call me by my given name? It is Joseph."

"Yes," she said, "Joseph."

"Jane," he said, smiling, "may I kiss you?"

She nodded and closed her eyes as he bent his head to hers. Their hands were still clasped. She had never been kissed before. His lips were cool, firm against hers. He kept them there long enough for her to become fully aware of his physical presence. She must grow accustomed to this and to a great deal more. It was not unpleasant. She realized as he lifted his head that she was gripping his hands very tightly.

He looked into her eyes before smiling. "There," he said. "Was it a terrible ordeal, Jane?"

She laughed, half in embarrassment, half in relief. "No, not at all," she said.

"I have committed myself to going to Templeton Hall next week," he said. "Joy and Wallace and the children are going also. Will you come too, Jane? We can get to know each other better in the country, and you can become better acquainted with part of my family. I would hate to go and know I would not see you for a few weeks."

Jane felt instant alarm. "Oh no," she said. "I could not possibly intrude on a house party."

"Nonsense," he said. "Fairfax is my best friend. We are almost like brothers. He will be delighted to have you come too and to have the greater chance to tease me. Besides, I have suggested to him that he invite Miss Jamieson. He will be more ready to do so, I believe, if you are going to be there too. Do say yes, Jane. Please.''

She shook her head and shrugged her shoulders at the same time. Words would not come.

He squeezed her hands and got to his feet, drawing her with him. "How stupid I am," he said, "inviting you to someone else's house party and expecting you to accept. Of course you are greatly embarrassed. The invitation must come from Fairfax himself. He will persuade you. He has great charm with ladies, does Fairfax. You will not resist his persuasions, my girl. Oh, Jane''—he squeezed her hands almost painfully— "what a very fortunate man I am. I can hardly believe it yet. All week I have been in terror that when I put the question you would refuse."

She smiled and leaned impulsively forward to rest her forehead against his neckcloth for a moment. "I am the fortunate one, sir," she said. "Joseph."

He tucked one of her hands beneath his arm and turned back in the direction of the music and the crowds.

Honor was in very high spirits. She had quite convinced herself that Fairfax had arranged it all himself. Why he would have made arrangements through his friend to escort her to Vauxhall and why he would do so after two weeks of making no attempt to see her, she did not stop to consider. It was sufficient for the evening that she was being seen by all the world in company with the most handsome man in London.

They danced a great deal. At Vauxhall the conventions did not apply. They were free to dance with each other far more than the two sets that were the limit at more formal events. And Honor liked to dance beneath the lights, where she could be seen and admired by members of the *ton*, cits, and lower-class people alike. They walked too, along the broader paths where the bulk of the crowds strolled. And they stopped to exchange civilities with numerous acquaintances, even those who were masked. Most of the masks at Vauxhall were worn for effect rather than to disguise.

And Fairfax finally had his kiss. She seemed eager for it. It seemed to be she rather than he who led their steps along dimmer, quieter paths after they must have been seen by most of the people in attendance that night. It was surely her footsteps that lagged more than his when they reached a particularly dark portion of the path. They both stopped, but was it she who exerted rather more pressure on his arm than he did on hers? Fairfax could not be sure. He knew only that he did not resist and that he despised himself even as he turned to her.

He kissed her hungrily, pulling her small, shapely body against his own, parting his lips over hers, trying —in vain—to tease her soft lips open. He wanted her. He would like to take her among the trees and . . . Fairfax straightened up and tried to steady his breathing without showing her how disturbed he was. Why take his anger out on her anyway? She was not its cause. And she was just an innocent young girl despite her flirtatious ways.

She was smiling up at him in what he supposed she thought a seductive manner. "Why, Lord Fairfax!" she said. "How you do take advantage of one."

"Pardon me, ma'am," he said, trying not to sound irritable or abrupt. "You are too lovely for your own good, I fear. Let me take you back to Lady Dart's box. It must be close to suppertime."

He could not see her very clearly, but she looked disappointed. "It is pleasant here," she said. "Very quiet and peaceful."

"And dangerous too, ma'am, I do assure you," he said. This time his voice did sound abrupt. He attempted to smile. "Your mother would not like you to be alone like this without a female companion. Let us go and find out if the orchestra will play another waltz."

But when they reached the end of the path and turned onto another, she pulled on his arm again. "Here are Jane and Mr. Sedgeworth," she said. "Ho, Jane, do come with us and dance. You have not done so all evening. And it is so wonderful to dance out-of-doors.''

Fairfax could feel himself stiffen and was powerless either to understand his own reaction or to do anything about it. Sedge was grinning at him as if he knew that the little Miss Jamieson had just been thoroughly and quite indecorously kissed. He was probably waiting for them to announce their betrothal. Damn Sedge! If he was not careful, Fairfax was going to put himself into a position of feeling obliged to offer for the girl. And he really had no wish to do so. He had found her chatter during the evening quite tedious, and when he had kissed her he had felt lust only, not any degree of tenderness.

He tried not to look at Miss Matthews. Sedge was still grinning. "This is an evening to remember, Fairfax," he said. "You owe me congratulations."

Fairfax's heart turned over within him. "Oh?" he said, one eyebrow raised.

"Miss Matthews has just made me the happiest of men," Sedgeworth said. "She has agreed to be my wife. Now, what do you think of that!"

Honor squealed and hurled herself at Jane. "Oh," she cried, "that is wonderful! I knew it. I just knew it. I am so glad. And I thoroughly approve. Oh, Jane, I am so happy for you. I am so happy." She hugged and kissed her cousin and danced her around in a circle. A group of young gentlemen who passed at that moment gave her openly appreciative glances.

The few seconds had given Fairfax the time necessary to recover from what had felt like a low and vicious punch. He held out a hand to his friend. "Congratulations, Sedge," he said. "I wish you happy. I am sure you will be. You dark horse!"

"How could I tell you?" Sedgeworth said with a grin. "She might have refused and I would have felt foolish in your eyes."

Honor turned from Jane and looked as if she would hurl herself at Sedgeworth too. She checked herself in time, but her eyes sparkled and her lips smiled. She held out both hands to him. "Mr. Sedgeworth, I am so glad that it is you who are to be my cousin-in-law," she said. "Is there such a thing? You are very fortunate to have Jane. She is a very special person, you know. But I think she is fortunate too. Congratulations, sir."

Sedgeworth, smiling, lifted her hands one at a time to his lips. Fairfax and Jane were left standing a little apart while this interchange was taking place. He turned to her, his face drawn and unsmiling. He held out a hand.

"My best wishes, Miss Matthews," he said. "You have chosen a good man. I wish you happy."

She put her hand in his and raised her eyes to his. Their hands remained clasped and their eyes locked for nameless seconds. What message passed? Fairfax wondered. He felt almost that he needed an interpreter. For the space of a few seconds their eyes penetrated beyond surfaces. They looked into each other's souls. He was left with a sense of deep grief and loss.

"Thank you, my lord," she said evenly.

He raised her hand to his lips and they broke eye contact.

"I have been persuading Jane to marry me this summer," Sedgeworth was saying, "so that I may take her traveling during the autumn. Provided the Continent is safe for travel by then, of course. But I think we can trust to old Wellington. If it is still not possible to travel there, we will go to Scotland, will we not, Jane?" He tucked her arm through his and smiled warmly at her.

"Wherever you wish," she said. "Almost everywhere in the world is new to me."

"Travel," Honor said. "Oh, lucky Jane! May I be your bridesmaid and accompany you on your wedding trip?" She laughed so gaily that they all joined in.

So that was it, Fairfax was thinking. She wanted something more glamorous from marriage than a home in the country and a ready-made family. She preferred Sedge and his adventurous life. He would not have thought it. It seemed he had misjudged Miss Jane Matthews from the start. And was she happy with her choice? She smiled and clung to Sedge's arm, but she did not appear as exuberant as he. And she studiously avoided looking at himself again.

"Fairfax!" Sedgeworth looked back at him as if he were about to announce some world crisis. "Jane has positively refused to say she will come to Templeton Hall next week. I have committed myself to coming with Joy and Wallace, yet I cannot possibly leave my betrothed here. Now you must give her a formal invitation so that she can see she will be quite welcome."

Good God! For perhaps a few seconds Fairfax viewed his problem, aghast. He could not have the woman at Templeton Hall. He would go mad. Yet there was no possible way he could refuse Sedge's request. It would not have occurred to Sedge, of course, to ask in private. He could not know that there was any possible objection to Miss Matthews' visiting the Hall. Good God.

"There can be no question of your refusing, Miss Matthews," he said to the back of her head. "Of course you must come with Sedge. I cannot do without his presence, you know, and he must not be asked to do without yours. I formally invite you to join my small house party at Templeton Hall next week. You will be very welcome, ma'am."

"Joseph!" she said in a stifled voice. "How could you put Lord Fairfax into such a very awkward predicament?"

He laughed. "He knows very well that I would do the same for him," he said. "I told you we are like brothers."

"And Miss Jamieson," Fairfax was saying, "if your cousin is to come, why not you too? Would you be willing to miss a few weeks of the Season in order to join my house party? Sedge's sister will be there to act as a chaperone. Shall I call on your mother tomorrow and ask her permission?"

Honor glowed up at him. "Oh, that would be divine, my lord," she said. She performed a few skipping steps. "What a wonderful day this is turning out to be."

She was still bubbling with excitement when they returned to the box and could hear that the orchestra was just beginning a waltz tune. No one else from their party had yet returned. "It is a waltz," she said, clasping her hands. "Mr. Sedgeworth, do come and dance with me. I wish to have a serious talk with you to discover if you really are suitable for my cousin." She giggled and hauled a smiling Sedgeworth off in the direction of the floor.

Jane sat down.

"Would you care to dance, Miss Matthews?" Fairfax asked.

She looked up at him, obviously quite as embarrassed as he. She appeared to be about to refuse, but she stood up and took his arm. Perhaps she realized, as he had, that silence while they were dancing would be preferable to silence as they sat side by side in Lord Dart's box.

They danced without a word for a while. He had never been physically aware of her before when he had danced with her. Now his hand at her waist registered her slimness. Her head reached above his shoulders. She was taller than most ladies. She moved with grace. There was a perfume about her that did not overpower but seemed to be a part of her. He had noticed it before without being quite conscious of the fact. Her brown curls were soft and shining.

"Does Sedge know that you are Jane Matthews?" he asked.

She looked up into his eyes, startled, a slight frown creasing her brow. Then she flushed deeply. "Yes, my lord, I believe he does," she said.

"I am glad," he said. "I knew you only as a commodity and a footstool, did I not?" He had not meant to sneer. In fact, he had not meant to say what he had at all. What was the matter with him?

She was still looking at him, her eyes wide and bright.

"I was angry," she said. "I spoke in haste. I am sorry. I did not mean to insult you."

Oh God, there were tears in her eyes. And they were in an infernally public place. He could not pull her into his arms here to comfort her. Did he want to anyway? She could not seem to look away from him. The tears were about to spill over onto her cheeks.

He pulled her arm through his and led her quickly from the floor onto a path that was a little darker, though fairly crowded with strollers. "I am sorry," he said. "There was absolutely no call for me to say that. It was quite unforgivable, in fact. Don't cry. Please." He handed her his linen handkerchief, which she took after some hesitation."

"I am sorry, Jane," he said again. "This should be one of the happiest nights of your life, and I am doing my best to spoil it for you. Please forgive me. You gave me a much-needed lesson in humility two weeks ago. I am not overused to rejection, and I am afraid I have been feeling rather angry with you. Let us be friends again, shall we? We were friends before I spoiled it all by offering for you, were we not? And we must be friends if you are to marry Sedge, you know. I quite refuse to lose his friendship, yet I must if I am at daggers drawn with his wife. Will you forgive me? And I do know that you are Jane Matthews, by the way. You are a very special person, I suspect, Jane. I envy Sedge. Have I set you to crying again? Come, I shall say nothing further. We shall merely turn around and stroll slowly back again. I see there are a few people in Joy's box now."

Before they reached the really public area in front of the dancing floor she had pushed his handkerchief into the pocket of her cloak. "Thank you," she said. "I should be happy to forget the awkwardness of the last two weeks. Will you really mind my coming to your home? I have never been more embarrassed in my life than when Joseph asked you so publicly to invite me."

He touched lightly the hand that was resting on his

arm. "Please come," he said. "Sedge will not want to part from you so soon, and I want to show off my daughters to you. I am sure you will like them. You see what a fond father I am? I refuse to admit that anyone may consider them to be brats."

Did he feel happy or miserable as he handed her into the box and took his place beside Miss Jamieson? He had not known that one could feel both emotions simultaneously and over the same subject.

# 9

The following morning when Jane awoke, she was convinced for one moment that she must be seeing an apparition. Honor was in her room, fully dressed, pulling the window closed to shut out the morning chill.

"Oh, you are awake finally, Jane," she said brightly. "I did not wish to waken you, but I am sure that in another minute my patience would have failed me and I would have been shaking you and yelling in your ear." She smiled broadly.

Jane closed her eyes again. "What time is it?" she asked.

"Past nine o'clock, slugabed," her cousin replied. "Do wake up, Jane."

"Past nine o'clock and you are up and dressed?" Jane said, eyes still closed. "Has Aunt Cynthia sent for the physician yet, Honor?"

"Oh, do stop teasing this minute and get out of bed," Honor said. "There is so much to talk about, Jane. I am so happy for both you and myself that I could leap from the window."

Jane swung her legs over the side of the bed and sat up. "What a very strange idea," she said. "Honor, do go downstairs. I don't believe I can cope with your high spirits quite yet. Give me a quarter of an hour. I shall be in the breakfast room by then."

"Well," Honor said, hands on hips. "What a happy newly betrothed lady we have here! Are you always like this when you first wake up? Fifteen minutes it is, Jane. I cannot possibly wait any longer. I am fit to burst. And of course Mama will not be up for at least another hour." She wafted from the room as if on wings.

Jane rested her head in her hands for a minute. How

many hours sleep had she had? Three? Four? She seemed to be making a habit of sleepless nights these days. Yes, she was newly betrothed. To Joseph Sedgeworth. How did she feel about that? Happy? She blanked her mind and tested her emotions. Yes, she was happy. He was a good man and an interesting companion. He respected her. He did not pretend to feel love for her, but he had an affection and a regard for her that amounted to almost the same thing. And she could feel the same way about him. Such a feeling was better than love. It was less painful.

It was not just a marriage of convenience for either of them. They would be good for each other. She would provide the companionship that he seemed to lack. He would provide her life with interest. She had never particularly craved travel and excitement, but she thought she would enjoy both with Joseph Sedgeworth. And she would have the emotional security of marriage.

She was not quite sure how she felt about the physical aspect of it. She could not say she had particularly enjoyed her first kiss the night before. But more important, she had not disliked it. She thought she would be able to perform her marriage duty without any great distaste. It might even be pleasant to know that one's person was desirable to a man. Perhaps they would have children. She did not know how Joseph felt about children, but she hoped that theirs would not be a childless marriage.

Yes, Jane decided, getting resolutely to her feet and crossing to her dressing room to select a dress, she had made the right decision. She was happy. She looked forward to seeing him that afternoon. If the weather was fine, he had said, he would take her walking after luncheon. And the weather was fine, though not sunny. She wanted to see him again in the light of day, knowing that he was now her betrothed. There was a lovely feeling of security about such a fact. He would be spending the morning, he had said, writing a letter to her papa. Strictly speaking, of course, he did not have to have anyone's permission to marry her, but he felt it a common courtesy at least to ask her father.

And next week they would be together almost all the time. They would be going to Templeton Hall. Of course! There always had to be something to come between a person and complete joy. She could tell herself with perfect truth that she had made the right choice, that she was happy to be betrothed to Joseph Sedgeworth, that she could expect a bright future of perfect contentment. It was all true. But at the back of it all was a dull ache. Viscount Fairfax. His daughters. Templeton Hall. Next week she would see exactly what she had rejected.

It was a nasty twist of fate that the man she had chosen to accept was a close friend of the viscount and that he had already arranged to visit Templeton Hall the following week. How she had been drawn into going there too, she was not quite certain. But there was no getting out of it now. Honor had been invited as a companion for her. Joseph had said that her presence was important to him, and Fairfax had agreed. And most important of all, perhaps, Fairfax had humbled himself in an apology to her and a plea that their friendship be resumed. She could not now refuse his invitation without making it seem as if she bore a grudge.

Jane twisted her arms to reach the awkward buttons at the back of her dress. She had chosen not to ring for a maid. She picked up a brush and began to tease some life into her curls.

She had found him so very attractive the night before. More so than ever. She had just agreed to marry another man, and yet she found herself aching with love for the one she had refused. It made no sense at all. When he had sneered at her on the dance floor she could have cried and cried. She had longed to put her arms up around his neck and her head on his shoulder and pour out all her feelings for him. She did not want him to misunderstand, to think her cold and calculating, perhaps.

And then had come his kindness. He had walked her away from the crowds so that no one else would see how close to tears she was. And he had spoken to her as if her friendship mattered to him, almost as if *she* mattered to him. He did know who she was, he had said. So he had understood what she had tried to say to him at the theater. He did know her as a person. She was not just any woman to him. She had tried very hard for the rest of the evening to be happy in her new betrothal. Indeed, she really had been happy. But all the time, throbbing away in the back of her mind, had been the knowledge that perhaps she need not have refused Lord Fairfax after all. She could be betrothed to the man she loved.

Useless thought! Jane dragged the brush through her hair and had to begin the teasing process all over again. It would not have worked anyway. Marriage to Lord Fairfax would not have worked. Always she would have fretted because her love for him far outmatched his affection for her. She could be quite contented with affection from Joseph. She would have always yearned for more than that from the viscount. There has to be equality of feeling in marriage, she persuaded herself: either love on both sides or respect and affection on both sides, but not a mixture. She had definitely chosen the right man.

"Jane!" The opening of the door and the voice sounded simultaneously. "You said a quarter of an hour more than twenty minutes ago."

"I am ready, Honor," Jane said with a smile. "Let us go and eat."

"Eat!" Honor said. "Who wants to eat? Oh, Jane. Templeton Hall for two whole weeks. And you betrothed to Mr. Sedgeworth. I could almost envy you if he were just a little more handsome. Though he is by no means unhandsome. He really does have a lovely

face, I noticed last night when I had a good look at him.
And a traveler. You are lucky, Jane. Just think of all the
places you will see."

"Not if this war takes place," Jane said. "The
situation sounds worse daily."

"Pooh," Honor said. "The Duke of Wellington will
make short work of old Boney in no time, you will see.
At least, that is what Henley says. And he should know.
Oh, Jane. Two weeks with Lord Fairfax. Is he not quite
the most handsome man you have ever seen?" She
giggled. "He kissed me last night. Most improperly,
too. He tried . . . But, no. I do not believe I could tell
you without coloring up quite uncomfortably. I told
him in no uncertain terms that he was taking advantage
of me. But I do hope he takes advantage again soon,
Jane. Not that I really liked being held quite so close. I
did not feel that I was in command of the situation."

Jane, inspecting the dishes of food in the breakfast
room, suddenly felt sick and picked up only a slice of
toast. Fairfax kissing Honor. Perhaps at just the
moment when she was kissing Joseph. Even the toast
looked too heavy for her stomach.

"He surely will offer for me after we have been to
Templeton Hall, do you not think?" Honor was saying.
"His intentions are really quite clear, I do believe.
Escorting me to Vauxhall last evening, dancing with me
all night, kissing me, inviting me to join his house party
for two weeks. He could hardly not ask. What do you
think, Jane?"

Jane broke her toast into small pieces and moved
them about her plate. "Is that what you want, Honor?"
she asked. "Do you really wish to marry Viscount Fairfax?"

"What female in her right mind would not wish it?"
Honor said. "I just hope he does not like spending all
his time in the country, Jane, and that he is not wholly
attached to those two babies. He could not possibly be
that staid, could he? No man who is that handsome

would not wish to cut a dash in society for at least part of each year.''

"I believe he does like to spend his time in his own home and with his children,'' Jane said quietly.

Honor pulled a face. "I suppose one cannot have everything one wants in life, can one?'' she said. "Now, if we could just combine Mr. Sedgeworth and Lord Fairfax, Jane, we could produce one perfect gentleman. The sense of adventure of the one and the looks of the other. Then we really could make a wager, Jane, to see who would have him, and we could fight to the death.''

No, Jane thought, if they could only combine the quiet domesticity of the one with the unthreatening physical presence of the other, then she would wager with any woman and fight for her man. She sighed.

"Jane,'' Honor said, "you are not in the dismals, are you? But of course, once one is betrothed it must seem irksome to have to wait for the wedding and the wedding journey. Are you going to be fitted for your trousseau before we go into the country? There will be little time afterward if you are to be married in the summer. Oh, do let me come and help you choose, Jane. You know I have an eye for color and design. And you must be fashionable if you are to go to places like Paris and Vienna and Rome. I am so very envious. Have my eyes turned quite green yet? Well, I can wait no longer. I do not care if Mama is cross as a bear when her sleep is disturbed. I have to go up to speak with her. Lord Fairfax is coming after luncheon to ask if I may accompany you to Templeton Hall.''

"Do you not regret all the balls and such you will miss for two weeks, Honor?'' Jane asked.

"Pooh,'' she replied. "There is no one exciting to make my staying here worthwhile. There is Henley, of course, but I really think he is too old. Do you not agree, Jane?''

She did not wait for an answer. She was already on the way to wake her mother.

* * *

Fairfax was eager to be gone. The five days between the Vauxhall party and his departure for Templeton Hall passed with fair rapidity only because there was plenty to keep him busy. There was business to attend to and shopping to be done. He had to take gifts home for the girls. There were people to visit and take his leave of. There were letters to be written, instructing his housekeeper on the number of guests and their servants to expect. And there was the visit to be paid to Sir Alfred and Lady Jamieson to arrange for their daughter to accompany Miss Matthews the following week.

He had some regrets for the haste with which he had issued the invitation. He hoped he was not tying his own hands. Would it seem to an unbiased observer that his invitation was a natural prelude to a marriage proposal? After all, she was the only unattached lady he had invited. But he reassured himself. It was perfectly natural that he invite her to accompany Miss Matthews, her cousin. He did not wish to be forced into marrying Miss Jamieson. She was extremely pretty and very lively. But he knew there could never be any real friendship between them. He would very quickly become bored with her company.

He was a little uneasy at the exuberance with which she and her mother received him the afternoon after Vauxhall. It seemed almost as if they were expecting an offer there and then. He must be very careful at home not to give the girl the impression that she was there as his intended bride.

He was still stunned by Sedgeworth's betrothal to Miss Matthews. Looking back, he supposed he should have recognized the signs. Those two had been quite friendly for some time, and clearly Sedge had invited her to accompany him to Vauxhall. But he had become so used over the years to believing that his friend was a confirmed bachelor that he had been taken completely by surprise.

He was equally surprised that Miss Matthews had

accepted Sedgeworth. He had assumed when she refused him that she was choosing a life of spinsterhood. To find only two weeks later that she had accepted his friend was a humbling experience. Yes, very humbling, he had to admit. When he really thought the matter over, he realized that his chagrin at being refused had a great deal of conceit in it. How could any woman refuse him? The question sounded quite dreadful when he put it in quite that way, but it was the way he had reacted nonetheless. And how could any woman prefer Joseph Sedgeworth to him? Again when he put the question into words in his mind, he fairly squirmed with embarrassment. Was he really that conceited? He had not thought himself so. But he must be.

Was that the image he had projected for Miss Matthews when he made his offer? Was that why she had refused him? Was that why she had accused him of treating her like a commodity? He had to admit, though very ruefully, that perhaps she had had some justification.

So he tried to be happy for his friend and for the woman he had wanted to marry. Why should she not refuse him if she wished? And why should she not choose to marry Sedge? He had to applaud her good taste. Sedge would be a kindly and a loyal husband. And she would not be tied down to a sedentary life as she would have been with him. He listened to Sedgeworth's enthusiastic praises of his betrothed without betraying by word or chance expression that he also had proposed to her.

And he tried to adjust his mind to thinking of her as his friend's betrothed. He no longer avoided her company but tried to concentrate on rebuilding the quiet friendship that had grown between them before he thought of making her his bride. He tried to prepare his mind for her presence at Templeton Hall and found after a few days that he genuinely looked forward to having her there. With Sedge, of course. He did not know Lord and Lady Dart very well. But he did know that he could expect some pleasant conversations with both Sedgeworth and his fiancée. And he wanted her to meet his daughters. Why, he did not quite know. Paternal pride, he supposed.

And it was to his daughters that his thoughts turned most during those five days, with an impatient eagerness to be gone. He was to set out a day before the others so that he would be able to welcome them properly to his home. On horseback he hoped to make the journey in one day. In that case he would have a two-day advantage over his guests.

"There will be a very good view of the Hall over to your right in just a minute," Sedgeworth said. He was bending from his horse's back in order to look into his sister's carriage, where the ladies rode. "It is built on a rise of land, a quite inspired choice of location, as you will see."

"Are we really almost there?" Honor asked. "I am frightfully relieved, as I do not mind saying. Not that this is not a very well-sprung carriage, Joy, but after two days on our delightful English roads, even good springs fail to disguise the bumps."

"Having to spend a night at an inn does not help matters either, does it?" Lady Dart said agreeably. "I always believe that inns must purchase their furniture from special manufacturers. Especially the mattresses. There must be competition to see who can produce the lumpiest."

"The gentlemen have all the good fortune," Honor said. "They have been able to ride all the way."

Jane did not participate in the conversation. She was watching the window on the right side of the coach, waiting for her first glimpse of Templeton Hall. She tried not to show her eagerness, but she could feel her heart thumping and her breath quickening.

And there it was. She sat forward and stared, oblivious now of the impression she might be making on

an onlooker. It was still a few miles distant but clearly
visible on a rise of land above fields and woods. It was a
strange mixture of architectural styles, Joseph had told
her. The original manor had been built in Elizabethan
times, but almost every viscount since had added
something. From this distance, however, it looked
massive and imposing.

The carriage rolled down a dip in the road and the
house was lost to view behind the roadside hedge. Soon
now, Joseph said, they would turn into the elm-lined
driveway that stretched for well over a mile before
reaching the house. She would see him again soon. It
was three whole days since she had set eyes on him.
Would he be outside to greet them?

Jane sat back in her seat suddenly, casting a conscious
glance at her two chattering companions. She had
realized the turn her thoughts had taken and was
horrified at herself. She must not allow such thoughts.
She had freely betrothed herself to Joseph, and she
looked forward to a good marriage with him. She must
forget this childish infatuation for their host. She must
guard against seeing him as anything else but her host
and her fiancé's friend for the next two weeks.

She closed her eyes briefly when the carriage turned
into the shady tree-lined driveway that would lead
eventually to the house. This might have been hers. She
might have been coming home now with her husband.
No. No! She resolutely opened her eyes and gazed at the
passing trees. She breathed in the scent of green
vegetation.

He was outside. The main doors, leading out onto a
cobbled terrace, were open wide. Two footmen were
visible inside, but their master was standing at the foot
of the steps, his hands clasped behind him, a smile on
his face. He must somehow have seen their approach.
Jane's stomach turned over.

Sedgeworth helped his sister from the carriage and
turned back to take Honor's hand. Somehow it was
Fairfax who helped Jane to the ground. He was smiling,

looking far happier and more relaxed than she had seen him look in London.

"I am so pleased to see you safely arrived," he said, his eyes smiling warmly into Jane's though he spoke generally to the whole group of travelers.

He turned away almost immediately to take Lady Dart's arm and lead her into the house. The others followed, Lord Dart turning to see that his children were being taken care of. They had been traveling in a separate carriage with their governess.

In the high tiled hallway beyond the great doors Fairfax presented his housekeeper, Mrs. Pringle, and his butler to his guests and had the ladies shown to their rooms so that they might freshen up before gathering in the drawing room for tea.

"Will you mind very much if my daughters come for tea too?" Fairfax asked before they left. "They are very eager to meet my guests. Of course, at the moment they have all the excitement of greeting three other children."

"Oh, I would just love to meet the little dears," Honor cried.

"I will not mind at all," Lady Dart said placidly. "Wallace and I are used to children around us. But our own must not be allowed down. They are always impossibly quarrelsome and irritable after traveling."

Jane said nothing.

The children were brought into the room by their nurse when they were all about to start their tea. They had evidently been dressed up for the occasion. Both were wearing frilled white dresses and spotless shoes. The elder girl had dark shining ringlets. She was not a pretty child, Jane decided, though she had strong features that suggested she would be handsome as she grew older. She was very much like her father. The younger child was just as much her mother's image. Her head was haloed by short, soft blond curls. She had a very pretty face with large hazel eyes.

"Ah," Fairfax said. "We have been waiting for you, poppets. Come and make your curtsies to our guests." He crossed the room to take a hand of each. The nurse quietly left the room.

Jane watched them, a strange leaden feeling in her stomach. Here was his past. These were the two children he had had with Susan. How could any other woman ever expect to have a part in his life? These two children must ever remind him of the great love he had lost. She was suddenly glad again that she had not agreed to become the second Lady Fairfax. She could not have borne to be so irrevocably in second place.

Fairfax brought his children to her and Sedgeworth last. "Now, here is someone who is not a stranger to you," he said. "Who is this, Claire?"

The younger child stared at Sedgeworth, smiled broadly, stuck a thumb into her mouth, and turned to hide her face against her father's leg. "Uncle Joe," she said through the double obstruction, and giggled.

"Are you going to sit on my knee today?" Sedgeworth asked. "Amy will, will you not, Amy?"

The older child walked closer and climbed gravely onto his knee.

"No," Claire said, wrapping her arms around Fairfax's leg.

He rested his hand gently on her soft curls. "This lady is going to marry Uncle Joe soon," he said. "Are you going to say good day to Miss Matthews, poppet?"

Claire peeped out from the safety of his leg and smiled around her thumb at Jane. Jane did not gush and coo at the child as the other two ladies had done. She kept her expression grave and quite slowly and deliberately winked at the child. Claire continued to smile.

"If I am Uncle Joe and Miss Matthews is to be my wife," Sedgeworth said, "she had better be Aunt Jane. Do you think I have made a good choice, Amy, love?"

Dark blue eyes regarded her seriously. Jane looked back as gravely. "Yes," the child said.

"And if you do not have the courage to sit on my knee, Claire," Sedgeworth said, "will you sit with Aunt Jane?"

The child continued to smile and cling to her father for a few seconds longer and then she let go and walked up to Jane's chair. She held her arms above her head. "Up," she said.

Jane leaned foward and lifted the tiny child onto her lap. She was really just a baby, she thought. She smelled of soap and powder. She sat looking up at Jane for a while, and her thumb crept back into her mouth. She seemed to be reassured by what she saw. She wriggled herself into a more comfortable position and laid her head against Jane.

Jane's arm went around the child and she looked up to surprise a strange expression on Fairfax' face. He smiled and turned abruptly away to ask Lady Dart if she cared to pour the tea.

# 10

**F**airfax slowed his horse to a walk when he reached the long lake that stretched in a wide crescent a mile to the east of his house. Why did water always look so much more beautiful in the early morning and early evening than at any other time? There was a glassy calm about it, its pale blue reflecting also the pink flush of dawn.

He was always an early riser in the country, especially in summer. It seemed to him that one who slept well past dawn missed the loveliest part of the day. This morning, though, he had been up even earlier than usual. Darkness had barely lifted when his restlessness drove him from bed and out to the stables for an early ride. He had ridden hard for a few miles and was now on his way home. However, it was still very early. There was little danger that he would be neglecting any of his guests if he lingered awhile longer. Most of them would probably not stir for another few hours.

Fairfax slid from his horse's back and tethered it loosely to the low branch of a tree. He wandered to the bank of the lake and looked out across it. It was quite erroneous to believe that nature was ever silent. Birds were singing far more loudly than they would later in the day. There was the faint stirring of the trees behind him. And even the water was making an almost imperceptible rushing sound, calm as it was. He breathed deeply of the cool air.

It felt strange to have houseguests again. Susan had frequently invited friends and relatives. Since her death —indeed, since the start of her final pregnancy— there had been no one except his mother for one month, and Sedgeworth. He thought he would rather enjoy entertaining. The Darts were easy to please. Their children seemed good-natured, if a little boisterous. Certainly his girls were excited by the presence of three playmates staying at the house. The only children they saw with any regularity were the Beasleys, children of the vicar, and the youngest of those was eight.

Then, of course, there was Sedge. Somehow he did not think of his friend as a guest. He was more like a brother. Fairfax was glad that they had not drifted apart during his marriage. Although they had not seen each other during those years, they had written regularly. And there were the two ladies. He believed he might find Miss Jamieson's presence amusing if he could just guard against giving the impression that he was her suitor. She had kept them all laughing with her chatter at dinner the evening before, and she had single-handedly organized a game of charades during the evening, though most of them had felt tired from the journey.

And then there was Miss Matthews. Jane. He almost hated to admit that he liked having her as his guest. When he had risen the day before to see that the sun shone, he had felt immediately glad that she would see Templeton Hall at its best. That his guests would see it at its best, he had corrected himself. He had seen the carriage approach along the main road before it turned into the driveway. And he had waited outside for it, as excited as any boy in anticipation of his first sight of her. Of all of them. He did not know quite how it had happened that he was the one to help her from the carriage when Sedgeworth was standing at the foot of the steps.

Claire had liked her. She was a shy child, willing to look at other people and smile at them, even talk to them sometimes. But she liked to cling for safety to him or to her nurse. She had gone to Jane Matthews with very little hesitation and had settled comfortably against her. She had been sleeping before they finished tea. He did not care to explore the feelings he had had the few times he had ventured to look at the two of them. Jane had held her comfortingly but without any affection. She had contributed as much as anyone else to the general conversation.

Indeed she had not acted toward the children with any of the demontrative affection of the other ladies. She had treated them as if they were quite normal people. One time when he had looked at her she was gently easing Claire's thumb from her mouth. And then she laid her hand briefly and gently against the child's cheek. She had not known that she was observed.

Fairfax bent to pick up a stone. He hurled it as far as he could out into the water. He picked up another, flatter stone and moved it around carefully in his hand before flicking it so that it bounced three times across the lake before disappearing from sight.

He did not wish to put into words in his mind the discovery he had made the day before. There was no point in doing so. He had had his chance to woo her. He had not handled it well. He was beginning to understand why she had refused him. He really had made his offer as if she as a person did not matter. He had given her reasons which were all selfish ones. She could make his own life and his children's lives more comfortable, he had said. It was no wonder she had felt like a commodity. He was appalled now by his own arrogance and by his overconfidence. It had not occurred to him that she might refuse. Of course, in his own defense perhaps he could say that he had not known at the time what he now knew about his feelings for her.

Well, he concluded, bending in search of another flat stone, it was too late to know now. She was betrothed to his best friend, and they were clearly well-matched. He must use this two-week period to adjust his mind to thinking of her as a friend. At least he would not lose her entirely when she married. He would see her as often as he saw Sedge, and he would hear about her from Sedge's letters. She would have an interesting life, more interesting than life with him would have been. He was glad for her. She would want children, though. He was sure she would want children. He was not so sure about Sedge.

But that was their concern, not his, he thought, with a sigh as he turned toward the building a little farther along the bank. It was a marble folly in the shape of a Greek temple. A rather grand structure, he had always thought, to be a boathouse and a bathing hut. He had always loved it, though. His grandfather had certainly had an eye for a perfect setting when he had had it built. He made his way toward it. He should check to see if the boats were in good repair. The girls would surely be pestering him soon to take them out, and his guests too would probably enjoy rowing on the lake.

Jane too was up early. She had asked to have a window left open the night before and had pulled back the curtains in her room after extinguishing the candles. Her room faced east. Dawn brought with it a pink glow into her room, followed by the orange rays of the rising sun. And thousands of birds housed in the woods at the bottom of the lawn that sloped away to the east must all have been singing as loudly as their beaks would stretch.

It was impossible to sleep longer, Jane decided at last, throwing back the covers from her bed and reaching for a wrap as the crisp morning air touched her bare arms. She crossed to the window and looked out. It was a beautiful day, and that was surely a lake of some sort beyond the trees. She had meant to ask Lord Fairfax the day before. She very badly wanted to go outside and walk around, perhaps even go down through the trees to discover what really was beyond them. But it was very early. There was probably no one about yet. Perhaps even the servants were not up. It was not seemly perhaps for a guest to wander house and grounds so early on the morning after her arrival.

Jane washed and dressed slowly and brushed her hair. But the lure of the outdoors was too strong. She decided to go quietly downstairs. If there was no one about and the door was still locked and barred, then she would creep into the library—she knew where it was—and choose a book to bring back upstairs until a more respectable hour. However, luck was with her. The front doors were standing wide open, and a maid was on her knees outside singing as she scrubbed the marble steps.

"Good morning, mum," she said, scrambling to her feet and bobbing a curtsy when Jane appeared in the doorway.

"Good morning," Jane said. "Please do not let me disturb you. Is it not a lovely day?" She breathed deeply of the fresh air.

"Yes, mum," the girl said. "It's going to be a scorcher."

"What is beyond the trees?" Jane asked, pointing to the east. "Is it a lake?"

"Yes, mum," the maid said. "A big one. There's a path through the trees."

"Thank you," Jane said. "I think I shall take a walk that way."

"Will you be having your breakfast first, mum?" the girl asked, looking as if she was about to get to her feet again. "Will I be going to Mrs. Pringle to tell her?"

"I shall eat later," Jane said with a smile. "Please carry on. I shall step down carefully this side so that I do not spoil what you have already cleaned."

The maid was singing again before she was quite out of earshot. Jane hoped Lord Fairfax would not mind her exploring on her own. She supposed it was an ungodly hour to be up. But she was always an early riser at home. Most of the year she slept with a window open and curtains pulled back. And how could one sleep when all the creatures of nature were very much awake and letting every sleepyhead know the fact? She loved the early morning. She could feel the dew seeping into her shoes now as she walked across the east lawn. She was glad it was a lake she had seen. There was nothing more calming to the spirit than an expanse of water.

It was far larger than she had expected. It was wide at the point where she emerged from the trees. And it stretched to either side, becoming narrower in the distance. There was a tree-covered island away off to the left. It was all very beautiful, as water always was early in the day. She would sit on the bank very quietly and let her mind soak up the beauty and peace of it all.

It could all have been hers. Part of her own home. Strange thought! She still found it difficult to believe either that Fairfax had made her an offer or that she had had the courage to refuse. She sighed. She must not dwell on the loss. Life was turning out much better for her than she deserved. Soon she would be seeing other countries or at least other parts of this country. There would be other places as beautiful as this on which to feast her eyes and her spirit. And Joseph really was a dear person. She had laughed at him the evening before. He had been on Honor's team for charades and had entered wholeheartedly into the game. Between them, he and Honor had made sure that their opponents had no chance of winning. And Jane had been one of their opponents. Honor had linked her arm through his after the game was over and giggled up at him.

"We make a very good team, sir," she had said. "Are you quite sure that as Jane's bridesmaid I may not accompany you on your travels? No? Well, I shall think of a way. I shall play on your sympathies or on Jane's before you leave. Perhaps I shall even steal you from her. Now, would not that be a coup?"

"Miss Jamieson, most-admired debutante of the year, running off with plain, ordinary Mr. Sedgeworth as he dishonorably abandons his trearful betrothed?" he said. "I fear the image is not nearly glamorous or romantic enough to tempt you, my dear."

Honor had sighed loudly and batted her eyelids before turning to Fairfax and taking his arm on some pretext.

"Little imp," Sedgeworth had commented with a grin, seating himself beside Jane and touching her hand briefly in an affectionate gesture.

Jane smiled into the water. She would be happy with him. And they would grow to love each other. Perhaps they would never be *in* love, but they would love nevertheless. She hoped they would have a child. She wanted to ask him how he felt about having children, but was always too shy to broach the subject. Yesterday he had seemed fond enough of Fairfax' girls. He had held the solemn little Amy on his lap during tea and had allowed her to play with his fobs and quizzing glass.

And she had held Claire. She had almost held her breath at first, expecting the chld to become restless and move away from her. Instead, she had snuggled close and fallen asleep. Jane doubted if there was any warmer happiness than holding a sleeping child in one's arms. Claire was very tiny and light, really little more than a baby. And so trusting to fall asleep in the arms of a stranger. She could have been the child's stepmother, Jane thought, and shook off the thought before it could develop further in her mind.

A snort behind her startled her and made her turn hurriedly. There was a horse tethered to a tree a little farther along the bank. She was surprised she had not seen or heard it before. It must have been there when she arrived. Where was its rider? She scrambled to her feet and looked around her. On her other side there was a small stone temple built at the lake's edge. She had only half-noticed it when she arrived. Was the horse's owner there? And was he Fairfax? Who else could it be? She turned toward the trees, almost in a panic to move away from there before she was discovered.

But it was too late. Before she had taken a step she was aware of someone coming out of the building, and she turned back to meet the startled eyes of Viscount Fairfax.

"Well, good morning," he called. "You are an early riser." He strode toward her across the grass.

"I am sorry," she said foolishly. "I did not mean to intrude. I could not sleep and thought I would come down here to explore. I had no idea you were here. I shall go back to the house."

"There is no need," he said. "You must feel free to do as you wish here. Do you often get up early? I hate to miss the early morning myself."

"I cannot miss it even if I wish to do so," she said. "The birds will not allow me to. But yes, I think it is the loveliest time of day. You have a beautiful home, my lord. I do not wonder that you like to spend your time here." She hoped as she said the words that she did not sound regretful.

"Would you care to walk a little way?" he asked, and waited for her to fall into step beside him.

He led her back the way he had come, strolling at a leisurely pace, his hands clasped behind his back. Jane held her shawl with both hands.

"This is a boathouse," he said. "Rather a grand structure for such a humble purpose, is it not? There are two boats for anyone who cares to take them out. We keep towels here too for swimmers. I sometimes swim here early in the morning. There is no more relaxing and peaceful exercise. You would not find it so, of course. You are afraid to put your head underwater." He turned toward her and gave her one of his unexpected grins.

Jane smiled back. "I believe I would find it more relaxing and peaceful to sit on the bank and watch," she said.

"Even if I swam past and splashed you?"

"If you were so ungallant," she said. "I should run to the boathouse and steal all the towels."

He laughed. "Let us move on," he said. "On the other side of the folly is what we have always fondly called the beach. It is merely a small area where the bank slopes down into the water. That is where I bring my daughters to swim. It really does not deserve the name, does it?"

Jane viewed the small shingled area. "I suppose anything is what one makes it," she said. "The folly, for example. I should firmly call it a temple if I lived here, and dare anyone to laugh at me."

If I lived here, she thought with some horror when it was too late to recall her words.

"Perhaps you will change your mind when you see a real Greek temple," he said. "I don't doubt Sedge will take you to Greece."

An awkward little silence stretched between them as they wandered across the beach.

"Will you like that?" he asked tonelessly. "Traveling, I mean?"

"I believe so," she said. "Though I doubt if we will travel soon. There is going to be war any day, is there not?"

"I fear so," he said. "The Duke of Wellington will have the fight of his life against Bonaparte, especially with so many raw troops and so many of our best still in America."

"Will he be defeated, do you think?" Jane asked.

"I do not know," he admitted. "But let me say this. If anyone can save Europe, Wellington is the man. Are you afraid of what will happen if Napoleon defeats him?"

Jane shrugged. "I suppose life will go on basically the same no matter what happens," she said. "But I would not like to think of having a foreign ruler."

"We must wait and see," he said. "There is no point in becoming worried before we need to do so."

"No," she agreed.

They strolled on in companionable silence. "There is my favorite childhood spot," he said at last, pointing ahead to the wooded island. "I believe I dug up every inch of it at one time or another looking for treasure."

"Did you ever find any?" she asked with a smile.

"Oh yes, always," he said, "though I did not realize it at the time. Childhood imagination is one of the greatest treasures a person can have. I want to make sure my daughters have a carefree childhood in which they can give free rein to their own imaginations. Did you have a happy childhood, Miss Matthews?"

"Oh yes," she said. "I was considerably younger

than my brother and sister, so I grew up essentially
alone. But I was never lonely. All of the moors were
mine. I did not usually play in quite your way. I used to
make up poems and stories as I roamed around.''

"Did you write them down?" he asked.

"Oh yes," she said. "I still do sometimes. You are
walking with a still-undiscovered Shakespeare, my lord.
My works will be discovered and published post-
humously, no doubt, and I shall become famous after
my death.''

"You mock yourself," he said. "Do you have any of
your writings with you? I should like to read some.''

Jane laughed in some embarrassment. "No," she
said. "I have not written since leaving home. And
nothing I have done is for anyone's eyes but mine. I do
not pretend to any great talent.''

"Be careful!" he said suddenly. "The bank is very
uneven here. It is easy to stumble.''

He took her firmly by the elbow at the exact moment
that Jane did indeed stumble awkwardly on a stone
hidden in the long grass. She fell against him and both
his arms went about her in a reflex action.

"Oh!" Jane said, looking up at him, startled. His
eyes looked very blue from so close.

There was a silence that stretched perhaps a second
too long for comfort. Jane blushed hotly, her breasts
registering instantly the hardness of his chest, her thighs
the firmness of his. It did not occur to her in that
moment to push away from him. His head bent toward
hers before he straightened suddenly and moved his
hands to her shoulders.

"My apologies, Jane," he said. "I should have
warned you sooner. Are you hurt?''

The sound of his voice released her from the spell that
had gripped her momentarily. She stood away from
him. "Oh no," she said a little breathlessly, "I just
twisted my foot a little. I should have seen the stone.''

He frowned in some concern. "Is your ankle
sprained?" he asked, kneeling beside her and reaching
out to test her ankle with his hands.

"No, not at all," she said, hastily withdrawing her foot. "Really it is nothing, my lord. The pain has already gone from it."

"Let us turn back anyway," he said. "Take my arm. And do not be afraid to lean on me."

Jane felt embarrassed, but she took his arm. She had thought he was going to kiss her. What an absurd thought! It had probably been the last thing on his mind. And she had wanted him to kiss her. In fact, for one moment the bottom had seemed to fall out of her stomach. It was a terrible admission to make to herself. She was being dreadfully disloyal to Joseph.

She should not have come to Templeton Hall. She realized that now. She had given in with very little struggle. And she had to admit, if she was to be strictly honest with herself, that she had come because she wanted to be close to Fairfax. She had wanted to see him in his home setting. She had wanted to meet his children. She was being very unfair. She was clinging to the security of a betrothal to one gentleman while indulging in an infatuation for another. She was trying to get the best out of both worlds. And she was being unfair to Joseph. Even now her body was soaking up the pleasurable sensation of being close to Fairfax. Her hand and arm were very aware of the firm muscles of his own arm. She could feel the heat of him along her left side.

"I am happy that Sedge has found himself a wife worthy of him," Fairfax said as they approached the beach again. "I have always been very fond of him, you know. We made our Grand Tour together when we were young pups. And he has been a great comfort to me in the last year since my wife died—first by letter and then in person. He never intended to marry, as he has probably told you. But he has met you, and I believe he will be happy with your companionship."

"Yes," was all she could think of to say. And then she added, "I think perhaps I am the fortunate one."

"Will he continue to travel indefinitely?" he asked. "Or will you persuade him to settle down after a year or two? Will you have a family, Jane? You should, you know. You are good with children.''

Jane could feel herself flushing. The topic she was too shy to broach with her betrothed was being raised in a quite matter-of-fact manner by Fairfax.

He turned to look at her when she did not reply. His hand came across to cover hers briefly. "I am sorry," he said. "I have embarrassed you. I did not mean to. Of course, your plans are none of my business. In my very narrow-minded way, you see, I was expressing my view that no one should be denied the pleasures of parenthood. I am quite besotted with my girls, as I am sure you have noticed." He grinned in that very unexpected way again.

"They are lovely," she said. "I might well decide to kidnap Claire when I leave here. I believe Amy takes some getting to know. She is solemn and reserved for so young a child, is she not?"

He was serious again. "Yes," he said. "She was at an impressionable age when her mother died. For Claire it was not so bad. She was still very much a baby. Amy needs a great deal of love and attention. I intend to give her both. I had hoped to give her a new mother."

He closed his eyes tightly for a moment and shook his head. He flushed quite noticeably. "Pardon me," he said. "Oh, pardon me, Jane. I had not meant to refer to the subject. Have I embarrassed you terribly? Please forgive me."

Jane dropped her head so that he would not see her face. She felt a raw pain in the back of her throat that she knew was the prelude to tears. She fought a silent battle with herself as they skirted the folly until they reached the grassy bank from which they had started their walk.

"I have embarrassed you," he said. "I am sorry, Jane. And I do wish you well. Sedge is a lucky man. You will make him happy. And you deserve better than to be tied to a man who has already had a wife and two children whom you did not bear. Forgive me for making you such an arrogant proposal in London. I do not blame you for becoming angry with me. You are a very special person and deserve more than a marriage of convenience.''

They had stopped walking. He laid his hands lightly on her shoulders and stopped to look into her downcast face. "I have not made you cry, have I?" he asked softly.

She shook her head and raised her eyes to his. "No," she said. "And thank you. I mean for inviting me here and accepting me as Joseph's betrothed. I . . . I hope your life here will turn out well. Perhaps soon you will meet another lady whom you can love, and then your daughters will have a mother. But I think at the moment their father is quite enough for their needs." She blushed at her own temerity.

He smiled into her eyes and leaned forward to kiss her gently on the cheek. "Thank you, Jane," he said. "Will you call me Michael, since you are soon to be the wife of my best friend?"

She nodded. "Yes, Michael."

He looked across to where his horse was still tethered. "I cannot lead Prince through the trees," he said. "I shall have to take him around. Shall I take you before me on the saddle?"

She shook her head. "No," she said. "I shall walk back. Thank you."

"I shall see you at breakfast, then," he said. "I wonder if anyone else is up yet."

Someone was, Jane saw as soon as she emerged from the trees. Sedgeworth was wandering in the formal gardens that stretched before the house. He waved when he saw her coming.

"Gracious!" he called when she came within earshot. "Are you up already, Jane? I thought you would be in bed for hours yet. I believed I was first up. Have you been to the lake? Lovely, is it not? Come and look at the flowers with me. And take a good long sniff of them. You know you are in England when you smell that particular fragrance."

He smiled and took her hand in a warm clasp as she

came up with him. He drew her to his side, glanced around him, and bent with a smile to kiss her on the lips.

"Do you always look as fresh and lovely in the mornings?" he asked. "Your cheeks are positively glowing."

"Yes, always," she assured him. "But then, do I not look lovely all day long?"

He grinned. "You are not fishing for a compliment, are you, Jane? I thought only your cousin used such tactics. She is quite a little imp, is she not? Yes, dear, you always look lovely to me."

Jane gave him a wide artificial smile and flickered her eyelids at him. He laughed and squeezed her hand.

# 11

"My dear Honor, not charades again tonight!" Lady Dart said wearily, setting her teacup back in its saucer. "We have played for the past two evenings, and you and Mr. Sedgeworth far outclass anyone else."

"Very well," Honor said gaily. "We will play on different teams tonight, will we not, sir?"

He raised his cup to her in a mock toast.

"Besides," said Lady Dart, not so easily mollified, "some of us spent the afternoon playing with the children and would prefer something a little more sedate this evening. Would you not agree, Jane? And Lord Fairfax? I need not ask you, my love. You were giving piggyback rides all afternoon and Gregory in particular is growing far too heavy for such games."

"How would an evening of music suit?" Fairfax asked, setting his own cup back on the tea tray and turning to his guests. "Shall we go to the music room?"

Honor was immediately enthusiastic. Jane was more quietly so. She had seen the magnificent pianoforte and the smaller harpsichord on a tour of the house the day before and had been longing for a chance to hear or even play the instruments. Mr. Sedgeworth, seated beside her, smiled.

"Jane has been promising to play for me," he said. "Now sounds like a good time, Fairfax."

"Well, if you will not consider me unsociable," Lady Dart said, "I believe I will stay here, my lord, and fetch my embroidery. I can think of no more blissful way of spending an evening."

Lord Dart announced his intention of fetching a book and keeping his wife company.

*Mary Balogh*

Honor took possession of the pianoforte as soon as they entered the music room. Fairfax stood behind the stool to turn the pages of the music once she had selected what she would play. Jane and Sedgeworth crossed the room to the harpsichord, which she proceeded to admire. It was a work of art in itself, its highly polished wood painted with scenes from mythology. She ran her hand over its surface.

"You must be tired, Jane," Sedgeworth said. "You were really very busy with the children while Fairfax was sedately rowing Miss Jamieson on the lake and I sitting idly on the beach. In fact, I had a very lazy time of it, did I not? I was still sitting idly on the beach when Fairfax joined in that very boisterous game of hide-and-seek."

"I enjoyed the afternoon," Jane said, "and I believe the children did too. It must be a rare event for them to have adults playing with them for so long."

"I am not sure of that," Sedgeworth said. "Fairfax seems to spend a large portion of his time romping with his daughters. You like children, do you not?"

"Oh, very much," she said, seating herself on the bench and smiling warmly up at him. "And a good thing too. Both my brother and my sister have families. I have been Aunt Jane for a long time."

Sedgeworth looked thoughtfully at her and smiled. "What power do you have over the little one?" he asked. "She climbed onto your lap and fell asleep again at teatime. She will not release her hold of Fairfax for anyone else."

"Claire?" Jane said. "We were outdoors, you know, and she had been doing a great deal of shrieking and running around. She was exhausted."

"Amy is the strange one," Sedgeworth said. "Very withdrawn and far too solemn for a four-year-old. Fairfax has been worried about her. Yet you seem to have befriended her to a certain extent."

"I showed her how to make daisy chains this afternoon," Jane said, "and she was very excited."

Her thoughts turned back to Fairfax' elder child as Sedgeworth directed his attention to the music being produced on the pianoforte. Honor was playing Mozart with precision though without flair.

During the morning of the day before, after her walk to the lake and encounter there with her host, she had accepted Joy's suggestion that they go up to the nursery to see the children. They had been besieged by three noisy youngsters all wanting to show their mother toys and books that they had found in this new nursery. Jane had moved away to observe Fairfax' chldren. Amy was painting, swathed to the chin in a large apron. Claire was standing before a bowl of soapy water in which she was bathing a doll, watched by her nurse.

"Say good morning and make your curtsies to Miss Matthews," the nurse said.

Amy muttered some words and bobbed a curtsy without looking up from her painting. Claire popped her thumb in her mouth and smiled around it. Jane crossed to her side.

"Are you bathing your doll?" she asked. "She is being a good girl and not splashing the water. What is her name?"

The child smiled around her thumb again. "Dolly," she said, pulled out the thumb, and covered her eyes with both hands.

"Perhaps her real name is Dorothy," Jane suggested. "Sometimes Dorothys are called 'Dolly' for short. Are you going to dress her, sweetheart? She will get cold lying in the water like that."

"I think her paint might rub off too," the nurse said with a smile at Jane.

Claire lifted up one garment from a nearby chair. "You dress Dolly," she said to Jane. And she stood in front of the chair watching wide-eyed as Jane complied.

Finally it was wrapped in a shawl. Jane put it against her shoulder and patted its back. "I think Dolly wants to sleep," she said. "Do you want to hold her?"

Claire put up her arms and was soon holding the doll

as Jane had and pounding its back. Jane crossed the room to Amy, who had made no move to join the noisy group around Lady Dart. Jane was careful to keep her eyes off the painting.

"May I see your picture, Amy?" she asked. "Or is it private?"

She did not think the child was going to answer. She continued to paint for a minute. Then she looked up with guarded eyes. "You may see it," she said.

There was the usual child's band of blue across the top of the paper and green across the bottom. There was the usual yellow ball in the top corner. Huge across the blank space between was a black witch, arms out-stretched, teeth yellow and jagged. Jane viewed it silently for a while.

"Tell me about the picture," she said. "That is a splendid large figure."

"That is *her*," the child said quietly and primly.

Jane reached down to touch the soft curls of Claire, who had put the doll down and come up to stand beside her and cling to her skirt. "Do I know her?"

Amy looked up, her eyes stormy. "Is Papa going to marry her?" she asked.

"Whom, sweetheart?" Jane watched the child intently.

"*Her*," Amy said. "The pretty lady."

"You mean Miss Jamieson?" Jane asked.

"Mrs. Pringle told Nurse he is going to marry her," Amy said.

Jane could no longer ignore the insistent pulling at her skirt. She looked down. Claire held her arms up above her head.

"Up," she said.

Jane smiled and stooped down to scoop the child into her arms. "I do not believe any such thing has been decided yet," she said carefully. "Why do you not ask Papa, sweetheart? Would you like Miss Jamieson as a mama?"

The child's cheeks flamed. "I do not want a mama!" she said fiercely.

Jane reached down with her free hand and touched the glossy ringlets reassuringly. It was at that point, while she was still searching for words to say to soothe the child, that Fairfax himself came into the nursery. Amy almost upset her chair in her haste to rush across the room into his arms. Claire smiled at Jane and pointed.

"Papa," she said, and Jane set her on the floor so that she too could scurry across the room to her father.

Their eyes met across the room for a moment and Jane felt herself blush. What would he think of her, in the nursery like this, holding and talking to his children when he had not even invited her to be there?

Claire had become almost embarrassingly attached to her, Jane thought, shifting her position on the harpsichord bench as Honor began to sing to her own accompaniment. That afternoon when they had all walked to the lake, adults and children alike, Honor had offered to carry the child. But Claire, thumb firmly in place in the middle of her smile, had scurried over to Jane and demanded with raised arms to be taken "Up." And she had, as Joseph had pointed out a few minutes before, climbed into Jane's lap during the picnic tea and fallen asleep there, though her father sat not far off, next to Honor.

Amy too had relaxed somewhat when Jane showed her how to make daisy chains. She had been moodily watching her father out on the lake with Honor before that. But she had actually smiled with delight when Jane joined the finished ends of the daisy chain together and hung it around Amy's neck. She had looked eagerly around for her father, seen that he was standing on the bank pointing out something to the elder son of Lord Dart, and rushed eagerly to show him her creation. Jane had been relieved to see that he immediately stooped down, examined the chain, and kissed his daughter before taking her hand and leading her toward the beach where the tea was being spread out.

And was he going to marry Honor? she asked herself now, looking from one to the other of them at the pianoforte. He had been attentive to her in the last two days, but his attentions did not seem quite like those of a lover. And would Honor accept him even if he did offer? The question would not even have been worth asking a mere few days before, but now Jane was not so sure of the answer. Honor had come to her room before dinner and sat to talk while Jane finished getting ready to go downstairs. It seemed that Honor was somewhat disillusioned with her handsome suitor—if suitor he was.

"Jane," she had said, "I begin to think you are right and Lord Fairfax is firmly attached to this home. I have never spent a more boring day in my life. Imagine being saddled with a parcel of children for a whole afternoon. I do not see why we should. Fairfax' children have a nurse, and Joy's have a governess with them. Why should they be with us?"

"But Lord Fairfax took you in the boat," Jane had pointed out.

"And did not say one word that could be construed as flirtatious or romantic even by the wildest imagination," Honor had said indignantly. "Really, Jane, I begin to think I am wasting two whole weeks of the Season. I am almost determined to say no when he offers for me. Your Mr. Sedgeworth has twice the charm of Fairfax. And is much more interesting. I think I might get him to elope with me. Would you mind very much?" She had giggled gaily. "But to be serious, Jane, it is mortally disappointing to find that the most handsome man in England is not also the most exciting man. I might have to settle after all for someone of lesser looks."

And Honor had been flirting quite shamelessly and quite harmlessly with Joseph, Jane thought. He very good-naturedly played up to her. Really, though, she felt that perhaps Honor was right. She should have stayed in London. She was not suited to be the second Lady Fairfax. And Jane hoped they would both realize the fact before taking the irrevocable step of marrying. She realized, of course, that her own opinion was not unbiased. The thought of Honor and Fairfax as man and wife was enough to make panic grab at her heart.

Fairfax watched Jane across the room, obviously deep in thought. Finally he deemed it time to call on her to play. Miss Jamieson was coming to the end of her third song.

"Miss Matthews," he said, raising his voice so that it would carry across the space between them, "will you play for us?"

Her face brightened. "Oh, I would love to," she said. "The pianoforte has a beautiful tone."

"Will you select some music?" he asked.

"No," she said. "I play all my favorite pieces from memory. Of course, it is a while since I have played seriously. I fear my fingers will be somewhat stiff."

"We will forgive a few mistakes," Sedgeworth said with a smile. "Come, Jane. Miss Jamieson has told me that you are very good. You have not confessed any such thing to me, of course."

She pulled a face at him as she seated herself on the bench. She sat for a few moments, Fairfax noticed, very straight-backed, her head bent, her hands loosely clasped in her lap. Both he and Sedgeworth stood behind her. Miss Jamieson had wandered across the room and was looking at a large canvas hanging on one wall.

Jane lifted her hands to the keys finally and began to play. It was a Beethoven piece that Fairfax could not identify. She did stumble over a few notes at the start, but then she played without error. And she played with feeling. She clearly loved deeply the music her fingers produced.

"Your cousin did not exaggerate," Sedgeworth said with admiration when she had finished. "You play extremely well, Jane." He sat down at the end of the bench next to her. "Why did we never hear you in London?"

"I do not play for an audience," she said. "Except this evening, that is."

"An audience?" he said, laughing at her. "Do you call your cousin and me and Fairfax an audience?"

She rose to her feet. "I want to hear Lord Fairfax play," she said.

Sedgeworth wandered across to join Honor before the large canvas while Fairfax seated himself and began to play, also without music.

"It is a Constable, is it not?" Honor said, not turning around. "It is quite glorious the way he captures nature."

"Yes, I believe it is," Sedgeworth said. "How did you know?"

"Oh," she said, "friends of Papa's have one that I saw last year. I was enthralled by it. He has a very distinctive style."

"You are a fraud, you know, Miss Jamieson," Sedgeworth said, amusement in his voice.

She looked back at him, eyebrows raised.

"How much have you studied about painting?" he asked.

"Me?" she said, eyes wide with innocence. "You know me, sir. A perfect ninnyhammer. I leave all—"

"—the reading and thinking to men," he completed for her. "Yes, you have said so before, my dear. Yet you recognized and seemed quite knowledgeable about a Holbein and a Van Dyck in the portrait gallery yesterday. And when teasing Jane and me about our future travels this morning, you revealed some knowledge of the Sistine Chapel that one would not expect a 'ninnyhammer' to possess. Before you blushed and looked self-conscious, that is. I believe you are a fraud."

"Well," she said with a bright little laugh, "I have always been interested in painting. Just one of my odd little amusements, you know."

"I wonder," he said, looking at her so penetratingly that she tittered and looked self-conscious again.

"Don't tell anyone," she said, "I had a governess once who criticized my watercolors by saying that they were too passionate. I would never attract a husband, she told me, if I appeared too knowledgeable or too emotionally involved in any activity. And she was right. Look at all the admirers I had in London. Jane did not have near as many. Oh!'' Her hand flew to her mouth.

"And do you value any of those admirers?'' he asked. "If you were to ask me, I should say that if all their brains were mixed together, one healthy one could not be produced.''

"But it is very pleasant to be so popular,'' Honor protested.

He looked at her with mock reproach until she giggled. "Well, anyway, it was fun for a while,'' she said.

"Have you seen the other Constable?'' Sedgeworth asked her.

"Here? In this house?'' Honor asked. "Where is it?''

"In the library,'' he said. "You did not follow the rest of us in there yesterday. You said something about books boring you, I believe.''

Honor blushed.

"Do they, by the way?'' Sedgeworth asked. "You probably read sermons each night to improve your mind, do you?''

She giggled. "I do assure you I do not,'' she said. "Not sermons, anyway.''

"Shall I take you to see the Constable?'' he asked. "It is best seen by daylight, of course, but if we take a branch of candles, we should be able to see it quite well.''

"Very well,'' she said. "But do not expect me to go into rhapsodies over the books.''

Fairfax came to the end of his piece of music and looked up to smile at Jane, who had stood quite still to one side of the instrument throughout.

"Men do have one advantage when they play,'' she said. "You have so much more power in your fingers than I do. I have never heard Bach sound quite so exciting. Please, will you play again?''

"Miss Jamieson and I are going to view the Constable

in the library,'' Sedgeworth called. "She thinks this one very pretty, Fairfax. We will see you later in the drawing room for supper?''

"In half an hour,'' Fairfax agreed.

Jane smiled at her betrothed.

"Bach sounds quite splendid played on the harpsi-chord,'' Fairfax said, getting to his feet. "Do you play the instrument?''

"I have only played it once,'' she said, walking by his side across the room, "when we visited my great-aunt years ago. I have never had another chance.''

"See if you agree with me,'' he said, seating himself at the harpsichord and beginning to play. He stopped after a couple of minutes. "Do you like the sound?''

"Yes, for bright, sprightly music it is perfect,'' Jane said. "May I try?''

She played Bach and appeared to have forgotten Fairfax after a few minutes. He crossed back to the pianoforte and picked up the same melody on its keys. He finished the piece with her.

She looked up and laughed. "We finished together anyway,'' she said. "The tones of the two instruments blend well together. Can we try something else?''

They agreed on a tune and played it through together, first one and then the other stumbling in the effort to keep in time with each other.

"I have another idea,'' Fairfax said after they had finished. "Have you ever played a duet on the piano-forte?''

"Goodness, no,'' she said. "Is it possible?''

"Come,'' he said. "You sit on this side of me and play the higher keys.'' He turned to pick a sheet of music from the pile on the table beside the instrument. "I shall play the lower part. It is not difficult most of the time. Just occasionally you have to encroach on my keys and I on yours. Shall we see if it can be done?''

Jane examined the music carefully. "It does not look difficult,'' she said. "I am ready.''

He got to his feet suddenly. "I am not sure I would want this overheard by anyone but us two,'' he said, crossing the room. "I see that Sedge left the door ajar. And I know why. One has to almost wrestle with it to close it and then is never sure it will open again."

He slammed the door shut, applying his shoulder to it as he did so, and turned back to the pianoforte with a grin. "Now for the performance of a lifetime," he said. He seated himself on the bench beside Jane.

They both kept their eyes on the music, playing carefully and without any finesse, concentrating merely on playing the right notes and staying in time with each other. Then they came to the parts where Jane had to slip her left arm beneath his to reach higher notes. By the time they arrived at the end of the music more than ten minutes later, they were both laughing helplessly.

"I do not believe we would find a place on anyone's concert bill yet, do you?" Fairfax asked.

"Perhaps as a comedy team?" she suggested.

"Actually," he said, holding up his hands before his face, fingers spread, "I think we did remarkably well. I ended up with four fingers and one thumb on each hand. How about you?"

She held her hands up also. "Remarkable," she said. "I do believe they are the same fingers and thumbs as I began with, too."

"Let me see," he said, leaning toward her and examining her hands. "Yes, you are right. At least I hope you are. I would not wish to lay claim to such slender, feminine fingers for my own."

He turned to laugh into her face, only inches away from his own. Jane. Jane with her eyebrows raised and her eyes dancing with merriment. Jane with her mouth curved into a smile. Jane flushing, the smile fading. As he could feel his fade too.

There was perhaps a single moment when he could have prevented what was about to happen, when he could have pulled back and made another joke. A single moment. Although perhaps not, as he admitted later when he had time to think it all over. He would have had to be superhuman to resist the temptation of the moment. He was alone with the woman he had grown to

love and in the near-privacy of a room with an
unmanageable door. Quite without premeditation he
was very close to her. And the space between them was a
powerful magnet that was not to be resisted.

He closed the gap between their mouths and kissed
her. But the invisible magnet was far too powerful to be
satisfied by that single action. His right arm went about
her, his left hand along her jaw. And his mouth opened
over hers, instantly demanding, instantly hungry for
more than a mere outer touch. And she responded as
instantly and as eagerly. Her shoulder dipped beneath
his and her arm came around him. Her other hand
reached for his shoulder. And her mouth opened
beneath his without any coquetry, any coaxing. She
gasped when his tongue plunged into her mouth,
exciting him beyond thought.

His hand was at her breast, a beautifully firm, small
breast. He wanted the warm smoothness of it in his
hand. He pushed ungently at the low neckline of her
gown and she shrugged the fabric away from her
shoulder and down her arm until he could lay his palm
against her hard nipple and caress the warm softness
around it.

He had her on her feet suddenly, pulled hard against
him, one hand cupped against the back of her head
while he covered her face with kisses and lowered his
mouth to her throat and her breasts, both now free of
her bodice. And back to her mouth again to ravish it
with his own. His hands went behind her waist and
moved lower, hard and straining, pulling her to him,
wanting her, aching and throbbing for her.

Jane. His beautiful Jane. His love. "Jane. Jane." He
could hear himself whispering her name against her
hair. He looked down at her, at her eyes dreamy with
passion, her mouth already swollen from his kisses, her
long, creamy throat, her lovely firm breasts. "Jane."
He looked back into her eyes. And knew suddenly with
jolting clarity what was happening.

His hands came up to clasp her bruisingly by the arms
and put her from him. He half-staggered across the

room until he leaned against the harpsichord. His fingers closed around it; his eyes and teeth were tightly clenched as he tried to drag his mind back to sanity, to force his body to obey his will.

When he turned back to her, his head felt cold, as if all the blood had been drained from it. Foolishly he tried to smile. "Jane, I am sorry," he said. "Oh, my dear, I am so sorry." She had covered herself already, part of his mind noticed.

She stared back at him, her eyes wide and bewildered, her hands crossed above the décolletage of her gown. Then she turned and fled, fumbling in panic at the door. It refused to open, and she rattled and tugged at the knob, one sob escaping her. Fairfax was halfway across the room to her before the door suddenly crashed back against her and she made her escape.

Fairfax closed the door behind her as far as it would go without resistance. He laid his forehead against the carved wood paneling. He loathed himself. He had been in the process of seducing a guest in his house, the woman he had come to love more than he had ever thought possible, the betrothed of the friend he thought of as a brother. A woman so innocent that she had not even known how to resist his advances. He closed his eyes. Jane. She was like a sharp pain cutting through his body. How could he say he loved her and yet dishonor her so and disgrace his claim to the name of gentleman?

He strode restlessly up and down the room, trying to impose some sort of calm on his mind, trying to compose the impossible speech of apology.

Outside the room Honor decided after all not to knock or push on the door, which was slightly ajar. She looked thoughtfully up the stairs, where she had watched Jane flee a few moments before. She could hear no music coming from beyond the door, yet Lord Fairfax was not coming out, either. She shrugged eventually and turned back to the drawing room and the tea tray, bright with the announcement that Lord Fairfax and Jane were too absorbed in their music to come for tea just yet.

# 12

"**A**unt Jane, look at us!"

"Aunt Jane, please will you read us a story?"

Jane smiled, weary as she was feeling. Joy, busy with letter writing in the morning room, had asked her if she would be a dear and look in at the nursery to make sure that the children had not driven their governess to distraction or murdered one another.

Gregory, the ten-year-old, was down on all fours giving Claire horseback rides. She was clinging to his fair curls and shrieking with helpless laughter. Amanda, the middle child, was trying, amid all the noise, to read a story to her five-year-old brother. Amy, not surprisingly, was on her own, working at her painting. The nurse and the governess were working their way through a small pile of mending and having a comfortable coze at the same time.

"Look at me, Aunt Jane," Gregory called again. "I am a horse."

"With a bruising rider on your back, I see," she said with a smile.

"Gee-up, horsey," Claire shrieked, pulling at his hair.

"Please, Aunt Jane," Amanda pleaded, holding out the book. "I have told Gregory to be quiet and he won't. And Miss George will not tell him to be quiet either. I cannot read when there is noise."

Jane sat down between Joseph's nephew and niece and opened the book on her lap. She put an arm around the young boy, who snuggled against her, and proceeded to read. She had not meant to stay, but how could one deny one's attention to children?

The story read, she crossed the room quietly to Amy, who was still intently at work. "May I see, sweetheart?" she asked. "Or is it a secret?"

The child looked up with an eager face. "I have been trying to finish before you left, Aunt Jane," she said. "It is for you."

"For me?" Jane said, moving around to Amy's side of the table.

Amy was putting the final touch to the painting—yellow rays coming from the inevitable sun in the top corner.

"Oh, Amy," she said, "how lovely it is. It is you wearing your daisy chain, except that this girl is not quite as handsome as you are. And look at all the daisies left in the grass. I shall be able to make a chain for myself out of those."

Amy giggled, the first time Jane had heard her laugh. "Silly!" she said. "They are paint. You cannot pick them."

"Ah, but I can imagine picking them," Jane said. "And that is far better because I can imagine picking them over and over again, even during the winter. Would you like to tell me the story of the picture and I shall write it down for you?"

The child's eyes lit up again. "I know how to write my name," she said. "I can write my name at the end of it."

Jane tugged gently on one glossy ringlet and went in search of paper and charcoal.

She was on her way downstairs half an hour later, having taken the picture and the story to her room, feeling considerably more cheerful than she had when she went up. Though there was no reason to, she thought gloomily. She still had all her problems to sort out and deal with. Sedgeworth rounded the bottom of the stairs and began to run up them two at a time. He did not see her until he was halfway up.

"Jane!" he said, reaching for her hands and smiling broadly. "You were in the nursery, were you? I have searched everywhere else. That was going to be my last port of call. Joy said she sent you there an hour ago but that you could not possibly still be there. Splendid news, dear."

Jane felt a lump in her throat as she looked into his happy face. She squeezed his hands unconsciously.

"The Duke of Wellington won a glorious victory in Belgium five days ago," he said. "Boney was completely routed and the allied army is chasing the French toward Paris. I think that will be the end of him this time, dear. England and indeed the whole of Europe are safe again."

"Oh," Jane said, "I am so glad. Were there many casualties?"

His expression became more sober. "Wallace's letter mentioned heavy losses on both sides," he said. "I fear it was a dearly won victory, Jane."

"Poor men," she said. "And poor wives and children and mothers left behind."

His expression softened and he lifted one of her hands to his lips and kissed the palm. "Dear Jane," he said. "How typical of you to think more of the suffering than of the victory. Would you like to come for a drive to the village? That is why I was looking for you. Your cousin has declared that she cannot live through another day without a length of yellow ribbon, and Joy has agreed that she would welcome the sight of a different human face for a change. Fairfax is shut up in the library with his bailiff, and Wallace is still busy writing letters. That leaves me for an escort." He grinned.

Jane smiled. "Will you mind if I do not come, Joseph?" she asked. "I did not sleep well last night and have been looking forward to spending the rest of the morning quietly outside."

"Of course I will not mind, dear," he said. "You are not ill?"

She shook her head.

"I must go then," he said. "Ten minutes ago your cousin declared to all the world that she would not wait five minutes longer."

Jane watched him run down the stairs as fast as he had come up them. What a very dear man he was. Why, oh why, could a person not choose whom she would love? Why could she only like him dearly and not love him at all? She sighed and continued her more sedate descent of the staircase. The sky was overcast today. It looked chilly outside. But she would not delay by going back upstairs for a shawl. She continued on her way down to the ground floor and out onto the cobbled terrace.

She wanted to go to the lake. She would be out of sight there. But she was afraid somehow that he would go there after he had finished with his bailiff. She walked along the graveled paths of the formal gardens, hardly aware of the beauty around her or of the heavy scents of the flowers. She made her way to the lowest level, where she knew there was a wrought-iron seat beneath a willow tree, out of sight of the house.

She knew exactly what she must do. But unfortunately it was so much easier to know what one should do than to do it. She was going to have to put an end to her betrothal to Joseph and leave Templeton Hall as soon as possible. She was going to have to return to Yorkshire and spend the rest of her life in seclusion and in single state. A very bright prospect indeed, she thought with a bitter little laugh.

She could not marry Joseph. She did like him a great deal, and they could have a good marriage. Could. But they would not. She could never be happy feeling as she did about his friend. And if she was unhappy, then ultimately he would be so too. She could best show her affection for him by breaking the engagement now before it was too late.

Besides, Jane thought, even if she could so school her mind as to forget her love for Michael Templeton, she could not marry Joseph. She had been unfaithful to him the night before. It was true she still had her chastity. But virginity was a relative state. Last night she had given her heart to Michael. She would have given herself if the setting had been more private or even right there in the music room if he had not stopped when he had. She had been beyond rational thought. She had allowed him to unclothe her to the waist. Indeed, she had assisted him, as eager as he to feel his hands on her naked breasts. She would have allowed him inside her body if he had chosen to take her. There was no point in trying to convince herself that she would have put an end to the embrace before that could have happened. She did not believe she would have.

So she had been unfaithful to Joseph in almost every way that mattered. And he had been in the same house at the time. Indeed, he might at any moment have walked back into the music room. She had offered herself wantonly to his friend anyway. She could not continue to behave publicly as if nothing had happened. That would not be fair to him. Even if he never knew that his betrothed and his friend had enjoyed a very unchaste embrace, it would not be fair to him to continue the engagement.

So she must tell him that she would not marry him after all. She really did love him in a very unromantic way, and she would hate never to meet him again, never to see his kindly face, or listen to his conversation. When the alternative to marrying him was to live a spinster life in the wilds of Yorkshire, it was very tempting to tell herself that she would marry him and spend the rest of her life making up to him for the dishonor she had brought him the night before. But she had to think of him first. He deserved a better wife than she could ever be. She was not worthy of him.

Of course, it was not going to be easy. Their betrothal had been publicly announced in the London papers. His sister and brother-in-law and his nephews and niece already treated her as one of the family. And he was fond of her, she believed. He would be hurt. And she would not be able to give him the real reason for breaking off the engagement. He would be left believing that somehow he fell short of her expectations. She desperately wanted to avoid giving that impression, but she had still not thought of the words she would say. Perhaps that was why she had not found the opportunity to talk to him that morning as she should.

And she must leave Templeton Hall. She should be packing her bags at that very moment instead of sitting idle in the garden like this. She should leave that very day. But oh, dear God, she would never see him or his children or this place ever again once she had left. She must be granted one more day during which to store conscious memories to last through the lifetime ahead.

Could she have been happy here? Could she have made him contented with her? Could she perhaps have made him love her just a little? She still could not understand his part in what had happened the night before. He did not seem the sort of man who would seduce a woman for the mere pleasure of doing so. And he appeared to value Joseph's friendship. The only possible explanation seemed to be that he had lost his head as completely as she had. But why would that have happened to him? She was not physically beautiful or attractive. He did not love her. Why, then? What other reason could there be? Would the same thing have happened if Honor had been sitting at the pianoforte with him instead of her? He had kissed Honor at Vauxhall. Had he kissed her like that?

Jane closed her eyes and lifted her face to the warmth of the sun, which was just now peeping out from behind the clouds. She had made a terrible mess of the last few weeks. She should have accepted Michael when she had the chance. She had thought then that having part of him would be worse than having nothing at all. She was not at all sure now that that was true. The future loomed ahead with terrifying emptiness. What matter that he had loved Susan and had only a leftover affection to offer a second wife? What matter that he would have married her only to care for his house and his children? She could have made that enough.

She loved his children. She loved all children, but there was something very special about those two little

girls. Probably because they were his. She could have
made happiness out of giving Claire the mother's arms
that any two-year-old still craves. And she could have
given Amy the loving attention the child needed to bring
her out of her shell. She would have loved to see her
gradually develop into a normal, happy four-year-old.
Amy, who looked so much like her father. And she
could have had children of her own perhaps. Hers and
Michael's. Now there never would be any children of
her own womb. Only other people's to love.

But she was giving in to self-pity, Jane decided,
lowering her eyes to the flowers at her feet. Other people
were about to suffer because of her selfishness and
folly. Honor too. She was going to be a problem. If
Jane were to leave, Honor would be expected to do so as
well. And Honor perhaps would wish to stay. Possibly
she still had hopes of becoming the second Lady
Fairfax. Even if she had definitely renounced her
interest in Michael, part of her Season in London had
been lost. And all because of Jane. Honor probably
would not have received an invitation to Templeton
Hall if it had not been for the betrothal of her cousin to
Joseph Sedgeworth.

Sometime today, Jane decided, she was going to have
to talk to Joseph and Honor. And perhaps Michael too.
If she were to leave his house, she must speak to him.
She could not just leave. And how was she to leave? She
and Honor had traveled down in Lord Dart's carriage.
The stage? Honor would never agree.

Her eye was suddenly caught by the sight of Fairfax
coming toward her along the gravel path. She jumped to
her feet in a panic, with some half-formed idea of
making her escape before he saw her. But she realized
almost immediately that he knew very well she was
there. She was his destination. She stood where she was.

"Good morning," he said with an attempt at a smile.
He looked as pale as she felt.

Jane said nothing.

"I saw you from the library window," he said. "I

came as soon as I was free. I owe you an apology."

Jane shook her head. "No, please do not," she said.

"I must," he said. He had stopped some distance from her. He stood now, his hands clasped behind his back. "My behavior last night was unpardonable. You are a guest in my house, Jane, and betrothed to my friend. You refused my hand when I offered it a few weeks ago. And yet I—"

"Please," she said. "Can we not forget it? I would rather not talk about it. I was as much to blame as you."

He shook his head. "No, don't think that," he said. "Do not blame yourself. I don't ask your pardon, Jane. I do not believe what I did was forgivable. But I wanted you to know that it will not happen again. I . . ." He took a ragged breath. "I suppose I have been lonely. It is more than a year since my wife died. And there you were, close beside me, lovely and full of laughter from our duet. I am afraid my need got the better of decency and courtesy and common sense. I thought I had better control of my instincts. But it will not happen again, Jane. You have my word on it. You need not feel afraid of me."

She stared at him wide-eyed.

"You are uncomfortable in my presence, I see," he said with that same twisted smile she had seen the night before and when he first arrived. "Perhaps you are frightened despite my assurances. I cannot blame you. I shall leave you to your quiet enjoyment of the flowers again." He bowed and turned to walk away from her back to the house.

Jane did not see him out of sight. The flowes, the sky, his retreating back: everything blurred before her vision. It was as she had thought, then. Pure physical need had driven him the night before. She had not admitted even to herself until this moment the desperate hope that perhaps he loved her as she loved him. How ridiculous she was. How very stupid!

\* \* \*

"So now you will be able to travel to the Continent on your wedding trip after all," Lord Dart said at the luncheon table.

"It seems so," Sedgeworth agreed, turning to smile at Jane. "It will be preferable to Scotland in the autumn anyway."

"You will be able to travel through Belgium to see where the battle took place," Honor said rapturously. "Did you say it was close to Brussels, my lord?"

"South of there," Lord Dart said. "Close to a village called Waterloo. Apparently his grace has decreed that the battle shall be called after it."

"The Battle of Waterloo," Honor said. "I do wish I could see the place."

Jane shuddered. "It is a mass graveyard, Honor," she said. "Do not glamorize it."

"But history has been made there, Jane," her cousin insisted. "Do you not believe that Bonaparte will be remembered as one of the greats of history?"

"Surely history can find worthier men to remember," Jane said.

"I do not believe Bonaparte is as bad as many people say," Honor said. "If other nations had not sneered so much because he has no royal blood, perhaps he would not have had to prove his worth by conquests. Is he so much worse than some of the other rulers of Europe?"

She caught Sedgeworth's amused eye at that moment and blushed hotly. "At least that is what Lord Henley told me in London," she said. "And he ought to know. I don't know, of course. I am a mere female. I am content to leave the thinking to the men of this world." She frowned crossly at Sedgeworth, who had mouthed the final words with her.

"I am merely thankful that the job has been done and we are at peace again," Fairfax said. "Though I grieve for the many good men who must have been lost to both nations."

"Joseph told you that the Reverend Beasley and his wife and older children have accepted your invitation to dinner this evening?'' Lady Dart asked Fairfax. "They are a very pleasant couple and the young people prettily behaved. And five younger children too. That is quite a family, my lord.''

Fairfax laughed. "You will probably hear Mrs. Beasley complaining that her husband gives away all their money to the poor despite the largeness of their family,'' he said. "But then she will assure you in the next breath that they live on love and that love is quite the best sort of wealth to possess.''

A very sensible attitude to take, under the circumstances, I am sure,'' Lady Dart said. "Are we to take the children out this afternoon again, since we are to have some adult entertainment this evening?''

"I must admit I have promised to take my girls swimming if the weather is warm enough,'' Fairfax said. "I hope none of you will feel neglected?''

"Mr. Sedgeworth,'' Honor said loudly, "you and I must console each other since everyone else seems to dote on the children. You must row me on the lake and show me that island. Unless you want to play hide-and-seek or make daisy chains, that is.''

Everyone laughed at the world of scorn in her voice.

"I am afraid I have not offered much in the way of entertainment for a young lady who is making her debut in society, have I?'' Fairfax said rather ruefully.

"Oh, no matter,'' she said. "Mr. Percival Beasley and Miss Cora Beasley both assured me earlier that they enjoy charades. We will see tonight if they can beat Mr. Sedgeworth and me.''

Lady Dart groaned.

"And Percy is really quite handsome in a very nineteen-year-old way,'' Honor whispered to Jane, who sat beside her. "I believe I have enslaved him already.''

Jane saw no possibility of having any of the serious talks she had planned, during the afternoon at least. She would have liked to excuse herself from the outing, but she did not want to draw attention to herself and perhaps dampen the spirits of some of the others. She stayed to the back of the group on their walk to the lake, talking to Gregory, who confided his indignation at still having to listen to a governess when he was all of ten years old. It would be two whole years before he would be sent away to school.

Amy, who had been walking sedately at her father's side, holding to one of his hands, dropped back after a while and took Jane's hand. Jane smiled down at her. The child said nothing but walked gravely on. Fairfax, looking back after a minute to see what had happened to his daughter, was surprised to see her hand in hand with Jane. He failed to catch the eye of the latter, though. Her head was bent down toward the eldest of Dart's children.

"Papa, Papa," Amy said, pulling at his coat when they had all reached the folly at the lake, "may we swim from the island? Please, Papa. It is so much more fun there."

"It would not be polite to abandon our guests to quite that extent, poppet," he said.

"Don't consider us," Lady Dart said cheerfully. "All my family has a healthy disgust of water. My children have plans of climbing trees and shooting down at savages, I believe. And I imagine Jane and I are unanimously elected as the savages, since I am sure we will not be fool enough to venture off the ground. Wallace will be delighted at the excuse, of course."

"Quite right, my love," he said cheerfully, shrugging out of his coat and proceeding to roll up his shirt sleeves.

"Please, Papa," Amy pleaded.

Fairfax looked down at his younger daughter, who was staring solemnly up at him, thumb in mouth. She smiled broadly around it. "Island, Papa," she said.

He grinned. "The island it is, then, poppets," he said. "Let us go and load up the boat with towels and dry clothes."

Honor and Sedgeworth were already settling in one of the boats. Honor was arranging her favorite yellow dress around her and raising the matching parasol.

Claire was tugging at Jane's dress. "You come too?" she asked.

"No, sweetheart," she said, touching the blond curls gently. "I am not as clever as you. I do not swim."

"Papa teach you," the child offered.

"Aunt Jane is afraid to put her head underwater," Fairfax said. "Perhaps we should teach her by taking her out in the boat and throwing her into the deep water. But I think not. She might drown, and then we would not feel very proud of ourselves, would we?"

"Aunt Jane can watch us," Amy said, looking eagerly up at her father. "I want her to see me swim, Papa. May she come?"

Fairfax looked somewhat helplessly at Jane. She opened her mouth to utter a very firm refusal.

"Oh, do go, Jane," Joy said from behind her. "I do not know why I did not think of it myself. You are forever spending your time entertaining the children. It is time you had a chance to relax. And the water is beautifully calm for the boat this afternoon. Go on. I shall be savage enough for these children. They will enjoy the opportunity to shoot at me. Thank heaven for imaginary arrows."

"Yes!" Amy shouted, jumping up and down in a greater show of animation than Jane had see in her before.

"Up," Claire was demanding of her, holding two arms skyward.

"Much rest from children Aunt Jane is going to have, by the look of it," Fairfax said. "And, Claire, poppet, I thought we decided at Christmastime that you do not have to be carried everywhere."

But Claire was in Jane's arms already and was not going to lose her perch without a struggle. She wrapped her arms around Jane's neck and laid one soft little cheek against hers.

"I can dive and swim on my back and my front, Aunt Jane," Amy was saying eagerly, clinging to Jane's skirt as Fairfax went in silence to load the boat and to pull it down into the water.

"It is going to be crowded," he said, "with one rower and three ladies. You sit very still beside Aunt Jane, Amy. And, Claire, don't move, poppet. Aunt Jane will hold you safe."

He was prattling, he knew. And he could tell from the look on her face that Jane was every bit as dismayed as he by the way she had been trapped into joining his family party. His palm still burned from contact with her hand as he had helped her into the boat.

# 13

"I suppose you wish you could go to Waterloo with your sketchbook and record the scenes of the battlefield for posterity," Sedgeworth said conversationally as he rowed Honor out onto the lake.

She twirled her parasol and lifted her chin. "I did not ask you to bring me out here so that you might insult my lack of feminine charms, sir," she said.

He laughed. "That governess must have been a real chucklehead," he said. "Who could possibly be interested in an empty-headed female who is good for nothing but . . . flirtation? I would not wish to be within thirty feet of a woman with nothing between her ears but empty air."

"How delicately you do phrase your meanings, sir," said Honor, giving the parasol another twirl.

"I have never seen you so much on your dignity, Miss Jamieson," he said with a grin. "Have I offended you? I did not mean to. I meant to compliment you. I have liked you much better since discovering that you are a fraud."

"Well," she said, her tone somewhat mollified, "I did not bring you out here to listen to compliments either."

"To avoid the children?" he said. "I must admit to a fondness for them all. It is pleasant, however, not to be 'Uncle Joe' every ten seconds."

"Not for that reason either," Honor said, the parasol positively whirling above her head.

"Very well, you have your wish, ma'am," Sedgeworth said, resting his oars and giving her the whole of his attention. "I am fit to bursting with curiosity. Why did you bring me out here, as you put it?

Though to my way of thinking it is I who have brought you out here. At least I have the oars.''

"I want you to discover that you are madly in love with me and cannot live without me," Honor said. "And I want you to persuade Jane to release you from your engagement."

"Ah, is that all?" he said. "Why did you not say so immediately instead of building such suspense, my dear Miss Jamieson?"

"I am serious!" Honor said dramatically.

He looked at her, and his eyes remained steadily on hers for several seconds. "I think you had better start at the beginning, if there is a beginning to all this," he said, the teasing inflection gone entirely from his voice.

"Do you love Jane?" Honor asked.

"She is to be my wife," Sedgeworth said quietly. "Of course I love her."

"Yes, I know that," Honor said impatiently. "But do you *love* her is what I mean. Are your feelings deeply engaged?"

"Forgive me," he said, "but is that not a private matter between Jane and me?"

"I need to know," she said, leaning forward in her seat. "If the answer is no, then I may proceed with Plan A. If yes, then I must move on to Plan B."

He did not smile at the absurdity. "Suppose you proceed with Plan A," he said. "It sounds quicker."

"Have you realized," she asked, "that Jane and Lord Fairfax are head over ears in love with each other?" He did not respond. "It is as plain as the nose on your face."

"What has led you to believe so?" he asked eventually. He picked up the oars again almost absently and began to row.

"I must admit that I did not really notice until last evening," she said, "though looking back, I believe it has been obvious for some time. When I went to the music room to call them for tea last night, Jane came rushing out of the room before I got there and dashed up the stairs. I do not believe she even saw me. And I do not believe she had a headache, as Lord Fairfax said when he came to the drawing room later. People do not rush when they have a headache. And when I listened at the music-room door, there was no music. Just silence. Yet Lord Fairfax did not come out either.

"I grant that is not a great deal of evidence. But I have observed them both closely today. They are both desperately unhappy, and they have a way of looking at each other, or not looking at each other, that tells a clear story."

Sedgeworth rowed several powerful strokes before he said anything. "I think perhaps your imagination has been overactive, Miss Jamieson," he said. "I cannot believe that either Jane or Fairfax would carry on such a . . . flirtation behind my back."

"Exactly!" said Honor. "That is why they are unhappy. It has obviously taken them by surprise. Do not take my word for it, sir. Observe for yourself later today. But if it is true, then you must set her free. And the best way to do that is to do as I say. Pretend that you are the one wishing to be released."

"Do you love your cousin so much that you are willing to become involved in such a way?" asked Sedgeworth. "I thought you were trying to engage Fairfax' affections for yourself."

Honor pulled a face. "I was," she admitted. "But appearances can be deceiving, you know. Behind the handsome exterior of Lord Fairfax lives a man whose way of life would have me screeching with boredom within a fortnight."

Sedgeworth smiled despite himself. "Then why are you willing so actively to intervene on his behalf?" he said. "And to doom your cousin to such a life of boredom?"

"But you are involved too, sir," she said. "You would be desperately unhappy, would you not, to discover too late that your wife and your closest friend love each other?"

"And do I matter to you, Miss Jamieson?" he mocked.

Honor opened her mouth to reply, blushed scarlet, and suddenly discovered something of remarkable interest to the right of the boat. "Look, the island," she said brightly. "We are quite close. Do let us land, sir, and see what is here."

"Nothing but trees and overgrown grass, I would guess," he said, turning the boat and pulling directly for the shore.

Honor vaulted out almost without the assistance of his hand. She left her parasol in the boat. She ran amongst the trees, swinging around some of the narrower trunks, determinedly gay.

"How marvelous!" she called back to Sedgeworth. "I would love to be marooned here—with the right gentleman, of course." She laughed brightly.

"It is a shame I tethered the boat so carefully then," he said, coming up to her just before she whisked herself away again.

"Will you please stop?" he said when he came close to her again. "There is more to say, Miss Jamieson. If you are right, and I follow your suggestion, what about the humiliation to you? Your cousin's betrothal is broken because of you, and then the gentleman escapes alone to the Continent."

"Well," she said airily, swinging around the trunk to which she held, "I could always marry you to make things look more realistic."

"Miss Jamieson . . . Honor," he said sternly. "Will you please stand still? I thought I had escaped children for one afternoon, yet here you are behaving worse than the pack of them all together."

She stood meekly still before him.

He looked at her searchingly.

"You know," she said, two spots of color high on her cheeks, "it may not be as bad as you think. I really am not such a ninnyhammer as I seem to be. I do not read as much as I ought these days, and I do not have a great deal of interest in music, but I know something about art and history. There are people who have said I have a definite talent in watercolor painting. And I always listen to any talk about state affairs, though I pretend to be playing with my curls or my fan or something like that. I would travel with you without complaint about inconveniences and be ever so interested in all the new people and places. Especially if you were to take me to Italy. And Greece! Oh, certainly if you were to take me to Greece. Home of all those handsome gods!''

"Honor," he said quietly, "are you proposing to me?"

"Yes," she said breathlessly, the two spots of color merging into one flood that covered her face and neck. Her eyes were on his neckcloth.

"Why?" he asked. "Because you wish to travel?"

"Yes," she said, raising her eyes boldly to his. "But more because I think I love you."

"Think?"

"Well," she said, "if you were to kiss me, perhaps I would be sure. Lord Fairfax kissed me once and I enjoyed it. But then I realized I had enjoyed it only because it was my first. Will you kiss me? Please? Joseph.''

"I am not free to do so, Honor," he said gently.

"Oh," she said. "But do you wish to? If you were free, would you wish to?"

He drew a deep breath. "So many strange things have happened in the last few minutes," he said. "I do not know what I think or feel. I suppose I have been growing fond of you in the last few days, but I assumed that I was growing fond of you as a cousin. I have a deep affection for Jane, and I do not yet know for certain that she wishes to end our engagement. I am committed to her."

"Yes," she said. "And I do not need to be kissed. I know. I do love you."

She looked very crestfallen.

"I want to kiss you, Honor," he admitted slowly. "That is not a cousinly urge, is it?"

She smiled.

"But I am not free," he said, "and I will not dishonor my betrothal. Or be unfair to you. We had better get back into the boat."

"Yes," she said. Then she brightened visibly. "I am not betrothed. I have no one to feel guilty toward. I shall kiss you."

And she stepped lightly across the distance between them and suited action to words. She twined her arms around his neck and put her lips against his. She kept them there for a long time. Sedgeworth did not move.

"There," she said gaily. "Now you know me for the hussy I am. First I propose to a betrothed man, and then I kiss him without his cooperation at all. That governess of mine would commit instant suicide if she knew. To the boat, sir."

He followed her back through the trees to the bank where he had tied the boat. The other boat was approaching, Fairfax rowing. Jane sat opposite him, her arm around one child, the other child on her lap. Sedgeworth smiled and lifted his hand in greeting. They looked like a contented family group.

"My daughters have persuaded me to come here to swim," Fairfax called. "You would not care to join us, I suppose, Sedge? Miss Jamieson can sit and watch with Jane."

Jane! Not "Miss Matthews" any longer?

"I think my valet would hand in his notice without more ado if I arrived back with these clothes wet," Sedgeworth called back. "No, Miss Jamieson and I will resume our very dignified row on the lake. Are you to be the audience, Jane?"

"Yes," she said. "Amy wants me to see her dive and swim on front and back. And Claire tells me she can swim, though I shall have to see it to believe it." She smiled down at the small child on her lap.

"Can swim!" Claire said indignantly. "Papa tell you."

"You certainly can, poppet," he said, stooping down from the bank and lifting her from Jane's lap. "Just like a cork. Aunt Jane is merely jealous because she cannot put her head under. Come, Jane. Take my hand and I shall try not to drop you in.'' He grinned at her, his hand outstretched.

"We will see you all later," Sedgeworth said. "I think we are going to row around the island to see what is on the other side."

"More water, Sedge," Fairfax said, "and more sky."

"We shall go and look anyway, my lord," Honor announced, her parasol firmly in place again.

Jane sat on the bank on one of the towels, hugging her knees. Fairfax and his children were already swimming in the lake, the little girls calling and shrieking happily. She did not care that she should have found some excuse not to come. She did not care about the embarrassment of the boat ride over, sitting facing Michael as he rowed, both of them brightly talking to the girls but not to each other until he had relaxed a little in the presence of Honor and Joseph. She did not care that later today she must tell several people that she would be leaving tomorrow.

She did not care. Now at this very moment she was living through an afternoon that she would remember for the rest of her life. Long after these girls were grown up and married, and probably long after Michael had remarried and produced sons to succeed him, she would live her life in Yorkshire, never seeing any of them again, perhaps never hearing of any of them again. But remembering. Remembering particularly this afternoon when they had come here, just the four of them, like a family.

She would dream now that they were a family. There could be no harm in it. No one but her would ever know and be hurt by it. And she was not likely to be carried from reality for long. She looked at Fairfax, laughing as he held Claire, showing her the correct arm movements for a certain swimming stroke. His white shirt clung to his arms and shoulders like a second skin, showing even at this distance the firm muscles beneath. His dark hair was wet against his head and forehead. She loved him. She looked at him and quite consciously loved him. And it was not just his extraordinary good looks that attracted her now. She loved the affectionate family man that he quite obviously was. For the first time she did not feel a painful jealousy of Susan, whom he had loved. She loved him, and she grieved with him in his loss. It should be Susan sitting here now watching her family, not she. She felt privileged.

She looked at the children and allowed herself to feel the full force of a mother's love for them. Michael's comparison of Claire in the water to a cork was an apt simile. The child was far out of her depth. Indeed, Jane had worried at first because they were all out of their depth as soon as they dived off the bank. There was no shallow water here. But Claire bobbed, floated, bounced, and even swam as if she had been born a water baby. And Amy swam quite gracefully back and forth in front of her father, constantly calling his attention to some new feat. And always he looked and made some comment or called encouragement.

His attention was wholly given to his children, Jane noticed. He must long to swim free, out into the calm sparkling water of the lake. But he did not do so. And she had dared think of him once as a selfish and an arrogant man! Jane swallowed a lump in her throat. For this afternoon he was her husband and the girls her children. She loved them.

"Aunt Jane!" Unnoticed, Amy had swum to the bank and was peering eagerly over its edge now. Her hair, lank and devoid of its ringlets, hung close to her head and down below her shoulders. She looked more than ever like her father. "I can dive right under. Watch me."

"Be careful, sweetheart!" Jane called, leaning forward with a smile.

Amy bobbed up, hands in the air, and disappeared below the surface, legs kicking up behind. Jane waited anxiously for what seemed an eternity until she reappeared a short distance away, shaking her head and shoulders like a wet dog. Claire was shrieking with laughter somewhere off to the left.

"I saw the stones on the bottom," Amy said, swimming back to cling to the bank again. "Do you think I am clever, Aunt Jane?"

"I am full of admiration," Jane assured her. "I would not dare do such a thing."

"Papa would teach you," the child said, but fortunately she did not pursue the idea. "Would you like to see me dive again?"

"Be careful," Jane said automatically.

Any drew in a deep breath and plunged again, a little bottom and two feet appearing for a moment. Jane watched in some anxiety the spot where she had disappeared. The child came up some distance farther out.

"Ouch!" she called. "I hit my head on the bottom." And disappeared again.

Jane scrambled to her feet, her eyes riveted to the empty lake, her heart beginning to pound heavily against her ribs, robbing her of breath. It seemed that she stood there for minutes before screaming out, "Michael!" and plunging headfirst into the water.

Instinct had led her to suck in a lungful of air. It did not occur to her in her terror to shrink from having her head under the water or from opening her eyes. She swam with the strength of near-panic out to the spot where she had seen Amy disappear, and tried desperately to find the inert form of the child on the stones at the bottom. When she was finally forced to the surface, she had drawn in a gasp of air to enable her to go under again before seeing Amy treading water, arms outstretched, just a short distance away.

Why she should have panicked just at the moment when she realized that no one else was in danger, Jane did not afterward know. But panic she did. The desperate breath she had drawn escaped her at the same moment as her head went under, and her hands clutched

at air. She came up sputtering and clawing at the water
in blind panic. She breathed in water as she went down
again.

And then there really was something solid to clutch
at, something that hauled her above the surface and
held her there. She clung on with a death grip,
struggling desperately to draw air into her lungs again,
finding it impossible to do so. She could draw it in only
as far as her throat, no farther. She fought.

"Steady, Jane. Steady," a voice was saying. "Don't
fight me, love. I have you. You are quite safe. Let
yourself relax. The breath will come. Steady, now."

She had fistfuls of wet shirt and flesh in her grasp.
And still the breath would not come beyond her throat.
It was Michael. Someone was crying out, "Aunt Jane!"
Her mind was clearly placing her surroundings, and she
tried to use it to impose calm on her body.

"Steady, love." His hands were firm at her waist. He
would not let her drown. "We are at the bank. I will
have you out of here in a moment."

And the breath came shuddering into her lungs,
setting her to coughing as if all her insides were about to
come up. And so she gasped and coughed and clung
with about as much dignity as a babe at birth, the clear
mind behind all the physical torment told her in disgust.

"There! You will live now," the warm, almost
teasing voice of Viscount Fairfax said against her ear.
And then the hands at her waist tightened and she was
lifted from the water to sit dripping on the bank.

While she coughed on, Jane was aware that he lifted
his two daughters out of the water too before coming
out himself.

"Fetch Papa the biggest towel," he said, and four
bare legs raced past her toward the dry clothes a short
distance down the bank. He knelt beside her, put an arm
beneath her knees, and lifted her legs onto the bank. It
had not occurred to her to do it for herself. "What were
you trying to do, Jane? Join the fun? You have ruined
your dress, I'm afraid. I like this one too. Pink suits

you." His voice was gently teasing. He was taking the towel from Amy with one hand and gathering Jane's draggled curls together at the neck and squeezing out the water with the other.

And then the final disgrace, that annoyingly clear mind told her as she put her hands over her face and failed to stifle a loud and quite unladylike sob.

"Jane!" he said, throwing the towel around her shoulders and pulling her against him. He was quite as wet as she, but there was warmth somewhere seeping through the fabric of his shirt to her cheek. "What is it, love? You have had a thorough soaking, but you are safe now. It must have been a terrifying experience for you. But I would not have let you drown, you know."

"I thought . . . I thought . . ." Painful sobs prevented her from getting the words out. "Amy . . . She hit her head."

"Did you, poppet?" she heard him ask. "Did you hurt yourself?"

"Only a little bit," Amy said. "Did Aunt Jane think I was drownding?"

"Yes," he said. "She dived in to save you." He lifted the towel from her shoulders and began to rub vigorously at her hair. "Let us get you as dry as we can, Jane, and back to the house before you take a chill. That was a very brave thing to do. Thank you, love." Perhaps he was unaware of the fact that he kissed her cheek as he said the words.

Jane pushed away from him and took the towel from his hands. "I made an utter fool of myself," she said. "I might have known Amy was safe. How could I have helped her anyway? I would have drowned us both." She hid her face in the towel as she rubbed at her hair. She began to shiver.

"Were those shrieks ones of enjoyment or fright?" a voice called from out on the water.

"Jane!" Honor shrieked. "You are soaked. You fell in. Oh, do pull in to the bank, Joseph."

Jane had recovered sufficiently to rather wish that she

could fall back into the lake and never come to the surface again. Soon she had three adults fussing around her, one child crying for some reason, and another standing silent and round-eyed with a thumb in her mouth.

"Sedge," Fairfax said, "Jane is soaked and has no dry clothes here. You must get her back to the house immediately. Miss Jamieson can come with us when we have dried off."

Jane's teeth were chattering. She had scrambled to her feet. "Oh, my dear, whatever happened?" Sedgeworth said, pulling off his coat to wrap around her. "Come. I shall have you back at the house in no time at all." His arm was warm and strong about her.

"I shall r-ruin your c-coat," she said, allowing him to lead her down to the boat and help her inside.

"Nonsense," he said. "We will leave my valet to worry about that." He untied the boat, climbed in, and took the oars.

"Here," Fairfax said, kneeling on the bank and reaching across to Jane. "Take my coat too, love, to put over your knees. And the towel to wrap around your head. Away you go, Sedge. There are two large blankets in the boathouse that we use for sitting on on the beach. Wrap Jane in one of those when you reach the shore."

Sedgeworth gave his friend a long and measured look before giving his attention to getting Jane to a warm house and dry clothes as quickly as possible.

Jane felt all the humiliation of having to face the exclamations and concern of Lord Dart and his family when the boat reached the shore. She felt very stupid. It was all just punishment for the fantasy she had been living out on the island, she thought. It was an afternoon she would remember for the rest of her life indeed! She recalled with deep mortification the way she had clutched at Fairfax and coughed and wheezed and sputtered all over him. She must have left bruises behind. How would she ever face him again even to say good-bye?

The thought sobered her considerably. She looked up into Joseph's eyes as he came rushing from the boathouse to wrap her warmly in a heavy blanket that smelled faintly musty. He put one arm firmly around her despite the audience that was dispensing sympathy and advice from close by.

"Take her straight to the house, Joseph," his sister advised unnecessarily. "And be sure that Mrs. Pringle prepares some hot milk for her. And a hot bath."

Jane allowed her head to drop wearily to his shoulder as they walked. "Joseph," she said, "I have ruined your afternoon and everyone else's."

He tightened his arm around her but said nothing.

She began to cry again and seemed powerless to stop herself. "Joseph," she said, "I am so very miserable."

"I know, Jane," he said, laying his cheek against the top of her head. "Don't worry about it now. We will talk later. Don't worry about it, dear."

She felt comforted and mortally dejected all at the same time.

# 14

Fairfax doodled with a dry quill pen on the leather of his desktop in the library. He should be on his way upstairs to get ready for dinner, as his guests had done fully half an hour before. They were even expecting outside visitors that night. He must be ready to receive them.

His mind was still not calm after the scolding he had been forced to give Amy when they arrived home. He hated having to be angry with his children. He had never hit either one of them and knew that they could never do anything so bad that he would do so. But occasionally he had to scold and punish. He would not be fulfilling his obligation to help them grow into mature ladies if he did not. But he derived as much pain and misery from the ordeals as they did, he was sure.

She should have known better already. She probably did. She had been upset at the time and not acting as she normally would, he supposed. She had been crying over Jane's mishap, blaming herself after realizing that Jane had been trying to save her. And even the child must have realized the good sense of sending Jane home with Sedge instead of forcing her to wait while they dried themselves and changed into dry clothes.

But she had not acted as if she had known. "I want Aunt Jane to come with us," she had wailed as Sedge rowed the boat away from the bank.

"Aunt Jane is going with Uncle Joe," he had said firmly. "We will see them back at the house. Run and get yourself a towel, poppet."

"I don't want *her* to come with us," Amy had said fully within Miss Jamieson's hearing. "I want Aunt Jane."

"Amy," he had said in the tone that his daughters usually did not argue with, or anyone else for that matter, "go and get a towel now, my girl, and not another word from you."

"I don't want to," she had wailed. "I want Aunt Jane."

He had taken her then firmly by the arm and marched her at a brisk pace over to the towels and dry clothes. She had screamed with mingled rage and fright. "Hush now, Amy," he had commanded. "Be a good girl for Papa and dress quickly. You do not need help, do you? I have to help Claire. We will talk about this at the house."

Claire had trailed after them, eyes solemn, thumb in mouth. "Amy cry?" she had asked. "Papa cross?"

He had hugged her before toweling and putting on her dry clothes. She had put her arms around his neck and kissed him wetly on the mouth. "Papa not cross with Amy," she had coaxed.

But he had been cross. He had had to walk over to where Miss Jamieson stood on the bank looking out across the lake, her parasol twirling above her head, and try to explain.

"Please pardon Amy's rudeness," he had said. "She was very upset. Jane dived in thinking she was drowning, you see, and Amy feels responsible. She forgot her good manners in the process."

"Oh, think no more of it," the girl had said airily. "I do not know how Jane does it, but she can always win the trust of children without even trying. I can't. But then, Jane loves children, and I think them horrid little nuisances most of the time. And now I have been unpardonably rude." She had laughed gaily. "Forgive me, please."

But that had not been the end of the matter. When they had got into the boat, Amy had refused to sit beside Miss Jamieson and had insisted on sitting at the bottom of the boat between his feet. Short of making a scene in which he sensed Amy would have begun screaming, he could do nothing. Claire had sat solemnly on Miss Jamieson's lap, but she had sat upright and silent, not snuggling against this girl as she did with Jane.

And so he had been forced to follow the children to the nursery as soon as he had ascertained that Jane was lying down resting, on the insistence of Mrs. Pringle and Sedgeworth. Amy, alone at her painting had cried as soon as she saw him and all the way to her room as he led her there by the hand. And there he had been forced to talk severely to her, knowing that the child was miserable and already punishing herself. And he had been forced to punish her so that she would know that such rudeness to a guest was a serious breach of the sort of behavior he expected of her. He had sentenced her to an evening spent alone in her room, dinner to be eaten in lone state, no painting or other amusement allowed.

And she was four years old! Sometimes it was hard to realize that. She was such a quiet, solemn child that she seemed older. And Claire's existence did not help. One tended to forget that the elder child was herself little more than a baby. He had to force himself now to sit doodling invisible patterns in order to prevent himself from going up to Amy's room again and telling her that an hour was long enough and she was free to go back to the nursery. Or from going to the kitchen and begging some treat from Cook to take up to his daughter. He hated having to punish.

He threw the quill pen aside and got to his feet. He wished to heaven he had never met Miss Jane Matthews. Why had he gone to that infernal ball of Aunt Hazel's? He had not wanted to go. And but for the accident of their meeting there, he doubted that he would have met her at all. He had not considered her beautiful when they first met—though how he could not have done so escaped his understanding now—and possibly would not have noticed her had he not been forced to do so. But of course he would have been attracted to that ninnyhammer of a cousin of hers under any circumstances, and through her he would have met Jane anyway. And loved her. One could not know Jane and not love her.

Dammit! And he was going to be late for dinner too if he did not rush. Just after he had been lecturing Amy on the good manners due a guest in one's home.

Honor was flirting quite outrageously with Percival Beasley and behaving for all the world as if she did not have a brain in her head. Jane would have felt quite sorry for the poor boy if she had not been so relieved on her own account. Apart from having to answer everyone's queries after her health when she came down to the drawing room before dinner, knowing that by now they would all know the full details of her stupidity, she had really escaped quite lightly.

The Beasleys arrived soon after she came down, and Honor went into action. She was wearing one of the finer of her ball gowns, altogether too elaborate for a dinner in the country, though young Mr. Beasley seemed not to think her appearance inappropriate for the occasion. He was soon stammering out an account of his first year at university to a wide-eyed, admiring Honor. Miss Beasley was gazing at her new acquaintance, the same age as herself, with almost openmouthed awe.

Jane found herself seated between Sedgeworth and Mrs. Beasley at dinner and listened with grateful attention to the almost ceaseless monologue of the latter. Mrs. Beasley was a large, comfortable-looking woman whose conversation centered almost entirely around her family and the endearing weakness her husband had of giving his money away to beggars.

"But there, my dear Miss Matthews," she said, turning to accept another spoonful of potatoes from a footman, "if we had more money perhaps we would have less love in our family. And where would we be without love? It is the greatest wealth one can possess, you know."

"I am sure you are right, ma'am," Jane agreed.

"Oh, take my word for it, my dear," the matron said. She lowered her voice and leaned closer to murmur confidentially, "Poor Lady Fairfax, you know. Had all the money in the world, dear lady. And as unhappy a person as you would care to meet. Poor dear."

Jane looked at her neighbor, startled.

"I don't believe dear Lord Fairfax was to blame," Mrs. Beasley said, continuing the confidence. "That poor lady could not love, I have always told the reverend. Spoiled as a child, no doubt. Always had everything she asked for and never learned to love. Poor lady. And such beautiful little babies that she could have loved. But there. It might have been different if she had had a boy. Another girl it was, you know. The one that killed her, I mean. Poor lady."

Jane felt uncomfortable and intrigued at the same time. She had never even dreamed of the possibility of Michael's first marriage being anything but perfect. But then Mrs. Beasley could not have known. Not really. She was very probably wrong. How could Susan not have loved Michael? And her two daughters. It was absurd to imagine that she had not. She had been bearing him another child when she died.

Mrs. Beasley turned at that moment to talk to Fairfax on her left at the head of the table, and Jane was free to talk to Sedgeworth.

"You look none the worse for your ordeal, Jane," he said. "Did you sleep?"

"I had little choice," she said. "You and Mrs. Pringle positively insisted that I lie down. What else was there to do but sleep?"

He chuckled. "Were we really such tyrants?" he asked. "If there is a chance later, Jane, shall we walk in the garden? We need to talk, do we not? And I believe we will both sleep easier tonight if we do not postpone it until tomorrow."

He knew, then. She had thought that afternoon that perhaps he had misunderstood and thought she was miserable merely over her wet state. But he knew. And he was still treating her with courtesy and even affection. Dear Joseph. Was she going to hurt him terribly? She knew he did not love her. Not in the way that a man can love a woman, anyway. But he had wanted to marry her. And from what he and Michael had said, it seemed that he had never thought of marriage before, had intended never to marry. She was really going to confirm him in his bachelorhood now.

She smiled warily. "Yes, you are right, Joseph," she said.

But it was much later in the evening before they could politely leave the gathering. There was music first in the music room and then charades in the drawing room. The latter was Honor's idea, of course, but the Beasleys greeted it with loud enthusiasm. Honor, with Percival Beasley on her team, won by a narrow margin, but only because Sedgeworth, the leader of the other team, seemed preoccupied, as Honor was loud in admitting herself.

"Go and fetch a shawl," Sedgeworth said to Jane eventually, when Fairfax had sent for the tea tray. "It may be cool outside by now. Jane and I are going to stroll in the garden for a while," he explained to the gathering.

"I say," young Mr. Beasley said, "what a perfectly splendid idea. Would you care to take a turn about the garden too, Miss Jamieson?"

"How delightful!" she exclaimed, fluttering her eyelashes at the young man. "Of course, I would be afraid to venture out at night without a gentleman to protect me. But with you, sir, I shall feel quite safe."

Sedgeworth could not prevent a secret smile, though he was not feeling particularly amused. He led Jane to the west side of the house, where there was a large rose garden, and was somewhat relieved to see a determined Honor leading her admirer into the formal gardens. The young pup was probably congratulating himself on his great good fortune.

He took Jane's hand in a warm clasp, and they walked in silence for a while. "So, Jane," he said at last, "you find that you wish to put an end to our betrothal?"

"Oh," she said, looking at him stricken. "It sounds quite dreadful when you put it into words like that."

"But true?" he prodded gently.

She stared at him. "It is not because I do not like and respect you, Joseph," she said. "In fact, I think it is because I feel a deep affection for you that I cannot marry you. I would make you unhappy."

"Yes, you would, dear," he said. "It makes me very unhappy to see you miserable."

"I feel so wretched," she said. "How can I do this to you? I was so sure that I wished to marry you and that I would be prepared to spend my life making you comfortable."

"Perhaps I do not wish to be comfortable after all, Jane," he said. "Comfort can be pretty dull really, don't you think? And don't blame yourself, dear. You were honest with me, remember. You told me at the time you loved another man. You cannot forget him?"

She shook her head.

"Is there any hope, Jane?" he asked curiously. "Will you marry him now?"

"Oh no," she said earnestly. "No. I shall never marry, Joseph. I did not decide to break my engagement to you only because I saw a more desirable chance for myself. I would far prefer to marry you than to face the life I must now face. But I could not do it, you see."

"My offer still stands, Jane," he said. "I will not ask more of you than you can give. If you wish to marry me, you must consider only our own desires. I have stated my wish to have you as my wife. On any terms that you dictate."

She stared at him. "How very dear you are, Joseph," she said. "You deserve a wife who will love you with a whole and devoted heart. I hope you will meet her someday. I really do. Thank you. But no. I cannot do it." She lifted his hand and laid it against her cheek. "I just wish I did not have to put you through the great embarrassment now of a publicly broken engagement. Oh, I do wish it."

He smiled. "I have never cared a fig for London gossip, Jane," he said. "You must not worry about that. What will you do now?"

"I shall leave tomorrow," she said. "The mail coach leaves at noon. It will be better than the stage for Honor."

He raised his eyebrows. "Miss Jamieson goes too?" he asked.

"Yes," she said. "I told her before dinner. She did not seem nearly as upset as I expected. She must be missing Aunt Cynthia and Uncle Alfred. And the life of London, of course."

He nodded. "You have told Fairfax?"

"No," she said. "I had hoped to do so tonight, but I shall have to leave it until morning now."

"Does he know, Jane?"

"No," she said, bewildered. "I just said—"

"I mean about your ending your engagement," he said.

"How could he?" she said. "I am only now speaking to you."

He looked searchingly into her eyes and nodded slightly. "Do you feel calm enough to go inside?" he asked. "I don't think I do. Shall we sit in the rose garden for a while? You need not make conversation if you would rather not. We are friends enough to sit in comfortable silence for a while, are we not, Jane?"

"Yes," she said.

They sat side by side on a wrought-iron seat, their shoulders touching, breathing in the heavy scent of the roses.

"Jane," he said, "I want to write to you. May I? I want to be sure that you are not terribly lonely and unhappy in Yorkshire. You are my friend, you know. And perhaps a little more than a friend."

"So I will share a little in your travels after all?" she said with a wan smile. "Is this just kindness, Joseph?"

"Not at all," he said. "I do not see my friends nearly as much as I should perhaps. But I keep them through my letters. I am quite an expert correspondent, you know. Ask Fairfax. I shall continue my friendship with both of you through letters. Shall I? Perhaps I shall be able to give you some news of each other now and then. And give you news of the children. You love them, do you not?"

She looked at him with some suspicion, but there was nothing in his eyes but his usual kindly smile.

"I would like to hear from you, Joseph, and write to you," she said. "Until you marry, that is. Not after that. I would not wish your wife to misunderstand."

He smiled and leaned across to kiss her very gently on the cheek.

"Do you not think Percy a handsome boy, Jane?" Honor asked later. She was curled up on her cousin's bed, her head propped on one hand, watching Jane pack her belongings for their departure the next day.

"Very," Jane said. "And a very pleasant young man too, Honor. Have you added him to your list of conquests?"

Honor giggled. "He tried to kiss me in the garden," she said, "and then spent all of ten minutes reviving me from a fit of the vapors and apologizing profusely. I really felt quite mean. It was mean, was it not, Jane?"

"What?" Jane said. "Is this a new Honor, feeling remorse at breaking a young man's heart?"

"Oh, it cannot be as bad as that," Honor said. "But I could not resist, Jane, when he was making such calf's eyes at me all evening. Of course, that was my fault too. I set my cap at him from the start. Poor boy. What I need, Jane, is an older man of firm convictions who will not put up with my nonsense but force me to behave more sensibly and responsibly."

Jane looked at her cousin suspiciously, her heart

slipping to somewhere in the area of her knees. "Fair-fax?" she asked.

"Heaven forbid!" Honor said with feeling. "I could never marry anyone so dull, Jane. Though I must confess I deeply regret his good looks. But what is the point of having a handsome husband if he never takes one anywhere that one might show him off?"

"Ah," Jane said. "So this older man is to be a future acquisition, is he?"

"Probably," Honor said. "Did you end your betrothal, Jane?"

Jane paused in her packing and looked at her cousin, her face troubled. "Yes," she said. She looked down again too late to see Honor's eyes light up.

"Was he very upset, Jane?" she asked.

"It is hard to say," Jane said. "He is so thoroughly the gentleman, Honor. With the emphasis on 'gentle.' "

"What did he say?"

Jane smiled. "Nothing that was not thoroughly noble," she said. "He wishes to write to me, Honor, and to retain me as a friend."

"Does he?" Honor said. "Jane, you did not tell me earlier why you decided to break off your engagement and leave here in such a hurry."

Jane shrugged. "Sometimes these things are hard to explain," she said. "Perhaps I would not be happy with his way of life, Honor. I do not believe I would like to live without a settled home. And I do not think Joseph would want children. I could not be married and not want babies of my own."

"You should marry Fairfax," Honor said carelessly. "He would probably want to do nothing but give you babies."

Jane hid her blushes by bending low over her valise as if to rearrange its contents. "Yes, I should," she said lightly. "Will you be glad to leave, Honor? There is not much for you here, is there, now that you are no longer interested in the viscount."

"Oh, I don't know," Honor said airily. "I could

always try to fix Mr. Sedgeworth's interest now that he is free again. If we were staying, that is.''

Jane laughed. "Poor Joseph," she said. "I do not think he would approve of your type of flirtation one little bit, Honor. Shall we go to bed? We are facing two days on the road, and I have no idea what the quality of the inns might be where the mail coach will drop us off. We must sleep as much as we can tonight.''

Jane closed her bags when Honor was gone and undressed for bed without summoning a maid. She did not believe she would be able to take her own advice. She would not sleep a wink tonight. She had severed her connection with Joseph already. It only remained to say good-bye to Michael and the children tomorrow morning. And then she would be gone. Forever. She would probably never set eyes on one of them ever again. And she was not going to dwell on it now. There had been enough of emotion in her life in the last few days. She had made her choices, and now she must learn to live by them. At least she would have memories. Many spinsters did not even have that much to make life tolerable.

She pulled back the curtains and opened one of the windows. She climbed wearily into bed and stared up at the canopy above her head, dimly visible in the moonlight. She would have Joseph's letters to look forward to. She did not think that he would neglect to write to her. He was a man of his word. She would be able to read about his travels. She would feel she had one interesting and dear friend outside the confines of her own neighborhood. And sometimes he would surely mention Michael and his daughters. She would know when he married again, and she would be able to follow the girls' growing up. It would be something. Perhaps he would not remarry. Perhaps she would never have to live through that painful news.

Jane slept very soon after lying down.

She woke up suddenly, feeling that something had woken her. She listened intently. A hand shook her shoulder again. She turned her head sharply, to find herself looking into a pair of eyes on a level with her own.

"Aunt Jane," Amy said. A sob followed the words.

Jane turned sharply onto her side and sat up. "Amy, sweetheart, what is the matter?" she asked. "Is something wrong?"

"Aunt Jane," the child wailed, and began to cry in earnest. She was standing barefoot in a long white nightgown, her hair hanging loose about her face and reaching to below her shoulders.

Jane swung her legs over the side of the bed and gathered the child into her arms. She felt like little more than a baby. "What is the matter, sweetheart?" she said, her mouth against the girl's hair. "Oh, you are cold. Come under the blankets for a minute and get warm. Then you shall tell me what is the matter. Is Claire sleeping?"

The child nodded and pressed herself against Jane, crying her heart out. Jane covered her warmly with the blankets and held her close until the sobs quietened to the occasional involuntary gasp and shudder.

"Do you want to tell me, sweetheart?" she asked.

"I hate her," Amy said. "I don't want Papa to marry her."

"Whom?" Jane asked. "Whom is Papa going to marry?"

"The pretty lady," Amy said. "Miss Jamieson."

"No," Jane said. "I don't think so, sweetheart. Papa is not going to marry Miss Jamieson."

"He made me stay in my room tonight because I was rude to her," Amy said. "And I was not even allowed to paint."

Jane smoothed the hair from Amy's forehead and kissed it. "Did he?" she said. "And were you rude, Amy? If you were, Papa punished you because he loves you and wants you to be the best little girl you possibly can be. It is not because he is going to marry Miss Jamieson."

"Promise?" the child begged, looking up with pleading eyes.

Jane hesitated. "I cannot quite do that, sweetheart," she said. "But I am as sure as I can be. Would it be so bad if he did? Would you not like to have a new mama?"

The child's eyes widened in horror. "No!" she said, and she began to cry again. "Not another mama, Aunt Jane. I don't want another mama. She will hate me!"

"Hate you?" Jane said. "Whatever gave you that idea, Amy? Mamas always love their little girls. Your mama loved you. Do you not believe a new mama would do so too?"

"No," Amy wailed. "Mama hated me. She said I was ugly and a nuisance and I wasn't a boy. She said Papa did not love me because I was not a boy. But that is not true. Papa loves me. He does love me, Aunt Jane, doesn't he? Papa does love me."

She was crying with loud sobs again. Jane hugged her close, rubbing a hand soothingly over her back.

# 15

J ane said nothing for a long while. She felt almost paralyzed by shock. And what could she say to undo the harm that a mother had done to a child who was no more than three years old when she died?

"Of course Papa loves you, sweetheart," she said eventually. "You do not really need me to say that, do you? You know it for yourself. And I know that Papa could not possibly love you or Claire one bit more if you were boys. Of course Papa loves you."

"Am I ugly, Aunt Jane?" the child asked, her sobs having subsided again.

"You certainly are not, Amy," Jane said. She chose her words with care. It was important to be quite honest with the girl, she knew. "You are not pretty either, you know, not in the way Claire is. But I am going to tell you something important. You are going to grow up to be a very handsome young lady. I will wager that by the time you are sixteen Papa will be beating the young men back from the door."

Amy snorted with mirth, her laughter somehow getting all tied up with a leftover sob.

"And handsome ladies usually stay handsome all their lives," Jane said. "Pretty ladies have to work hard to keep their prettiness once they grow older."

"Older than twenty?" Amy asked.

"Yes," Jane agreed gravely.

"Aunt Jane," the child asked, her hands playing with a button on Jane's nightgown, "do you love me?"

"Well, Amy," Jane said, her voice amazed, "of course I do. Did you not know it without asking me?"

"Do you love Claire more than me?" Amy asked timidly.

"No, I do not," Jane said.

"She is prettier than I am," said Amy.

"Yes, she is," Jane agreed. "And you are more handsome than she. But I will tell you a little secret, sweetheart. I would love both you and Claire even if you were as ugly as . . . As what?"

"A wicked witch?" the child suggested.

"A wicked witch," Jane said. "And I would love you equally. You and Claire are very different from each other, and both of you are very dear. You do not ever have to compete with Claire, you know."

"Complete?"

"Compete," said Jane. "Try to be better than her. That is what competing is. You do not have to do it. Always be yourself, sweetheart, and everyone worth caring about will love you."

"Aunt Jane, may I sleep here tonight?" the child asked timidly.

Jane kissed her forehead. "Nurse will be worried if she finds you missing," she said. "I shall carry you back to your room, shall I, and tuck you into bed?"

Amy started to cry again. "I don't want to be alone again," she said. "I couldn't paint or read or talk to anyone. And Papa was very cross."

"Lie here for a little while then, sweetheart," Jane said, hugging her close again. "I shall take you back later."

"Will you come here often when you are married to Uncle Joe, Aunt Jane?" Amy asked. "Please!"

Jane closed her eyes and rested her cheek against the top of the child's head. "I shan't be able to, Amy," she said. "But it has nothing to do with you. Or Claire. I shall always love you and think of you, but I cannot come here again. Will you love me and think of me too?"

"Always," the child said, snuggling closer. "When are you going, Aunt Jane? I don't want you to go."

"Tomorrow, sweetheart," Jane said.

Amy said nothing, but continued to cling tightly.

After several minutes Jane could tell that she was asleep. She did not know quite what to do. The child must be taken back to her room, or at least the nurse must be informed of her whereabouts. But Jane did not want to risk moving for a while and perhaps waking the girl again. She would wait quietly for perhaps fifteen minutes and then see if she could move without disturbing Amy.

She held the warm little form of the sleeping child in tender arms. Poor little girl. If her story was to be believed, she had had all confidence in herself destroyed by a selfish and bad-tempered mother. It seemed almost incredible to think of Susan that way, but she supposed that it was possible. She had not really known the beauty, after all. And a girl who had been made so much of by the *ton* might have found the responsibilities of motherhood irksome. Especially if she had her heart set on producing an heir.

Had Michael shown disappointment with her for giving him daughters instead of sons? Had she then taken out her unhappiness on her elder daughter? But no. Jane could not possibly believe that. His love for his daughters was so obviously deep and genuine that it could not hide a dissatisfaction with their gender.

For the second time in one day her image of the marriage that had existed between Michael and his wife had been challenged. Could the marriage have been less than perfect? If Susan had resented her children and Michael loved them, there must have been some friction between the two of them, surely. Had he known of the way she treated Amy? How could one tell a three-year-old that she was ugly and a nuisance? And how could one tell a daughter that she should have been a son? It was no wonder that Amy was solemn and withdrawn and hostile to any female who might become another mother.

Jane felt a twinge of gratitude that she had not accepted Michael in London and returned to Templeton Hall as his bride. She might never have won Amy's trust under those circumstances. And what would happen to the little girl now? She would have Michael's unconditional love, it was true, but would it be enough? Would she ever quite get over her distrust of women? Would he understand his daughter well enough to choose his next bride with special care?

Was that why he had chosen her in London? Jane wondered with sudden shock. Was that why he had not looked for beauty or love but for good sense? Had he recognized in her a woman who would love his children? Had he put their happiness even before his own? And she had thought him cold and selfish because he had not put her feelings first! He had left his children for several weeks, a parting that she now knew must have been painful for all of them, in order to bring them back a mother who would give them the security of knowing themselves lovable. And he had chosen her!

Jane swallowed. Suddenly, being chosen for such a reason became infinitely more precious than being chosen for love. He had been willing to trust her with the upbringing of his children, whom he loved more than himself. What a mess she had made of her life and of his and the children's. She had thought she knew all the answers back in London. She had prided herself on saying no to him and asserting her own worth as a person. She knew nothing. She was only now learning something about the selflessness of love. Now, when it was far too late.

Jane's eyes closed as she laid her cheek more comfortably against Amy's head.

Fairfax was standing at the window of his bed-chamber, his hands thrust into the pockets of the dressing gown he had put on against the chill of the night. He looked out on the formal gardens, illuminated by the light of an almost full moon.

He supposed he should go back to bed and try to sleep again. It must be well into the morning hours. But he hated to toss and turn in bed. Better to be on his feet, tired though he felt.

He could not stop thinking about the previous day. He really had not wanted Jane to go to the island with them. He had wanted to stay clear of her. But she had come, and his treacherous heart had not been able to treat her as just another guest. All the way across in the boat he had drunk in the sight of her sitting before him with Claire snuggled close on her lap and Amy cradled in her other arm. She had given an equal show of affection to both children. So many of his acquaintances favored Claire because she was more obviously lovable.

He had found himself, at first involuntarily and then quite deliberately, imagining that she was his wife and that they were taking their family for an afternoon outing. He had been very careful not to frighten her again. Not by word or gesture, he felt, had he given her any inkling of the direction his thoughts were taking. But he had dreamed nonetheless. She had looked very pretty sitting on the bank when the rest of them were in the water, hugging her knees and watching the children with a smile.

And then that stupid misunderstanding that had almost drowned her. He really had dropped his guard at that point. He hoped that she had been too overwrought at the time to notice that he had several times used an endearment instead of her name. He even had a memory that made him turn hot and cold, of calling her "love" in Sedge's hearing. He had not realized it himself until the boat was already pulling away from the island.

He would always hold as one of his most treasured memories the image of Jane screaming out his name and then diving into the water to save Amy. When she was terrified of water covering her head! And when she must have known that he could be there in moments himself. If only she loved him as she loved his children! Fairfax laughed somewhat harshly. Perhaps he should have lured her to Templeton Hall before making his offer and used her love of the children as a persuasive force. Perhaps then she would have taken him as part of the bargain. He could have no doubt that she did love his daughters.

But then, he thought, Jane loved all children. That was the type of woman she was. She romped and played with Dart's children too when the opportunity presented itself. And why should she not? They were to be her nephews and niece when she married Sedge. Soon perhaps she would have her own child. He hoped Sedge would give her one. It would be an irony of fate if Jane Matthews had to go through life childless. He knew that Sedgeworth was not greatly fond of children himself. But perhaps he would change when he married Jane and became her lover. He would want to give her a child then.

Fairfax turned from the window. It made him feel almost physically sick to think of Sedgeworth making love with Jane. He remembered how she had felt in his own embrace the previous night—was it only such a short while ago?—slender and yielding, her mouth unexpectedly hot with passion, her breasts small and firm in his hands. He could not bear the thought of anyone else, even his friend, touching her like that, touching her with even greater intimacy, possessing her body. He could almost kill at the very thought.

He gritted his teeth and shook off the thought. It was Sedge who should be wanting to kill. Sedge had the right to all the intimacies he had claimed for himself the night before.

He thought of Amy. It was anxiety about her that had originally had him tossing and turning in bed, unable to sleep. She was four years old. A baby. And for a momentary rudeness to a guest, committed when she had been in an emotional state, she had been sentenced to a lonely and idle evening in her room and to bed straight afterward. He had not even had the chance to hug her and assure her of his love and forgiveness at bedtime. She had been asleep already, curled up on top of the bedcovers, looking in the relaxation of sleep the baby she was. She had not woken even when he lifted her and tucked her beneath the covers.

Should he be feeling this guilt? Had the punishment

been too harsh? He was so afraid of spoiling his daughters, of being overindulgent and having them grow up to be selfish, bad-mannered ladies that sometimes he felt he was overstrict. Yet he loved them so very much. And he had to be both father and mother to them. Even when Susan was alive she had had little time for them, and he had often feared that when she was with them she was not showing them adequate love. Amy had not once cried after Susan's death, though he had thought it important to tell her the truth instead of inventing some lie about her mother having gone on a visit for a while.

It was no good, he thought, glancing reluctantly at his bed. He would not be able to rest until he had seen the child again and was sure she was sleeping peacefully. What four-year-old would not be sleeping peacefully at this ungodly hour of the night? But there was no point in arguing with himself. Go he must, to make sure that the nightmare image of the child crying alone into the darkness had no basis in truth.

He smiled when he saw Amy's empty bed. The child had the intelligence to understand what he had meant by an evening of solitariness. During the night she had felt free to creep into Claire's bed in the adjoining room. He was glad. She would have felt comforted to feel Claire's warmth. He lowered his candle and shaded it with his hand again as he moved quietly into his younger daughter's room.

Ah, he thought as he gazed down at the chubby face of Claire, her mouth open, her thumb on the pillow close by, the night had not been quite so happy for Amy. His heart felt heavy again. Had she crept into her nurse's room for comfort, or had Nurse heard her crying perhaps and come to her? At least it was a comfort to him to know that the child was warm and safe in someone's company. He turned to leave and cursed under his breath as his foot caught and overturned a chair that stood close to the door. He stood quite still for a few seconds, but Claire appeared not to have been disturbed.

He almost collided with the nurse as he went back into Amy's room.

"Oh, my lord!" she almost shrieked. And then in a loud whisper, "I thought you was burglars."

"I am sorry, Mrs. Cartwright," he said, closing the door into Claire's room. "I was just checking to see that the girls were safely asleep. Did you take Amy to your room, or did she go there herself?"

"My lord?" she said blankly, and looked across to Amy's empty bed.

"Amy *is* with you?" he said, a note of anxiety in his voice.

She stared at him wide-eyed.

Well over half an hour of increasingly frantic searching ensued before Fairfax and Mrs. Cartwright started to look in the more unlikely places where Amy might be.

"She must have gone outside," Fairfax said, his voice beginning to sound decidedly shaky. "We will have to arouse all the servants and have the grounds searched. There is nowhere else in the house she can be. We have looked for her in all the daytime apartments and in the rooms of the other children."

"She is very fond of Miss Matthews," the nurse said doubtfully. She was dabbing at her eyes with a large handkerchief that was already half-sodden.

"We cannot wake her up at this hour," Fairfax said. "But we must. We cannot continue searching without further help. Mrs. Cartwright, will you wake Miss Matthews first, please, before we disturb anyone else? Perhaps she will have some idea about Amy's whereabouts."

He waited outside the door until Mrs. Cartwright came to look out at him, crying harder than ever.

"Here she is, my lord," she sobbed. "Bless the good Lord. She is sleeping in here with Miss Matthews."

He elbowed her aside and was inside Jane's bed-chamber without a single thought to the impropriety of such an action.

\* \* \*

Jane came fully awake as soon as the gentle knock sounded on her door, and was quite aware of the fact that she must have fallen asleep with Amy still in her arms. She sat up with a panicked feeling of guilt as soon as she saw the children's nurse entering the room with one candle lifted aloft. How unpardonable of her. The nurse must be frightened half out of her mind.

"She is here, Mrs. Cartwright," she whispered hastily. "Amy is here. She is sleeping."

But instead of rushing forward as Jane expected, the nurse turned back to the door, said something, and was almost immediately pushed to one side. And Fairfax was in her room, clad in a dressing gown, his eyes wild with anger or relief, she was not sure which.

Jane sat almost paralyzed on the bed, making no move either to get up or to cover herself. She stared stupidly. He stopped when he was close to the bed and blew through his cheeks. His eyes were on the still-sleeping form of his daughter.

"Thank God," he said. "Oh, thank God."

Then he looked at Jane, a long, narrow-eyed look. With so much to say by way of explanation, she could think of nothing to say at all.

"Mrs. Cartwright," he said quietly, turning back to the nurse, who stood inside the door, "can you carry Amy back to her bed? I don't think she will waken. I shall come to check on her in a few minutes."

The nurse bustled over to the bed and carefully picked up the child while Fairfax crossed the room to set down his candle. Amy muttered some protest, but she did not wake up. She nestled her head against the ample shoulder of Mrs. Cartwright. They left the room.

Jane was still foolishly kneeling on the bed. She could not see Fairfax' face as he came back toward her, the candle behind him. "I fell asleep," she said lamely.

She knew as soon as his hands reached for her what his face must look like. He was furiously angry. He lifted her from the bed as if she weighed nothing at all and set her on her feet in front of him.

"Did you come here deliberately to wreck my home and plague my life?" he said. The sound came from between his teeth.

"Michael," she said, "I can explain about—"

"I am sick of your interference," he almost snarled at her, cutting her off in the middle of a sentence. "Do you think I am so incapable of loving and caring for my own children that you must be forever playing mother? Interfering where you are not needed and not wanted? Do you think that no one could care for Amy tonight but you? Did you imagine that she would not be missed? And did you imagine that her nurse and I would not be sick with worry for her safety? Do you think you are the only one who cares?"

"Michael . . ." she said and gulped loudly.

"Be quiet, madam," he said. "How dare you come here like this and try to take my children's trust away from me and undermine my authority with them. How dare you! You would have none of me when you were given the opportunity. Yet you have inveigled your way into my home and into the hearts of children you do not want as a permanent charge. Have you given a moment's thought to their feelings when you leave here to begin your travels? Do you know what it must be like for a child to begin to feel loved and to be abandoned again? You are a selfish and an interfering woman!"

Jane stood mute before him, her eyes huge with unshed tears.

"I want you away from here," he said. "Immediately. Tomorrow. I do not care what explanation you give Sedge. Make up whatever lie you wish, or tell the truth if you will. But I want you away from here. Do you understand me?"

"Yes, my lord," she whispered.

He stared at her for a long moment. At least, she assumed he stared. She still could not see his face clearly. She looked back, so terribly miserable that she could not even cry or say anything to defend herself any longer.

He reached for her suddenly. "Oh God, Jane!" he

said viciously. It was almost like a curse. "Jane." He pulled her roughly against him and his arms came about her like iron bands, squeezing the air from her lungs. "What a monster I am. There is a good explanation for this, is there not? She came to you?"

"Yes," she said dully.

"She was miserable because I punished her?"

"Not for that reason only," Jane said. "She is terrified of losing your love. And terrified that you will marry Honor."

"Oh God," he said.

"She is not sure that she is lovable," she said. "I could not turn her away. I did not want to do so. But I did intend to take her back once she was soundly asleep. I fell asleep." Her voice was quite toneless. "I am sorry, my lord. I know you must have been quite frantic."

"Jane," he said. "Jane, you have so much love in you—for my children."

He pulled his head back to look down at her and then lowered it toward hers. His arms tightened again and his lips brushed hers. His mouth was open. But it was the merest suggestion of a touch. He shuddered and put her sharply away from him. He turned his back on her and put a hand up to his face.

"You must go, Jane," he said. "I am appalled at my own lack of hospitality. I have never before ordered a guest from my house. But you must go before I do you some mischief. And I do not want you back here when you are married to Sedge. I don't want to see you again. Not for a long while, anyway. Make what excuses you must, but send him here alone when he comes. Or keep him away too. I want you to leave tomorrow. I shall make arrangements for a carriage and servants to protect you on your journey if you go alone. Tomorrow, Jane. Or today, rather. You must go."

"Yes," she said. Her voice sounded surprisingly calm to her own ears. "Make the arrangements, my lord, and let me know through the servants or Joseph. I will say good-bye now."

He wheeled around. "Good-bye?" he said. "Yes.

Good-bye, Jane.'' He took a deep breath. "Thank you for caring for my daughters. Even at the risk of your life yesterday afternoon. Be happy. Please.''

He held out his hand to her, but he withdrew it again before she could react, turned abruptly, and left the room without another word.

Jane closed her eyes. The end. No more. Never again. She would never set eyes on him again. Never hear his voice. Never touch him.

Never. Not ever. For all eternity.

She could not cry.

# 16

H onor declined the pleasure of accompanying Jane to the nursery the next morning to bid farewell to the children. She declared her intention of taking her leave of the adults instead. Sedgeworth was in the breakfast room with his sister and brother-in-law. Honor did not stay long there before going to the library, where she had been told Fairfax was already busy. When she came from there, Sedgeworth was pacing the hallway.

"Ah, Mr. Sedgeworth," she said gaily for the benefit of the butler and one footman who were also there, "do escort me to the rose garden. I shall be cooped up in a carriage for two days. I simply must have some fresh air and exercise first. I have half an hour, I believe, before the carriage has been summoned."

He bowed and offered his arm. "I am sorry your visit has to be cut short like this," he said as they stepped down onto the cobbled terrace.

"I do not really understand it," she said, taking his arm. With the other she held and twirled the inevitable parasol, a blue one this time to match her muslin dress. "Why is he letting her go?"

"Several events have happened quite suddenly," he said. "They probably need some time apart before coming to any decision about their future."

"We were not wrong, Joseph, were we?" she asked. "I am quite sure that they love each other."

"Yes," he said. "I believe you are right. But we cannot interfere further. They must decide for themselves now what they will do."

"Well, I think it a horrid inconvenience," Honor said, "that Jane and I have to leave like this. Until Lord

Fairfax insisted on sending for his carriage this morning, we were going to travel by the mail coach. Imagine! Mama would have had a fit of the vapors when she heard.''

He touched briefly the hand that lay on his arm as he led her through the archway into the rose garden. "I shall miss you," he said. "Both of you."

"Will you, Joseph?" she asked, looking up at him and forgetting for the moment to twirl the parasol. "I thought you might be glad to be rid of me. I was dreadfully forward yesterday, was I not?"

"I was honored, my dear," he said. His eyes twinkled suddenly. "What a delightful pun, though quite unintentional. Did you mean what you said?"

"Oh yes," she said airily. "I really do love you. And I mean to have you if I can. Consider yourself fairly warned, Joseph. Of course, I suppose I will not have the chance if you do not come to see me again."

He took the parasol from her hand and fumbled with the handle until he had closed it. He tossed it onto the grass at their feet and took both her hands in his. "I will certainly come to see you, Honor," he said. "I shall be in London next week when Joy and Wallace return home. I cannot say more than that now. My mind is still in a whirl from the breaking of my betrothal and my loss of Jane. I truly am fond of her, you see."

"Of course you are," she said soothingly. "And she is fond of you too, Joseph. But you do not love her, do you?"

He smiled slowly. "I do not quite know this term 'love' that you young ladies use so earnestly," he said. "You are very beautiful, dear, and very full of vitality. And you have a lively and intelligent mind too when you choose to use it. I find myself attracted to you. But just yesterday, dear, I was planning marriage to your cousin. I cannot be sure of the state of my heart so soon afterward."

"You are very cautious," she said, frowning suspiciously at him. "Are you telling me as gently as you can that you want none of me? If so, I wish you would come out and say so, so that I might the sooner persuade myself that I do not care a fig for you and start looking about me again."

He could not suppress a laugh. "You would too, would you not?" he said. "I think that after all you are in many ways more sensible and practical than Jane. No, Honor, I am not trying to tell you anything. I am telling you as truthfully as I can that I believe I might grow fond of you, that I know I may find myself unwilling to go on in life without you at my side. I just need a little time, dear. Do I ask too much?"

She smiled brightly. "Oh no," she said. "I know that you will miss me when I am gone. And when I see you again next week, I shall dazzle you with a new gown and tease you with the names of all the admirers who have been pursuing me since my return. And you will admit then that you love me as I love you. Kiss me now or the carriage will be ready and there will be no time for it."

"I should not take such liberties until I can feel ready to offer for you," he said gently. He reached out and touched her cheek lightly with his fingers.

To his surprise, tears sprang to Honor's eyes. "Yesterday I was forced to kiss you," she said. "And you were behaving with such loyalty to Jane that I might as well have kissed a marble statue. You did not move a muscle. Am I going to have to kiss you again? I need to feel wanted, Joseph. Just a little bit. I know you do not quite love me yet or wish to marry me, and I know that perhaps you will not. But I have to leave you within the next few minutes, and I feel miserable about it. I want to feel your arms around me so that I can cry a little and not have to be forever putting on this show of being lighthearted and not having a care in the world."

She really did not need to end this monologue. Even before she had finished speaking, his arms were tightly about her and one hand had gone to the back of her head to bring it against his neckcloth. And she could not have continued the speech. Her voice was already wobbling almost beyond her control.

"Oh, my dear," Sedgeworth said, "I am a selfish, unfeeling brute, am I not?"

"Ye-e-es," Honor wailed.

"Of course I love you," he said, his cheek against her hair. "Oh, of course I love you, Honor, you little imp of mischief. How could I possibly not? But I am being selfish. Quite honestly, I am terrified. I have never felt this way before, have always somehow scorned people who did. I am very fond of Jane, but I chose her with my head. I know she would be a good companion and wife. With you I am being pulled by the heart, and I am frightened of the vow it is calling me to make. But of course I love you. And when you have finished crying and soaking my neckcloth, I am going to kiss you. But you might be sorry. It will not be a gentle or passionless kiss."

Honor raised an eager face to his, wet cheeks and red eyes notwithstanding. "Is that a promise?" she asked.

"Imp!" he said. "I will never again know a moment's quiet peace if I marry you, will I?"

"I shall try my best to see that you don't," she said, beaming. "I promise, Joseph."

He kissed her then and was every bit as ungentle and passionate as he had threatened to be.

Honor clung to his neck when it was over. "Must I go now?" she asked wistfully.

"I think it is time we walked back," he said. "The carriage will be here soon, and I must say good-bye to Jane." He stooped to pick up her parasol and gave her his arm again. "Are you very dejected, love? I am too, you know. But a week is not a very long time. I shall come to speak with your papa as soon as I return."

"Will you?" she asked, her eyes lighting up. "Oh, I do love you, Joseph. And that is very surprising, really. I always swore that I would marry only a very handsome man."

She giggled when Sedgeworth suddenly shouted with laughter.

\* \* \*

Lord Dart's children were just getting ready to go walking with their governess when Jane entered the nursery. They all hugged her and bade her a noisy farewell before leaving. The nurse was bustling around tidying the room. Claire was standing in the middle of the floor, large solemn eyes watching the loud departure, thumb in mouth. Amy sat at a table, a book open before her.

"Up," Claire said, raising her arms when she realized that Jane was looking at her.

Jane picked her up and hugged her. "Where is Dolly today?" she asked.

"Dolly sleep," said Claire.

"Are you going to give me a hug and a kiss?" Jane asked. "I have to leave very soon."

Claire hugged Jane's neck and offered puckered lips to be kissed. "Aunt Jane go away?" she asked.

"Yes, sweetheart," Jane said, drinking in the sight of the pretty little face and the soft blond curls.

"Come back 'morrow?"

"No," Jane said. "I can't come back, sweetheart. Aunt Jane has to go far, far away."

"Claire go too?" the child asked, brightening.

"No," Jane said, kissing her. "Claire has to stay to keep Amy and Papa company."

Claire stared back a her. Her thumb crept to her mouth. Jane smiled and set her gently down on the floor again. The child trailed after her when she crossed to the table where Amy sat looking at her.

"Aunt Jane," she said, "I don't want you to go."

Jane stooped down so that she was on a level with the child. "I have to go, Amy," she said. "But you will remember what I said last night, will you not? You are a very special little girl, and you are going to grow up to be a handsome lady."

"And you love me?" Amy asked, gazing anxiously up into Jane's eyes.

"And I love you, sweetheart." Jane laid a gentle hand along the child's cheek. "And remember that

Papa loves you too. Even when he is sometimes cross with you. Papa will never stop loving you, no matter what happens.''

"I don't want you to go," Amy said again, and her bottom lip thrust out and began to tremble.

Jane put her arms around the child and lifted her up. She could think of nothing to say that was both true and soothing. "I love you, precious," was all she said eventually as she put Amy down again and turned to leave.

"Amy cry?" she heard Claire say as she closed the door behind her.

Finally they were on their way. All their good-byes had been said, and the carriage was moving down the shady driveway. Jane closed her eyes, discouraging talk, though the move seemed unnecessary; Honor was unusually quiet.

She did not feel any pain. Not yet. She knew she would soon. And it was going to be a dreadful pain because there was no hope in it. No hope for anything but a long and dreary future. But she could feel nothing now. There was just too much to be felt. Her mind and her heart could not cope with the load, but had mercifully decided not to function at all.

There was the good-bye she had said to the children, the final parting from Joseph. And of course there was the fact that she had not seen Michael that morning. She had known she would not see him. It would have been too dreadful if she had. But still there had been the threatening panic when the time appointed for the arrival of the carriage approached and he had not appeared. And then the carriage had been there, and Joseph and Joy and Lord Dart had crowded around them, the men handing them inside. And then the departure. And no Lord Fairfax.

Well, it was over now. Better to have it over, the worst known and in the past. However bad the pain would be when it finally hit her, she was at least on the road to recovery. Nothing could possibly happen to her in the future worse than what had happened in the last few weeks. That knowledge was some comfort, Jane supposed.

She pulled off her bonnet and tossed it onto the seat opposite. At least they would travel in comfort. And in safety. Lord Fairfax was sending two servants as outriders in addition to the coachman and footman who rode with the carriage. She looked around her at the opulent luxury of the green velvet interior. His carriage. She would still have this slim contact with him for the rest of today and much of tomorrow. She leaned back in her seat and closed her eyes again. He must have sat in this very place numerous times.

Honor sat very still, her hands clasped in her lap, her eyes watching the trees outside the window.


Sedgeworth tapped on the library door and opened it to peer inside. "Are you busy, Fairfax?" he asked. "Oh, Amy is here, is she? Is this a private interview? Shall I take myself off?"

"No," Fairfax said. "Come in, Sedge." He was sprawled in a leather chair close to the marble fireplace, Amy on his lap, her head against his chest, one hand playing with the buttons on his waistcoat. "Are you feeling better, poppet? Do you want to go back upstairs while I talk with Uncle Joe?"

She buried her face against her father for a moment but climbed obediently from his knee and left the room.

"I feel like a fish out of water already," Sedgeworth said. "You did not come out to see them on their way, Fairfax?" It was a quite unnecessary question.

"How could you let her go on her own with only her cousin for company?" Fairfax asked. "I fully expected you to go too, Sedge."

"With whom?" Sedgeworth asked guardedly.

"She is your betrothed," Fairfax said. "I would have thought your place was with her, especially on a long journey, even if you do feel some obligation to stay with your sister here."

Sedgeworth frowned, puzzled. "You are talking about Jane?" he asked. "She did not tell you?"

"Tell me what?" Fairfax went very still.

"She asked to be released from our engagement yesterday and decided that she must leave today," Sedgeworth said.

Fairfax was sitting foward in his chair. "Your betrothal is at an end?" he said. "Why, for God's sake?"

"I naturally assumed that Jane would have told you when she came to inform you that she was leaving today," Sedgeworth said. "What reason did she give you?"

"She didn't," Fairfax said. His face was tense. "Why the end to the betrothal, Sedge?"

Sedgeworth gave his friend a measuring look. "I rather gathered that she loved another man," he said.

"And she is going to him?"

"Going from him rather, Fairfax," Sedgeworth said. "I thought perhaps he had decided he did not want her."

Fairfax jumped to his feet. "They have left already?" he asked. "Has she gone, Sedge?"

"Almost half an hour ago," his friend replied.

"Oh God!" Fairfax said. "I shall need my horse, Sedge. And a coat from my room. And they will need to know in the kitchen that I shall not be home for luncheon. The Darts will have to know that I will not be here for a while." He was pacing agitatedly from desk to door and back again, his hand to his brow. "Will she have me, Sedge? Do you think she will have me?"

"I think perhaps you had better ask Jane that," his friend said, some amusement creeping into his voice.

"I have," Fairfax said. "I have asked her. And she said no."

"What?" said Sedgeworth. "Jane said no? Are you quite sure?"

" 'No,' does not sound anything like 'yes,' Sedge. She said no. And then she said yes to you."

"You mean you made her an offer before I did?" Sedgeworth said, incredulous. "And she refused you, Fairfax?"

"Will she have me now?" Fairfax said, his pacing increasing in speed. "Is there any chance that she has had a change of heart? Oh God, I cannot live without her, Sedge. And last night I had the audacity to stand there in her bedchamber and order her to leave my house."

Sedgeworth stared. "Look, old friend," he said after a pause. "You go upstairs and fetch your coat. And mine too, if you please. I shall see to having our horses saddled and sent around."

"You are coming too?" Fairfax asked, frowning. "Will you not find the meeting awkward under the circumstances, Sedge?"

"Someone will need to take Miss Jamieson out of the way while you have your talk with Jane," Sedgeworth said.

"You would do that for me?" Fairfax said. "Entertain the beautiful ninnyhammer? You are a true friend, Sedge. Can we overtake them within the hour, do you think?"

"Not if you keep pacing the library floor, my friend," said Sedgeworth.

Fairfax sat down suddenly and stared guiltily at his friend. "I am being dreadfully selfish again," he said. "What about you, Sedge? What does her loss mean to you? And how will you feel if I immediately go chasing after her?"

"Strangely, I would be pleased," Sedgeworth said. "I love you both, Fairfax, and you belong together. And I do not love her in the way you do. I can continue loving her in my way after she is married to you. Get out of here now, will you?"

Fairfax, descending the stairs two at a time, two coats

over his arm, stopped suddenly and took the stairs two
at a time back up again. He made his way quickly to the
nursery. He was just in time. Amy stood all ready for
the outdoors. Mrs. Cartwright, also clad in bonnet and
shawl, was in the process of tying the ribbons of Claire's
bonnet beneath her chin.

He hurried across to his daughters and knelt in front
of them. The nurse retreated to the other side of the
room. "Listen," he said. "I am going riding with
Uncle Joe. What would you say if I brought Aunt Jane
back with me?"

"Aunt Jane come back?" Claire asked, her eyes
lighting up.

"But she has gone away, Papa," Amy said. "She said
she could never come back."

Fairfax took her by the arms. "I am going after her,"
he said. "I cannot promise that I can persuade her to
come back. But I am going to try. Do you want her to
come back, poppet?"

"But she will go away again," Amy said.

"Aunt Jane go away 'morrow?" Claire asked.

"I am going to ask Aunt Jane to stay for always,"
Fairfax said carefully. "I am going to ask her to marry
me."

"She is going to be my mama?" Amy asked.

"Yes, if she will agree," Fairfax said.

"Aunt Jane be my mama too?" Claire asked.

Fairfax tousled her curls with one gentle hand.
"Would you like that, Claire?" he asked.

The child smiled broadly and put a thumb in her
mouth. "Yes," she said, and continued to smile.

"Papa." Amy reached for him, and he hugged her
against him. "Aunt Jane will not stop loving me if she is
my mama. Will she?"

"I think Aunt Jane will always love you, poppet," he
said. "Even if she never sees you again."

"That is what she said," Amy said doubtfully. "And
Aunt Jane says I am not ugly. She says I am handsome
and that is better than being pretty. And she likes me
being a girl."

Fairfax understood in a flash all the fears and doubts that had made his daughter a sullen and withdrawn child for so much of her life. And she could only have learned to see herself as ugly and worthlessly female through the eyes of Susan. He held the child away from him and looked deeply into her eyes.

"Perhaps Aunt Jane will not come back with me," he said. "I don't want you to set your heart on seeing her again, Amy. But if she does not come, it will be something to do with me and nothing to do with you. She loves you and Claire. And if she becomes your mama, she will only grow to love you more. Do you believe that, poppet?"

"Oh," Amy said almost in a wail, jumping up and down suddenly. "Go and fetch her, Papa, or she will have gone too far and you will never catch her. Claire, Aunt Jane is coming back. Aunt Jane is coming back. And she is going to be our mama. Mama is coming back, Claire. I am going to paint a picture for Mama for when she comes home. I am going to paint her jumping into the lake."

"Mama?" Claire said, looking wide-eyed up at Fairfax. "Mama coming home?"

When Fairfax left the room, not sure if he had done more harm than good by his impetuous visit, Amy was already pulling off her cloak and bonnet and carrying her paints across to the table. Claire, thumb in mouth, was watching her.

The coachman had been given instructions to change horses at the Red Lion Inn. And Honor was hungry, the luncheon hour being already past. But it seemed a tedious delay to Jane to have to stop there and avail themselves of the private parlor the servants had been instructed to hire for them. The very thought of food was enough to nauseate her. She wanted now to be back in London, to send away the coach that was her final link to Fairfax, and to start living her life again.

It was foolish to think that life held nothing else for her. It was going to take a long time to recover from the emotional upheaval of the past few weeks, but recover she would. She wanted the healing to begin, but it would not begin as long as there was one thread connecting her life with Fairfax'.

"Tell me, Jane," Honor said, having ordered a large luncheon to be sent to the parlor, "do you have any regrets about Mr. Sedgeworth? About leaving Templeton Hall? And the children?"

"Yes to all three," Jane said briskly, removing her bonnet and setting it down on the window seat. "But not about anything I have done. I could not have made Joseph happy. Better to make him perhaps a little unhappy now rather than to see him wretched for the rest of his life."

"Do you think he will marry anyone else, Jane?" her cousin prodded. "And would you be hurt if he did?"

"No, I think not," Jane said. "In fact, I believe I would be delighted if he did marry. Only I would worry that perhaps he had married someone who was not worthy of him. And I should never know for sure because I will not write to him, you see, or allow him to write to me after he marries."

"And what sort of a wife would you consider worthy of him?" Honor asked.

"Oh, let me see." Jane sat down at the table and rested her elbows on it. She set her chin on her clasped hands. "Someone very quiet and sensible. And intelligent. And someone who would not mind having no fixed home for most of each year. And someone who did not crave children."

"I think he would be dreadfully dull with such a female," Honor said. "I think he needs someone who will tease him out of his quiet, rather unsociable ways. Someone who will lead him a merry dance, perhaps."

"Poor Joseph!" Jane said with feeling. "He would hate that."

Honor looked rather smug, but since a tea tray was brought in just at that moment, Jane did not notice.

"I still think it a great shame that one of us did not

win that wager you refused to enter into," Honor said. "Imagine our letting a perfectly gorgeous gentleman like Viscount Fairfax escape both of us, Jane. We should be ashamed to raise our heads in public."

"I thought you had decided he was far too dull for your tastes," Jane said.

"Yes, but handsome, Jane," Honor sighed. "He would not be too dull for you, of course. You like the sort of life he leads. I really think it was poor-spirited of you not to try at least to fix his interest. I would quite willingly have renounced my claim on him to you, you know, once I realized that he was not for me." She spoke gaily. She watched carefully.

"Well," Jane said with a smile, "our chances are over, Honor. I am afraid we will both have to settle for lesser mortals. Quite frankly, I am perfectly happy to know that I shall never see Viscount Fairfax again. He is just too handsome for a woman's peace of mind, is he not?"

"Oh, Jane," Honor said rather crossly. "When shall I ever get anything but calm good sense out of you? I do believe my dinner is here. And about time too. I am starved."

She turned expectantly to the door, on which a brief knock had sounded. "Do come in," she called.

The next moment Jane had scrambled to her feet and made for the window almost as if she had every intention of casting herself through the panes into the stableyard below. Very calm and sensible behavior, Honor thought as she stared openmouthed at Viscount Fairfax standing in the doorway and Joseph Sedgeworth in the hallway behind him.

# 17

"**M**y lord!" Honor exclaimed. "Mr. Sedgeworth."
Fairfax came further inside the room, though
he still held to the handle of the door. Sedgeworth
walked past him into the room and smiled at Honor. He
looked somewhat uneasily at Jane's back.

"Miss Jamieson," he said, "would you care to walk
out with me for a short while? The afternoon is really
quite pleasant and the village picturesque."

"No!" Jane said involuntarily, turning a flaming face
to the group.

"Did you ride all this way after us to take me
walking, sir?" Honor asked. "I must confess myself
flattered. Though your timing could be better. I am
awaiting my dinner, and I am starved."

"No, I did not ride all this way merely to show you
the wonders of an obscure English village," Sedgeworth
said, giving her a significant look. "Fairfax has some
unfinished business with your cousin."

"Oh," said Honor, seating herself at the table and
looking up eagerly at Fairfax. "Do you, my lord? Let us
hear it, then. It must be important if you have come
after us all this way. Does it concern the carriage? I
must compliment you on it. We have not felt the least
bit shaken about in it. Have we, Jane?"

"Miss Jamieson," Sedgeworth said. "Our walk?"

"Ah, yes," Honor said. "Do you come too, Jane?
Perhaps a walk will help you work up an appetite. Jane
is not hungry, you know, my lord, although it is well
into the afternoon already and she had no breakfast. Is
that not foolish? One would almost think she was not
enjoying the journey or wishing to return to London.
But how foolish of me! Of course, if you have caught up

212

with us so soon, you must not have stopped for luncheon yourselves. Shall I call a servant so that you may order something too?'' She smiled dazzlingly at the two gentlemen. Jane was examining her hands.

Sedgeworth crossed the room purposefully to pick up Honor's discarded bonnet from a table in one corner. He held it out to her. ''Do you wish me to put it on for you?'' he asked, all politeness.

''No, thank you,'' said Honor. ''Gracious, you are so eager to be gone with me, sir, that I almost begin to tremble for my safety. Perhaps I should sit here until Lord Fairfax has finished his business with Jane so that she may come as a chaperone.''

She was tying the ribbon on her bonnet into a bow beneath her chin as she spoke. She looked provocatively at Sedgeworth, but the look seemed to assure her that it was time she moved. She smiled mischievously at Jane and triumphantly at Fairfax, and swept from the room.

''Honor,'' Sedgeworth said as they stepped from the inn into the cobbled stableyard, ''was that a foretaste of the way you plan to behave if and when we are wed?''

''Yes,'' she said, grasping his arm tightly and smiling into his face. ''Don't you think it was enormous fun, Joseph, to see their faces? I thought Lord Fairfax turned a decided shade of purple, or was I deceived by the shadows of the room? And Jane must have been counting the hairs on the backs of her hands. She was certainly concentrating on them hard enough.''

''Could you not feel the tension in the room?'' Sedgeworth asked. ''Yet you must stay and tease them into thinking you have about as much intelligence and sensibility as that fencepost over there.''

She giggled and did a little jig by his side. ''Oh, Joseph,'' she said, ''I shall be returning with you and will have a whole week left at Templeton Hall to enslave you and make sure you do not change your mind.''

''If you were wise, my girl,'' he said feelingly, ''you would travel as far away from me as you can for the next week and hide so that I will forget what a troublesome imp you are until after I have made my offer and it is too late to withdraw honorably.''

"You are teasing me," she said. "But you are a little bit serious too, are you not, Joseph? I am so glad. I will lead you a merry dance, I promise, but I want to know that there are limits beyond which I dare not push you. And there are, are there not?''

"I shall probably develop the routine of beating you once a week whether you deserve it or not," he said, "just to keep you within the bounds of decency.''

She giggled. "How did you persuade him to come?" she asked. "He looked so very solemn and handsome when he burst into the room, Joseph, that I could almost have wished that it were me he was pursuing. What a waste of good looks, alas! But he is too dull for me.''

"I am afraid you are going to just have to get used to my very ordinary looks, my dear," Sedgeworth said, patting her hand. "And I do not want you even flirting with all the handsome devils you will meet on our travels, or I shall take you back to my much-neglected home and lock you up there for the rest of our lives. Understood?''

"Understood, Joseph," she said meekly. "I shall cast down my eyes demurely whenever I suspect that a gentleman approaching might be handsome. And everyone will comment on what a sweet little mouse of a wife you have. Of course, I might see nothing but floors for the next twenty years, but you are worth the sacrifice.''

"Ah, I see I am taming the shrew already," Sedgeworth said. "Let us try this laneway out into the country, Honor. It looks more attractive than the village street.''

"Oh yes," she agreed with some enthusiasm. "And far more secluded. Once we have turned that bend, you will be able to kiss me, Joseph. How delightful. And I thought I would have to wait a whole week!''

* * *

Fairfax shut the door behind Honor and Sedgeworth and stood with his back against it. Jane looked up slowly from her hands.

"Jane," he said quietly, "why did you not tell me?"

"About what?" she asked foolishly.

"Why did you not tell me that your betrothal to Sedge is at an end?" he asked. "I did not know until he told me so himself this morning after you had left."

"I did not have an opportunity to do so," she said. "Last night did not seem the appropriate time, and I did not see you this morning."

"Last night," he said. "Jane, will you ever forgive me? I behaved abominably. Not so much in telling you to leave. I had to do that for my own protection and yours. But making those stupid accusations. I have been insanely jealous of you with my children. They have both grown fond of you. Claire will sometimes come to you rather than me, especially when she is tired and needs to be held. And Amy has learned to smile and become a young child again when she is with you. Last night I was badly frightened when I discovered her missing. I suppose I had to take out my frustration on someone. And you were there in my path. I am sorry, Jane."

She was examining the palm of one hand, tracing the lines with a finger of the other hand. "I understood," she said. "I was a little upset, but I was not angry with you. Indeed, you had reason to be angry with me."

"And do you understand why I had to send you away?" he asked.

Her finger moved in a circular pattern around her palm before she looked up at him.

"Do you understand that if you had remained I could not have stayed away from you?" he asked. "That sooner or later I would have been touching you again, molesting you as I did in the music room? And you were betrothed to my closest friend. I could not live with myself or the temptation, Jane. I had to send you away."

"I was leaving anyway," Jane said. "Honor and I were going to return to London by the mail coach."

"Yes," he said, "I know that now. And that troubles me, Jane, and has me standing here, in fear and uncertainty. Why did you break off your betrothal? Why did you do so and not tell me? And plan to leave my home the following day?"

Jane was looking at her hands again. "I love Joseph," she said. "I mean, I love him as a dear friend. I could not marry him because I could not offer him a whole or an unbruised heart. It would not have been fair to him to trap him into such a bond."

"And where is the part of your heart that is not yours?" he asked quietly. "Who has bruised your heart, Jane?"

She shook her head and said nothing.

He took a few steps farther into the room. "Until a few weeks ago, I had a great deal of confidence with women," he said. "Is it conceited of me to say that I know I have been blessed with more than my fair share of good looks? When I was younger I don't believe I ever thought consciously about the fact that I could attract any woman I wanted. But the few times I put the matter to the test, it always proved true. You did me a great deal of good, Jane. You set me completely on my ear when you refused me. I could not believe it was true. I had not realized that I was so arrogant. But you were quite right. I was. Now you have made me into a tongue-tied boy, and I am not sure that that is so good."

"I believe I was wrong on that occasion," Jane said quickly and breathlessly. "I have seen since then just how very selfless you are in your love for your children. You had every right to ask whomever you wished as a second mother for them. And you were quite honest with me. You told me your reason for choosing me. I was the selfish one, wanting to be appreciated as a person. I can see now that your daughters mean more to you than even your own happiness."

"I am not sure that you are right, Jane," he said. "If the children had chosen a woman different from the one I have chosen, I am not sure I would give up my choice in order to secure theirs. I am not sure at all. My children love you and want you as a mother. I love you and want you as a wife. I do not have to make the choice between them and my own happiness."

"Oh!" Jane looked up into his eyes, her own bright with unshed tears.

"You saw fit to deny my suit a month ago," he said. "I would not harass you now. Tell me if the turn this conversation is taking is repugnant to you, Jane. If it is, I shall stop immediately and go out to find Sedge. We will return to Templeton Hall and you will never be troubled by me again."

He looked at her in anxious inquiry.

"I love you," Jane almost whispered. "I always have."

"Always?"

"Five years ago," she said, "when you courted your first wife, I loved you terribly. And spent the years between persuading myself that it was merely infatuation. It probably was, but it revived immediately when I saw you again this year."

"Jane," he said, his eyes puzzled as they gazed into hers. "Why? Why did you say no to me? And why yes to Sedge?"

"It is easy to agree to marry when there is love on neither side," she said. "Joseph and I like and respect each other. I could not marry you knowing that to you I was a mere convenience, a new mother for your children. Not when I loved you so. And when I knew you had felt that kind of love for your first wife."

He came closer to her and placed his hands on her shoulders. He laid his forehead against hers. "Jane," he said. "I was blind. Very, very blind. I think I must have loved you even when I first offered for you. I must have. I abhor the thought of being married to someone I do not love. I think perhaps I fell in love with you at the

library that day. Do you remember? When you became
so indignant at poor Pamela for marrying Mr. B.? You
were so serious, just as if they were real people who had
just ruined their lives. But I would not admit the truth. I
was so afraid of falling in love."

Her hands were smoothing the intricate folds of his
neckcloth.

"I fell in love with Susan," he said. "Deeply, head
over heels in love. And then when it was too late, we
both discovered that we did not really love at all and
that we did not even have enough in common to make
us friends. I do not blame Susan. Poor girl! For four
years she lived a life that she hated, and she died a
dreadful death, for which I shall always feel in large
measure responsible. But I did not love her, Jane. I was
very unhappy for three of those years. And so I was
afraid of falling in love with you. But the reverse
happened this time. When it was too late, when you
were betrothed to Sedge, then I discovered that I loved
you. I do love you, my dear. I am not just *in* love with
you, though I must confess that I am that too."

"Michael," she said, and swallowed hard, "is it true?
Can it possibly be true?"

He turned his head so that his lips met hers, raised his
head, and looked deeply into her eyes. He smiled.

"I want to kiss you and kiss you until we both have
no breath left," he said. "But first I want to hear your
answer, Jane. Will you marry me, love? I will be deeply
honored, believe me. I cannot promise you a life of
great excitement, but I can promise that you will be
deeply loved by three people. And by me most of all.
Will you, Jane?"

"The children?" she asked. "Will they accept me,
Michael? Amy is terrified of having a new mother, you
know. She is afraid that a mother will not love her."

"I went to them," he said, "before setting off in
pursuit of you. I wanted to be sure that they would be
glad if I brought you back in order to marry you,
though I was almost sure that they would be. I left Amy

jumping up and down in her excitement and telling Claire that Mama was coming home."

The tears finally spilled over from Jane's eyes. "And Claire?" she asked.

"Claire merely sucked her thumb and asked me if Mama was coming home," he said. "We really must break her of that habit, you know, Jane. She is two years old already."

Jane giggled suddenly and brushed at her tears with the backs of her hands. "I suppose I had better say yes," she said, "or I might be dooming Claire to sucking her thumb until she is twenty."

"Yes, Jane?"

"Yes," she said. "Oh yes, Michael. I want to marry you more than anything else in the world." She threw her arms around his neck and hugged him.

"God, how I love you!" he said. "My lovely, sensible, kind, courageous Jane. And very desirable. I really do not know how I stopped myself in the music room that night, you know. I wanted you more than I have ever wanted anything in my life. And you felt it too, did you not? When we are married, you are going to spend all night and every night in my bed, and I am going to teach you to enjoy sleepless nights and endless passion. Will it be hard for you?"

Jane buried her face against him.

He laughed and hugged her closer. "I am putting you to the blush, am I not?" he said. "You just wait, my love. Oh, you just wait. I want to love you and love you, Jane. I want to put my child in you."

She lifted her head finally. "You will want an heir, Michael," she said. "I hope I can give you a son." Her cheeks were flaming.

He drew a deep breath and let it out slowly. "Come and sit over here, love," he said, and led her to an old but large and comfortable-looking chair and settled her on his lap. "Listen, Jane. Perhaps I am unnatural, but I have never really understood this obsession many men seem to have with producing heirs. I have numerous male cousins, all of whom are perfectly respectable and capable of taking over my title when I am gone. It is not essential to my peace of mind that it go to a son of mine.

"I want to have children with you, Jane, because I love you and I want us to have that experience together. And I shall be delighted if we have a son. I shall be equally delighted if we have a daughter—or half a dozen daughters. Gender does not matter. How could I resent your presenting me with a daughter when you yourself are female and I love you so dearly? Please, my love, don't ever become anxious about what so many women conceive of as their duty. Susan was obsessed with having my heir. That is why she died in childbed only a year after Claire was born. If you and I are blessed with children, they will be at least two years apart. And you will find me quite inflexible on that matter, Jane."

She laid her head on one of his shoulders and put a hand on the other. "Yes, my lord," she said.

"Are you making fun of me, Jane?" He peered around into her face. "Is there any other matter we need to settle before that kiss? I do hope not, because I want to kiss you quite thoroughly and I am afraid that if we postpone it much longer, Sedge and your cousin will be back here. In fact, I think him quite heroic for having kept her out of here so long. I find the girl rather amusing myself, but I can readily imagine that she is not Sedge's type at all."

"No," Jane said, "I do not believe there is any other matter to settle, Michael." She turned her face up to be kissed.

It really was a blessing that the parlor door was unlocked and Sedgeworth and Honor expected back any minute, they both agreed sensibly later that evening when they were sitting in a very similar position in the library of Templeton Hall. Otherwise the embrace might very well have got out of hand, as the evening one certainly did. As it was, Jane's lips were quite noticeably swollen after it was over and her mouth thoroughly ravished by an ardent and ungentle tongue. And her breasts were left taut and tender to the touch from the caresses of his hands, which somehow found their way down inside her dress.

"Jane," he said over and over again as his mouth wandered over her face, along her throat, and always back to hers. "Jane, how beautiful you are. Oh, yes, love, yes. Here, darling, so lovely, so warm and soft. We must be wed soon. As soon as I have written to your father and had a reply. Soon, Jane. I cannot wait long. Soon. And then . . . Oh, then, Jane . . ."

She said nothing but his name, often repeated. But soon, yes, her mind and her kisses and touches assured him. Soon and perhaps sooner. She could not resist him. She would not resist him. She was his from this moment on. Her thoughts might be irrational during these minutes of delirious passion, but she had no interest in bringing them back to rationality. She loved him and she would trust him with her life. And with her honor too. She was his now. A wedding would only set the seal of law and religion on what had already taken place between their hearts.

Perhaps it was as well that she did not give these thoughts utterance there in the inn parlor, though perhaps she did later that evening.

There was the sound of heavy footsteps and loud voices in the passageway outside the room. The footsteps stopped, but the voices continued for a whole minute, accompanied by some throat-clearing and one high-pitched giggle before a firm knock sounded on the door.

Fairfax laughed and set Jane on her feet. "I wonder they did not hire a bugler to come before them," he said. "Do come in, Sedge and Miss Jamieson, before all the other guests demand that you be thrown out for disturbing the peace."

"Well," Honor said impatiently as soon as Sedgeworth opened the door, "did we stay away long enough?"

"By no means," Fairfax said. "But we must not be

greedy, I suppose. You may both congratulate us." He wrapped an arm around Jane's waist. "Jane has consented to become my wife."

"What!" Honor squeaked. "What a very unexpected surprise, my lord. I never would have guessed that such an event was in the offing."

Sedgeworth took one of her hands firmly in his. "You are a lucky man, Fairfax," he said. "And, Jane, you must know how very happy I am for you, dear. Yours will be a very suitable match. I believe it might be more appropriate for me to ask for your condolences than your congratulations. I do believe that I am about to offer for this little imp here. My life might never know a moment's peace again."

Honor beamed fondly at him while Jane and Fairfax both stared, speechless.

"It is quite true, you know," Honor said. "I have changed my mind, you see, Jane. I have decided to marry for love, after all. And once I decided, Joseph did not have a chance of getting away from me. I always get what I want, you see. But he will not be sorry. I can see that you both believe he will be. You are wrong. I shall show you. Joseph will be the happiest married man there is, even including you, my lord. And I shall prove it to you all."

Sedgeworth pulled a large linen handkerchief from the pocket of his coat and handed it to Honor. "She really is a reformed character," he said. "This is the second time today she has turned on the waterworks. I have great hopes of making a subdued lady out of her yet. Now, don't cry, love. Fairfax and Jane will be over here within the minute to hug you and kiss you and wring me by the hand. All they need is that minute to recover from the shock of knowing that a thoroughly dull dog like me has captured your heart."

"Silly! I am not crying because they have not come over here," Honor said crossly, blowing her nose loudly in the handkerchief and then appearing not to know quite what to do with it. "It is just that I am so hungry that my stomach is threatening to become an orchestra pit, and yet no one here has enough sense to order luncheon—or tea or dinner or whatever meal seems appropriate to the moment."

"Oh, Honor," Jane said. "That is surely the most sensible thing you have said in a long time. I am positively starved too. In fact, I'll wager we all are. And yet all we can think of to talk about is love."

"Well, Sedge," Fairfax said, releasing Jane's waist and crossing to the bell pull. "At least one comforting fact has become evident. We will both have wives who will put our creature comforts before romance. And their own, of course. It is quite an anticlimax, is it not, to be dreaming of roast beef or mutton after the events of the past few hours? Now then, Miss Jamieson— Honor, if I may—shall we proceed to that hug and kiss before the poor landlord comes and is shocked by the sight of us?"

"Oh," said Honor, holding out her arms to him, her eyes shining, "and I have just promised Joseph that I will not flirt with any more handsome men. But he will have to excuse me this time, for he is kissing Jane."

Jane laughed. "Would we not give a very misleading picture to the landlord if he did walk in just now?"

"Let us change partners again, Sedge, shall we?" Fairfax said. "And at least restore some measure of respectability to this scene. Come here, Jane. Where you belong, love."